Praise for
THE KONKANS

A Publishers Weekly Best Book of the Year

"*The Konkans* is a humane book...D'Souza and his narrator are on the side of love, tolerance, and familial respect, and against cruelty, racism, and imperialism."—*New York Times Book Review*

"Promising...D'Souza is mining territory ripe for novelization, tracing through his characters an upheaval still under way in America's hierarchies of class and social status."—*New York Observer*

"The author, a savvy storyteller with a clear, soulful voice, just knows good source material when he lives it. What he has created—with an appealingly unfashionable simplicity—is a rich, warm, personal yarn."—*Entertainment Weekly*

"Francisco tells the stories bereft of either editorializing or sentimentalizing, and yet he fills the reader with emotion over the very humanness of these very likable characters trying desperately to find a place that feels like home in this very American story."
—*San Antonio Express-News*

"Chicagoan D'Souza (*Whiteman*) spins this amusing, cross-cultural tale of Francisco D'Sai...colorful and engaging."
—*TheMorningNews.org*

"With both humor and pathos, D'Souza has written an engrossing story of characters caught in a clash of past and present from which they can't escape."—*Booklist*

"Every page yields its pleasures—D'Souza is a natural."
—*Kirkus Reviews*

"With this moving portrait of a mixed Indian-American family...D'Souza puts a fresh spin on the theme of cultural alienation, and he achieves something even more universal as he shows how the characters are alone together in their family."
—*Publishers Weekly*, starred review

"This vibrantly written novel, with colorful descriptions of India and the experiences of new immigrants in America, alternates between the hilarious and the heartbreaking; highly recommended."

—Library Journal

"Captivating storytelling...much like a sunset walk on the beach. Words in his hands blended the verdant colors of India with well-sewn threads of suburbia into an enduring tapestry of diversity and familial love. A fictional family you'll be glad to know."

—ArmchairInterviews.com

Praise for
WHITEMAN

*Winner of the Peace Corps Writers Organization's
Maria Thomas Prize for Best Novel*

Finalist for the Young Lions Fiction Award

Florida Book Awards' Gold Medal in General Fiction

*The American Academy of Arts & Letters
Sue Kaufman Award for Best First Fiction*

A St. Louis Post-Dispatch Best Book of 2006

"Ultimately, what makes *Whiteman* so affecting is D'Souza's understanding of what it's like to fall in love with people who will never be like you, with a place that will never be home, and with a troubled continent that—despite your best intentions—you can do nothing to save."—*People*, Critic's Choice, four stars

"It's the quality of vision that makes D'Souza's novel notable and, for a first book, unusual...In original, unfussy prose, *Whiteman* suggests, with force and restraint, why a young American serving abroad, however haplessly, might not relish the prospect of having to return home."—*New York Times Book Review*

"Quirky, seductive, and funny...the author has acquired the arts of a master storyteller, and each little tale nestled in this novel has an intoxicating, fireside charm. Some of the tales are sad or spooky or bawdy, but all of them seamlessly combine the ancient allure of folklore with a modern, Western literary elegance."—Salon.com

"A powerful debut novel, full of insight and sly humor. This is a visit to Africa you will not soon forget."—*St. Louis Post-Dispatch*

"Taut and nervy, so natural and alarming in its telling that it is tempting to wonder how many experiences Jack and his creator—who was a Peace Corps volunteer in Ivory Coast—share."
—*Denver Post*

"*Whiteman* has its terrifying moments, but it also has laugh-out-loud humor, steamy sex, lyrically beautiful descriptions, and enough insight into the West African cultures Jack encounters to satisfy an anthropologist."—*St. Petersburg Times*

"A subtle but damning response to the assumption that Western aid is all-benevolent."—*Entertainment Weekly*

"*Whiteman*, an intimate and unabashed account...reads with a startling honesty."—*Minneapolis Star Tribune*

"*Whiteman* is the tale...of chivalrous acts and the search for love, of witchcraft and genies, of isolation and war, of storytelling and language."—*Sarasota Herald-Tribune*

"To read D'Souza's debut novel is to be plunged into the precarious—and authentic—existence of the foreign relief worker...alternately amusing, sexy, moving, and, when war erupts, frightening."—*Library Journal*

"An exceptional account of West African village life, written with enormous affection and you-are-there immediacy...Africa may be ultimately unknowable for the author, but this nonfiction novel, his debut, represents a thrilling partial discovery."
—*Kirkus Reviews*, starred review

"The book has a very real, immediate, nonfiction feel to it."
—*Los Angeles Times Book Review*

"D'Souza makes humor, danger, and chaos occupy the same page like old friends, and his characters speak with a musical cadence that brings them alive."—*Arizona Republic*

"Promising...the real surprise of the novel is its fearless treatment of Jack's sexual relationships with local women...D'Souza skillfully counterpoints Jack's sojourn with his stateside existence, yielding unexpected motivations for Jack's work and his liaisons."
—*Publishers Weekly*

"Sad, scary, and funny... *Whiteman* is absorbing."
—CurledUp.com

"Tony D'Souza has written a frank, funny, humane novel full of true news about the intermittent tragedy that is contemporary Africa. The illuminations, seductions, and ultimate costs of the narrator's adventurous assimilation into West African village life are presented with sensitivity, and with great drama, in tersely lyrical prose."
—Norman Rush, author of *Mating*,
winner of the National Book Award

"*Whiteman* captures the marvels and mysteries of an alien culture seen through an outsider's eyes. D'Souza is an astute talespinner, alert to the diverse stories of the human tribe. I was fascinated from the opening scene to the final word, which was—what else—*Africa*."—Kim Addonizio, author of *Little Beauties*

"*Whiteman* is a full-hearted antidote to Conrad's *Heart of Darkness*, a worthy and illuminating sequel to Chinua Achebe's *Things Fall Apart*, a seductive call-and-response to Naipaul's *A Bend in the River*. Surely Tony D'Souza's amazingly artful first novel was born in a literary state of ancestral grace. Africa has not been loved with such fierce intimacy since Isak Dinesen."—Bob Shacochis

The KONKANS

Books by Tony D'Souza

Whiteman
The Konkans

The KONKANS

Tony D'Souza

MARINER BOOKS
Houghton Mifflin Harcourt
Boston   New York

First Mariner Books edition 2009

For information about permission to reproduce selections
from this book, write to Permissions, Houghton Mifflin
Harcourt Publishing Company, 6277 Sea Harbor Drive,
Orlando, Florida 32887-6777.

www.hmhbooks.com

An excerpt of this novel appeared originally in *Playboy*
magazine.

Library of Congress Cataloging-in-Publication Data
D'Souza, Tony.
The Konkans/Tony D'Souza
p. cm.
1. Konkans (Indic people)—Fiction. 2. East Indians—
United States—Fiction. 3. India—Fiction. I. Title.
PS3604.S66K66 2008
813'.6—dc22 2007015303
ISBN 978-0-15-101519-1
ISBN: 978-0-15-603493-7 (pbk.)

Text set in ITC Galliard
Designed by Linda Lockowitz

Printed in the United States of America

VB 10 9 8 7 6 5 4 3 2 1

For my uncle
storyteller

PART 1

The Pig

A long time ago, my uncles bought a pig. I was a few months old at the time. I'd like to say that my uncles bought the pig to herald my birth, but no, it was instead to celebrate the feast of St. Francis Xavier, my namesake and our family's patron saint, the man who had brought Catholicism and the roots of Konkani, my uncles' language, to the western coast of India, where they and my father were from, in the early sixteenth century. My uncles had been in America less than a year, my father, four years. My mother was born in Detroit, had spent three years in the Peace Corps in India, where she'd met and married my father.

My uncles were rowdy, debonair young men in the Indian way, not like my father at all. My father was a replica of my grandfather, a police commissioner in Karnataka state, a man as hard as granite with the old Portuguese work ethic as sure in him as his tightly clipped mustache. There was a photo album in our house devoted just to pictures of him, and whether he was in his captain's uniform with the sash and epaulets and his

Lee-Enfield rifle on his shoulder, or whether he was in his rat-tan chair on the porch of his house in India in a white T-shirt and *lungi* wrap with one hand raised on his cane, he never cracked a smile. That's what my father was like, too.

But my uncles did not have the burdens on them that my father did as a firstborn Konkan son, and they liked to drink and dance and joke and chase women. My mother says that the transition to American life was hard for all of them, but the pictures of my uncles from that time don't support that idea. In picture after picture, my uncles flank my father, smiling like boys up to something, while my father does his best impression of a senator. For two years, my uncles lived in the basement of our house on Nelson Street, and then my father got fed up with them and sold the house, and we left Chicago for the suburbs. My uncles were then on their own.

The one uncle was named Samuel Erasmus, but my father renamed him Sam when he arrived, and the other was named Lesley Wenceslaus, but my father renamed him Les. This was to help them fit in to America. When they got off the plane at O'Hare in 1973, they were both sporting Fu Man-chu mustaches that swept the edges of their chins, because an American kung fu film had been all the rage in India the year before, and knowing nothing of America other than that, they'd grown those mustaches to get ready for their immigration to it. No one else wore mustaches like that in their town in southern India, so everyone had known what they were up to and where they were going. According to my uncles, they became very popular with girls.

The first thing my father said to his brothers at the airport, even before "Welcome," which he never said, was, "Those mustaches have to go." He stopped at a Walgreens on the way home to buy disposable razors, and before they could even sit down to their first American meal, meat loaf with ketchup and mashed potatoes, which my mother, newly pregnant with me, had prepared for them, they were in the basement bathroom shaving while my father looked on with his arms crossed.

"You don't know anything here. Do you understand me? You do not know one single thing."

"Fine, Babu, you are right," they said together. "Tell us every small thing and we will do it."

"Be quiet and don't make a lot of noise."

"Yes, Babu, that is what we will do."

The fact was, my father did not want his brothers in America, did not want anything from India following him into his new life here. My father was something of a prig, and though it wasn't his fault, there it was. My grandfather had spent the family's money on educating him, and while the rest of the children ran about the streets of Chikmagalur in their bare feet just like the Hindu and Muslim kids did, my father went to a Catholic college in Mangalore on the coast, and then worked for a number of years as a clerk at Standard Chartered Bank in Bombay. He always had the finest shirts and trousers, and had been a member of the British-organized Chikmagalur Boys' Cricket Club in his youth. My father wanted to be a British gentleman above and beyond all else, and when the opportunity of my mother came along, he took that as a ticket to the United States, the ersatz Britain.

But my uncles were the dust and chaos of real India, and when they wrote on my grandfather's urging that they'd like to come, my mother snatched the letter from the trash where my father had tossed it, and she filled out the paperwork to sponsor them. This threw my father into a rage. His specialty those days was swearing through clenched teeth and thumping his chest.

"Don't you respect me, Denise? Didn't you take a vow to support me in all I do?"

"I don't remember saying that I would be your slave, Lawrence," my mother told him, "and besides that, I want mine to be a life of family. When I married you, I married your family. If they want to come over, then it's our duty to help them. Why should you be the only one in the world who gets to live here?"

My mother was headstrong and brave, with slender arms and long blond hair that she wore in a ponytail. She'd gone to India for a lot of reasons, primarily to get away from her family, and secondly because she had believed in John F. Kennedy's vision of the world. While there, she had first fallen in love with the country and its people, and later, just before she was scheduled to leave, with my father. My father could read and write and had a salable education. My mother would probably have been happier married to an oxcart driver or laundry washer, but her poor roots had made her practical about the realities of the world, and in marrying my father, she'd brought home with her the one living-and-breathing souvenir of that place who could also get a job in America. Sponsoring over my uncles was done to spite him, a return to what she really loved. Many were the nights that my mother drank and sang and talked Konkani with them while my father glowered in his study, pretending to pore over paperwork for his position as a corporate insurance manager with the multinational Hinton & Thompson, but really grinding his teeth at all that noise, which reminded him in an uncomfortable way of where he was from and who he in fact was.

My mother prepared the basement of the house on Nelson Street for my uncles' arrival with happiness and cheer. The house had been cut up into rentals before my parents had bought it, and there wasn't much for her to do, really, but wipe a wet sponge along the sink and toilet, and hang yellow curtains over the half windows to make that basement seem like a home. There was a cement-stairway entrance to the basement apartment from the garden, where my mother grew tomatoes, cucumbers, and peppers in trellised rows, as well as a stairway inside that led to my parents' kitchen. Just before they came, my father had a workman install a lock on the door at the top of the stairway to the kitchen, and all during their first weeks in the basement, my uncles had to go out through the garden and up onto the porch to ring the bell like visitors if they wanted to see my parents. Then one afternoon my mother opened the front door and saw my uncles shivering in their undershirts in the spring rain, and she made my father give her the key and unlocked the door in the kitchen for good. Whether it was a wise decision or not, from then on the door was open, and my uncles came and went through the house as they pleased.

As men in India, my uncles weren't used to cooking for themselves, had never really done it, but in their reluctance to let go of their birthplace in this new nation, they began to cook Indian food for themselves in their basement kitchenette. This involved sautéing onions and garlic in oil and browning curry powder and meat in frying pans. The odors soon pervaded the whole house through the opened door and drove my father crazy. The other thing my uncles did down there that pissed my father off was they played Indian music on the turntable my mother had bought for them, and sang and danced and drank to it in their underwear night after night. The noise filled the house, and as they'd lie in bed together with me gestating in my mother's womb, my father would clench his teeth in the dark and say, "You see, Denise? What did I tell you? Why did we come here if everything will be as it was before? My clothes stink of it, I can feel them looking at me at the office. Why did I come here if everything I hated about it is dancing in my basement?"

My mother would rub my father's shoulder. She'd say, "It's not forever, Lawrence. Besides, we need a little more life in our lives than we've been having."

"Who's not living, Denise?"

"You're not, Lawrence. If it wasn't for your brothers, you'd be nothing but work, always trying to fit in, never anything but worry and unhappiness."

"I was happy before they came."

"You could be happy that they are here."

"I would be happy if I was allowed to be a normal American."

"I'm sorry to tell you this. A normal American is the one thing you'll never be allowed to be."

What could my father do but grind his teeth, get up from the bed, and close himself up in his study? In there, he would sit in his leather armchair in a cloud of anger that he could only get a grip on by drinking scotch neat. Sometimes my mother would rise from bed in her nightgown to knock on the study door, enter it, kneel, and rub my father's feet to soothe him, and other times she would lie where she was and not sleep and let the night play out as it would. My father was not a violent drunk, he managed himself best when left alone. No matter how much of the bottle he needed to salve himself, he would always be up in time to catch the train downtown for work, and though his resentments against my mother and his brothers were growing in him, he kept them to himself.

"We love you, hey, our Babu." My uncles would tromp up the stairs with beer bottles in their hands and rub his head and shoulders like masseurs as he sat to his dinner of steak and boiled potatoes. "Our big brother, we are grateful for all you've done, bringing us to America, making a place for us in your home."

"Go back downstairs and turn down that Hindu nonsense," my father would patiently tell them and chomp his food, and after a little more laughter and a last singing of *"E puri kon achi?"* (Whose Daughter Is She?), the Konkan young man's national anthem, my uncles would do that. Neither had jobs at that time, and my father was supporting everyone.

But the last thing, the linchpin thing, that kept the household, and my father, together in those early days after my uncles' arrival was my grandmother's gold.

To help my father and mother get started in America, my grandfather had told my grandmother to collect her gold jewelry, everything save for her wedding ring, and sew it into the lining of my mother's suitcase, underneath where my mother would put her folded underwear. Even my grandfather knew that my mother's white skin and blond hair would not raise a customs inspector's suspicion, and so my mother returned to America after three years in India with my father on her arm and four and a half pounds of filigreed and finely worked bangles, earrings, nose rings, and necklaces wrapped in cloth and hidden in the lining of her suitcase. Both the Indian and American customs inspectors made my father dump all his shirts and socks out onto the steel counters, while my mother held her heart in her throat, and enough gold in the suitcase in her hand to make a down payment on a house. And once my father had sold the jewelry to a Sikh silk–and–dry goods trader on Devon Avenue, that's exactly what they did.

So though my father didn't really want his rowdy brothers living in his American basement, in the end he was too beholden to his family not to let them. And though they never talked about it, my uncles knew my father was beholden as well. For the most part, when they first arrived, they followed his rules. They also soon had jobs, Sam as a washing machine salesman at Polk Brothers on Belmont, and Les at an industrial printing press in Elk Grove Village. Then I was born, and the winter of '73 settled in with rain, and then they bought the pig.

Sam was the planner, and Les was the one who went along. They were both in their midtwenties, Sam a year older, full of life the way young men are at that time. If they had stayed in India, their lives would have been resplendent with friendships and flirtations, the last before their marriages, which my grandfather would have arranged. But they were in my father's basement in Chicago, and they both understood that their lives here would not be like that. With the money they'd begun to earn, they bought a secondhand Cutlass Supreme, blue with a burgundy interior, which they filled with smoke and music and Puerto Rican girls from the neighborhood, whom they drove about the city.

There were not many Indians in America at that time, certainly not in Chicago, and people took my uncles for Mexicans, as they did my father. My father hated this and would shake his head and turn his back in his suit on the lost laborers and nannies on the "L" train home, who took him as sympathetic, one of them among all those white people, asking him, *"Disculpe, caballero, donde está el* Montrose?*"* but my uncles didn't mind. Ours was a mixed Hispanic neighborhood near Wrigley, and drinking on the porch with the neighbors in the evenings, my uncles quickly learned enough Spanish to joke and fit in, and to have enough Ramons and Eduardos coming around looking for them to make my father slap his hand to his forehead in anguish. Aside from their jobs, my uncles learned how to sell stereos and speakers out of the trunk of their Cutlass, how to dance to mariachi music at neighborhood *quinceañera* parties, how to walk down the street with a lope, and they filled their closet with clothes. They'd sneak their girlfriends into the basement after my parents had gone to bed. The giggling that came up through the vents made my mother smile and long for her own youth, which she felt had passed, and sent my father to his study.

Though they were in America and succeeding in their way, my uncles missed India as much as my father did not, and when it was time for the Feast of St. Francis Xavier, my uncle Sam hatched a plan. They would buy a pig. They would slaughter the pig in the laundry room in the basement and have fresh pork for a traditional *dukrajemas* curry. Everyone in the neighborhood would be invited, they would play *"E puri kon achi"* for them, and teach them how to dance to it. They would even invite the parish priest. Slaughtering a pig would honor the saint and be in keeping with the traditions of their people. There weren't many things to distinguish the Catholic Konkans from the hordes of Hindus and Muslims they lived among in India, certainly not their skin color, which was exactly the same. Their religion and the meat it allowed them to eat were the paramount things that identified them as a people in this world. The Americans ate turkey, the Mexicans hit piñatas. The Konkans cooked *dukrajemas* pork curry and sang *"E puri kon achi."*

But where to get a live pig? In India, they had grown up with chickens and cattle and buffalo and pigs all about them, but in America there seemed to be none of these things. So Sam went to his friend Javier, who supplied them with stereos to sell, and Javier told him to go to Maxwell Street. A black man, Walter Johnson, had a rib stand there, and that's where Javier's family got pork for their parties.

"You tell him the day, Sam, he'll kill the pig in the morning. Then you go and pick it up and it will still feel warm. So cheap, like half the price. You'd think everybody would do it that way. But no way. These white people, they like to think you can eat without having to kill anything. They want to think every dirty thing is clean, have everything packaged up."

"But we need a living pig," my uncle said and shook his head, and Javier made a face down at him from his porch.

"A live pig? What are you going to do with a live pig?"

"Butcher it for the feast of our saint."

"You know how to butcher a pig?"

"People butcher pigs in India," my uncle said.

"What saint is that that needs you to kill a pig?"

"Francis Xavier."

"What did he do?"

"He made us into Catholics."

"What were you before that?"

"Hindus and Muslims."

"No shit? Sounds like he saved your life. You need a pig? I'll call Walter. He's got to have a live pig stashed somewhere. Anyway, this is America. Money's the only thing that matters here, so if you've got the money, you'll get your pig."

My uncles gathered together forty-five dollars in cash, and following Javier's directions, drove downtown to Maxwell Street the Saturday morning before the feast. The sky was gray and overcast, heavy like a low sheet of slate, and the city was becoming cold again in that unbelievable way it had been when they'd first arrived. Sam drove, as was their way, and all down Lake Shore Drive, the traffic was light and pleasant and Sam and Les smoked Pall Mall cigarettes and listened to the De-Paul game on the radio. They didn't know the ins and outs of basketball yet, and their love of cricket made this fast game hard for them to follow. Who could appreciate a point when a point was scored every instant? But too, this was America, and it was good to follow American sports now, and though they found basketball strange, they liked the energy of it, the nonstop running, the leaping bodies, which is what America was to them.

Their plan was to get a pig, put it in the trunk, bring it home to the basement, and slaughter it in the laundry room, next to the washing machine, where the drain in the floor would let the blood run out. They would play music a bit louder than usual to cover the sound from Babu, who they knew would not like it. But never mind, Babu would like it once he smelled the rich flavor of the simmering curry. Never mind, too, that neither of them had ever slaughtered anything. They had made it to America and had jobs and lives here. If they had been able to manage that, then they could manage to kill a pig. Also, Sam had seen the low-caste Konkan butcher slaughter many pigs when he'd been sent on errands by their father through the streets of Chikmagalur to buy parcels of meat for their Sunday meals.

"Samuel, I don't think that Babu likes it that we are here," Les said to Sam as they drove. "At first I could understand it because we did not know anything. But now we know many things about living here and still Babu seems embarrassed."

"Babu is Babu, Lesley. Who can know what goes through his mind? He is very busy with his work and his family. The pressures he feels are different from ours."

"But Samuel, I feel that Babu doesn't like us personally, that he never liked us. When we were boys, he was always away, and when he would come home, I could see that he was angry. He did not like it when we would touch his clothes, don't you remember? Many times I felt that he did not even know my name."

"Who knows the name of the third-born son, isn't it, Lesley? So what? Who knows the name of the second? Life is different here. Babu wants to make his own life in his own house without worrying about the flies that land in the chutney."

"That is it, Samuel. Babu makes me feel like a fly. But what is life if there aren't flies?"

"There aren't flies in America, Lesley, haven't you seen?"

"I ask myself, 'Would I be the same about it if I was Babu?'"

"We can't think that way. When we have white wives and houses of our own, then we can say if what Babu does or doesn't do is or isn't right. Until then, he can only be our Babu."

"Even family is different here."

My uncle Sam nodded, looked out the window at the gray expanse of the lake, didn't say anything.

My uncle Les went on. "Family here is just one man and his wife. No brothers, no cousins, no uncles and aunties and uncles' aunties and aunties' uncles. A place without uncles, can you imagine? Life is lonely here, Samuel. We would be happier if we were at home, isn't it?"

"Who knows what it is to be happy? Were you happy there with no job, with no room of your own? Were you happy with one pair of shoes? Were you happy to be married to some third Noronha daughter with one glass bangle and a lazy eye? Anyway, it is not now for a long time. For now we are at Babu's. We must do our best. Babu will be Babu, and we will be Les and Sam. We can make and save money, and then we can decide. Who is to say that next year we won't be in Chik-magalur, opening a sweetmeats shop together? For now let us learn this thing basketball and all the other things so that when it comes time to decide, we will know what is good for us and what is not."

They quieted and let the game fill the car, and the announcer spoke quickly with words they did not know, and raised his voice in a babble of syllables they could not follow except to know that something definitive and important had happened in the game, and they cheered, Sam unfurling his fingers on the steering wheel, and Les tapping the dashboard with his hands like beating a drum, and the announcer was silent so they could only hear the murmuring of the crowd, and then the announcer said in a new voice, "That's it, folks. The finale. What's surely the last nail in the hometown coffin."

Maxwell Street at that time was an open-air bazaar of second-hand electronics, knockoff designer shoes, food stalls, junk, and trinkets to rival any great market in the Third World, and the vendors and shoppers came from every corner of it. It was a carnival of simple commerce, people haggling over single pairs of socks in eleven languages. There were blues musicians and scat singers, a clown selling helium balloons. And then there was the food: chitterlings and collard greens, corn on the cob and Polish sausages. Latkes, pierogis, tamales, churros. Pickles and pickled pigs' feet, pickled beets and eggs. Halfway down was Walter Johnson's barbecue stand, the man in a big white cowboy hat, a red feather tucked in the band, his pockmarked face, his height and muscled arms. Around his waist was an apron streaked with soot and sauce, and before him at the wide and steaming grills, boys in sneakers hopped and blinked at the smoke, sweated, struggled to keep up with the long line of customers: blacks, Mexicans, Asians, whites, all the working-class people of Chicago, a heated battle to trade dollar bills for rib sandwiches wrapped in foil. Walter Johnson lifted racks of sizzling baby backs with tongs from the long grill choked with them, briskly hammering the cleaver through bone as if chopping onions, all the while urging on his troops with occasional clipped commands. The new Sears Tower rose up over everything, an obsidian obelisk to the city's achievements.

Sam and Les waited in line with cigarettes tucked behind their ears, trying to seem more comfortable in this place than they really were. They were two thin young men with limbs and waists so slender, their denim jackets and jeans billowed around them like bags. Of course they didn't see themselves that way. When they got to the head of the line, the boy taking orders with his pad and pencil said to them, "Rack or rib? Spicy or reg?"

My uncles furrowed their brows. It was hard enough understanding the Americans, but they could hardly make out the blacks at all. "We want to speak to Mr. Johnson," my uncle Sam said and folded his arms, and Les stepped in close and folded his arms, too. "He is waiting for us. Expecting us even. Javier called him about the purchase of a pig."

The boy looked at them a moment, furrowed his brow back. "What did you say to me?"

"A pig," my uncle said.

"A what?"

"We want to buy a pig!"

The boy pointed his finger beyond them, looked past them. He said, "Next in line! Rack or rib? Spicy or reg? Hey Walter, these two belong to you."

"Back here," the big man bellowed, and waved them over with his cleaver. Then he whacked it quickly through a rack, gathered the pieces with a swipe of the blade, tossed them in a pan. He did this all the time he spoke to them. "You the guys who want a pig? Javier's friends? Javier warned me you wouldn't be your everyday beaners. You boys ever tried these ribs?" When my uncles shook their heads, he whacked the tips off the end of a rack, drowned the meat with dark sauce from a squeeze bottle, pushed it toward them. "Put that in your mouths," he said, and they did. Being people who knew something of spicy food, they rolled their eyes, nodded their heads in surprise and pleasure.

"You like the spicy, hey?" the man said and smiled.

"We like the spicy very much," my uncles told him.

"You know that's pig meat, hey? It ain't dirty for you?"

"We eat pig," my uncles said.

"Then you can't be Pakistanis. Isn't that right? Pakistanis are Muslims and can't eat pig. So you have to be something else. Indians? Now I know that Indians don't eat cow. But you're telling me they'll eat pig?"

"No, the Hindus will never eat pig or cow. We are another kind of Indian. We eat cow and pig. But first we eat pig, and then we eat cow. We are not Hindus or Muslims. We are Catholics. We are Catholics from India."

Walter Johnson shook his head as he blinked his eyes from the smoke. "Thank god somebody over there eats pig. Tell all your cousins to come over here and buy my ribs."

"The Catholics of India are unfortunately very few."

"A few from here, a few from there. That's all we need to get by. Come back after things have calmed down and I'll fix you up with a pig."

My uncles ate rib sandwiches and walked about Maxwell Street looking at the young women pushing strollers as they shopped, at the men on the corner playing jugs and spoons, and my uncle Les said to my uncle Sam under his breath, "With the first one, all that I could think was that he looked like a monkey," and my uncle Sam said back, "*Naka*, Lesley. That is not a good way to think. You won't think that any longer once you begin to see them. But where you work, you do not get to see them."

"You get to see them at your work, Samuel?"

"One delivers parts to the store. I see others. But they don't go into the suburbs."

"They are not allowed, is it?"

"They are allowed. But I listen to how the people talk. Technically, they are allowed by the law. But the whites do not give them jobs in the suburbs."

When the lunch rush was over and the boys were scraping off the grills, Walter Johnson took off his apron, adjusted his hat, came to my uncles, and they could see his alligator-skin boots. There was a place they had to go, he told them. My uncles led him to their car.

All along the Dan Ryan south, he asked them questions about India and what they were doing here. Wasn't there any work in India? There wasn't. Did they bring women with them? They hadn't. So what did they do for women? They dated Hispanic women. Would their father be happy if they married Hispanic women? Probably not.

Walter Johnson said, "At one time, there was nothing in Chicago but blacks and Jews and Italians and Irish. But now there are all these new breeds. All those Jews and micks and Italians and Polacks aren't anything anymore but just white. Sure, they all still talk all their individual talk. But those days are done and gone. Because now we got beaners and Chinks and Nips and gooks and I don't even know what to call you boys. Ever been to the Southside before? It's all chocolate down here. All the way to Indiana. You got your Louisianans and Mississippians and Alabamans and holy rollers and Nation of Islam, but as soon as a white guy comes walking down the street, that's the end of it. Then we're all black. Pig-eating Indians, hey? We've got to think up a good name for you. A nice nasty name so you can fit in."

Soon enough they were at Seventy-seventh Street, and Walter Johnson guided them to a line of brownstones a few blocks from the expressway. It was all black people here, young men walking in groups, mothers leading children by the hand, and people crossed the street every which way, it seemed, except at the corners. The buildings were neglected and broken, some of the cars on the curbs had flat tires. They turned down an alley and a gang of stray dogs looked up at them from sniffing something and ran away. Walter Johnson told them to stop, led them around the garage, through a chain-link gate, and into a muddy yard. In the back of the yard and built against the fence were a few slated stalls lined with chicken wire. Pigs grunted in the shadows of the stalls.

"You have raised these pigs here," my uncle Sam said as he picked his way on the boards through the mud of the yard. He saw children watching him from a back window of the house, and when the children caught him looking, the curtain furled into place.

"This is just where I hold them. I've got a guy on a farm near Normal who brings them up to me. I hold them here a few days, then kill them in the garage. What kind of pig are you looking for? A shoat? A hog?"

My uncles looked at each other, didn't know what those things were.

"A big pig or a little pig?"

"A big pig. A pig for forty-five dollars."

Walter Johnson whistled. He said, "That's a pretty big pig. You sure you want a forty-five-dollar pig?"

My uncles Sam and Les looked at each other. They had come all this way. They had even come to the Southside when Babu had told them never to because of the danger. If they were going to do all of this, then why not do it big? Big like coming to America. Big like life here was. They looked back at Walter Johnson. My uncle Sam said, "We want the big pig."

Walter took off his cowboy hat, hung it on a nail on the side of the stall, shucked off his leather jacket and folded it on the top. Then he rolled up his shirtsleeves and picked up some lengths of rope that had been lying in the mud. "Last chance," he said and looked at them over his shoulder, and my uncles folded their arms and nodded. Then he unlatched the stall door and ducked into it. For some long moments there was squealing, curses from the man, and then there was one loud squeal, and it was quiet. Walter came back out of the stall clapping his hands together to clean them, and he spit to clean his mouth. He took the forty-five dollars from my uncle Sam's hand and put it in his pocket. Then he put on his jacket and hat again. He said to them, "Go on in and get your pig."

The pig was big and angry, bristles raised on its back in a ridge, glaring at them with an angry eye. It huffed through the cheeks of its tied-off mouth, its muscles flexed under its skin. The legs were trussed together in a bunch at the hooves, and even despite that, the pig kicked, turning itself on its side in the dirt. Some smaller pigs squealed in the far corner. It took the both of them to drag that pig out of the stall and into the afternoon, and Walter gave them a metal pipe to run between the pig's legs. Then they lifted the pig on the pipe to their shoulders, their jaws clenching from the weight. The pig bucked as it swung in the air, the pipe ground into their bones. Then Walter led them out the way they'd come, and they dumped and locked the pig in the trunk.

"It is truly big," my uncle Sam said as he clapped his hands clean, his face drained of color from the labor.

"I like to satisfy my customers," Walter Johnson winked and said.

"The ropes will stay tight?"

"They're wet. The more that hog struggles, the more they'll bite. You're nervous now, ain't you? You're the one who asked for that pig."

"I am not nervous. It is only that the pig is big."

"Big angry pig. But big or small, they all die the same. Stick him. He'll be dead. But he'll also still be big."

As a last thing after my uncles got back in the car, Walter leaned in the driver's side window, smiled, and said to both of them, "Go home and butcher your pig. We'll settle the rest of the business the next time I see you."

"The rest of the business?" my uncle Sam said.

"The rest of the business. When you're done eating that pig, come down and have a rib sandwich. Then I'll tell you your nasty name."

The sun broke through the clouds enough on the ride back that my uncles were able to crack the windows, and the downtown buildings gleamed in the new sun with all their glass and steel. There were many things to like about America, my uncle Sam admitted to himself as he smoked. There were jobs here, yes, and money to be made, but also America was open and fresh and new in a way that India could never be. There was space to move and breathe, even in the city, and too, despite the sense of loneliness he, like Les, felt at times, it was good to be away from the stifling rules of family. In America, each one could be whoever they were. His older brother Babu could put on his suit and go to work, his friend Javier could wear his tattoos and drink Mexican beer on his porch. Walter Johnson could wear his hat and boots and keep pigs in his yard. And as for him, the possibilities were opening as much as the sky was. He was happy and knew it. My uncle Sam understood then that he had left India for good.

Les said, "What if they could see us now, hey, Samuel? Papa, all of our friends? In our own car? Driving so fast? All these other cars? A pig in the trunk? Such riches here, hey? It is good what has happened to us, isn't it, brother?"

"It is good," my uncle Sam said and tapped ashes out the window.

"That man was a very nice man. So what if at home they call them monkeys? What have they ever seen at home?"

"If they call them monkeys at home, it is only because they don't think that they might also be called something."

"Today was good. Now we have our pig! But it was a bad day, too. Now I am thinking that Babu is right. We have learned many things. But also, maybe not much. Maybe we should listen to Babu more, Samuel. Maybe we should be more quiet."

"Babu knows much more than we do. From now on we will listen to him until we know exactly what will be our way."

My uncles had indeed managed to get their pig, but in their exuberance to achieve that most important thing, they had forgotten to plan for all the other little things that went into the making of a proper *dukrajemas* pork curry. For one, they needed vegetables to accompany the meat. And for two, they needed special spices for the flavor. First they drove all the way up to Devon Avenue, and Les spent some time in one of the new Indian spice shops, coming out with packets of curry powder, cardamom, and cloves. Then they turned south again, to shop at the Jewel supermarket on Western, which was the one on their way home.

They parked the car. Sam patted the trunk to calm the pig— which wasn't making any noise—through the time that they would be inside. Both Sam and Les liked going to the super-market because they knew they could count on seeing young women there. They loaded their handbaskets with onions, gar-lic, potatoes, cauliflower. They followed one bouncy-bottomed girl in yellow track pants up the liquor aisle, and after winking at each other about it when she turned the corner, Les took down a gallon jug of Gallo Chablis, carried it by the ring. Then they pretended to be looking at rigatoni as a girl in sunglasses came down the pasta aisle, nudging each other in the ribs once she'd passed because of the size and sway of her breasts. They also didn't put any pasta in their basket, because it wasn't a food that they yet ate.

"Did you find everything all right?" the checkout girl asked without really looking at them, and Sam said, "Yes, very, very well, thank you." Then there was a commotion in the lot, and everyone in line turned to look.

Even from the doorway, my uncles could sense that some-thing wrong was happening, and they stopped with their pa-per bags in their arms to take it in. People were streaming past them and out of the store, stock boys in their aprons, the women they had looked at, the checkout girls in their striped uniforms, shoppers from all around. What did my uncles have left to do but step forward slowly, as though in a dream, toward the flashing lights of the police cruiser, toward the gathering crowd, toward the place where this new thing was happening, which was exactly where they needed to go?

The squad car was parked behind their Cutlass, blocking it in, and two officers were working a long metal bar together, trying with all their might to pry open the trunk. Women held their hands to their mouths, men looked on with knitted brows. Cars on the street slowed in a line as their drivers gaped. And because they knew all of this belonged to them, my uncles moved forward like sleepwalkers. The crowd parted for them, each new set of eyes fell on them in their slow march. Then they heard the squealing of the pig exactly as all those other people did: as a human being, a woman, screaming to be let out.

My uncle Sam dropped his grocery bags. He yelled, "It is a pig! It is only a pig!" and sprinted forward.

The policemen drew their guns. The crowd sucked in its breath. Les stood in place with the onions from Sam's bags bouncing around his feet.

The officers were in shooting stances. They shouted, "Stop!" My uncle stopped and raised his hands. They shouted, "Take out your keys!"

Squad cars peeled into the lot, lights whirling. A helicopter crested the apartment building across the way and choppered overhead. People ran over in groups from across the street, they hung out of the surrounding buildings' windows. Even a passing bus came to a stop with hands and faces pressed against the glass. My uncle Sam took out his keys, and the cops motioned him toward the trunk. Listening to the pig, he wondered himself if it hadn't somehow turned into a woman. Had he and Les somehow kidnapped a woman? What would happen to them if they had? Why had he ever gotten involved in this stupidity with the pig? Why had he ever come to this country? His trembling fingers somehow fit the key in the lock, turned it, and the trunk popped open. The pig was still a pig.

———

Wouldn't it be nice to think that after that big scene, my uncles could have gotten themselves home, the pig in the basement, the knife wiped across its neck, and that would have been the end of that? It wasn't.

My father was working in his study, my mother trimming and covering her roses in the garden for the coming winter. My uncles were still trembling from what had happened at the supermarket, my uncle Sam's ears still burning from his dressing down by the cops. But, too, they had gotten away with one. The police hadn't written them a ticket.

My mother heard the squealing as soon as my uncles turned into the alley; she took off her gardening gloves and ran to the fence. Of course it had to be my uncles, she knew, she only hoped she could contain whatever they were up to before it managed to upset my father. Any illusions about the Feast of St. Francis long since over, my uncle Sam already knew all the trouble he'd be in once he opened the trunk to show the pig to my mother. When he did, my mother took one look at the furious animal, wrung her hands, and said, "Lawrence isn't going to like this at all."

My uncles were exhausted now, on the verge of panic. If they had thought my mother would help them, now she wouldn't, and the only thing that could save any of this was if they could get the pig into the basement and turn up the music before my father noticed any of it. They pulled the pig out of the trunk by the rope wound around its feet, dumped it in the alley. Its squealing drew the neighbors from their homes, the children running in close, the women with their hands in their jacket pockets and laughing to each other in Spanish. My mother opened the gate and my uncles dragged the pig into the yard. Even in this, their muscles ached. Why had they thought to get a pig so big? And just as my father stepped out onto the back porch because of all of the noise, the pig's kicking and my uncles' pulling caused the rope to break. What remained was a hundred-and-fifty-pound bristling razorback with nothing on its mind except hurting something as badly as it itself had been hurt. My mother leaped up onto the fence as the pig banged against it, my uncles dashed onto the porch just as my father stepped inside and locked the door. The pig clambered up the steps; my uncles hopped over the railing. The pig trampled through the trellises of my mother's garden; my mother whacked at it with a stake. The neighbors leaned their elbows on the fence to watch; my uncle Les ran into the garage and came out with a hammer. "Lead it here, Sam," my uncle Les called, and my uncle Sam, whom the pig was chasing, ran past his brother. My uncle Les raised the hammer and with the practiced eye of someone who had never swung a hammer like that before, hit the pig in the snout when he'd been aiming between its eyes. So first blood was drawn by the humans, and all the neighbors cheered. But second blood was quickly drawn by the pig because it slammed my uncle Les into the wall of the garage, and when it realized it couldn't bite him with its tied-off mouth, it reared and pawed my uncle's head until my uncle Sam rushed in and tackled it, serving his own penance then on his back at its hooves.

I'd like to say that this display went on for a long while, to the vast delight of everyone. And in fact it did for a time, with more running of my uncles, leaping of my mother, furious charges of the pig, mud progressively caking one and all to the cheers of the assembled crowd. Then two loud shots rang out, and Javier stood over the pig with his gun. He nudged its face with his toe to make sure, then put the gun in his pocket and waved everyone home.

My uncles were muddied and bruised, their heads hanging lower than they ever had. From the porch, my father stared down at them. He let the silence gather all around him. Then he said, "Are you happy, Samuel Erasmus? Lesley Wenceslaus, are you happy? It was not hard enough already and now we are fools before all these people? Go and take your pig. Butcher it. I hope you choke on it. Because you are going to eat every last bit of it if you want to go on living in my house."

My uncles ate very little of that pig. Who knows what the roots of their plan had really been? Certainly it had to do with who they were in America, what they were feeling about themselves in it at that time. But perhaps, too, it was simply their desire to remind themselves that they were Konkans.

They knew as little about butchering a pig as they had about killing one, and so with the help of Javier's nephews, the pig was hung by its forelegs from the beams of Javier's garage, gutted and quartered by their deft hands, and while my uncles did curry a shank for the Feast of Francis Xavier, the majority of the meat ended up in tacos and tamales all around the neighborhood. Soon enough, my father told my uncles of his plan to sell the house, to move to the suburbs, and just as soon as he had told them that, my uncle Les joined the navy.

But my uncle Sam didn't. In time, long after his bruises and pride had healed, he found his own apartment. He visited us once a week, on Saturdays, to hold me in his arms and talk to my mother. My father wasn't yet ready to speak to him, and my uncle understood that.

My uncle Sam began to move about the city as though it belonged to him. Now and again he'd drive down to Maxwell

Street to have a rib sandwich at Walter Johnson's. The first time that he did, Walter Johnson called him out of line.

"Hey there, Sam, how did it go with that pig?"

"It went okay."

"I've finally decided what it is I've got to call you," Walter Johnson said and winked.

"What is it?" my uncle said back.

"Dot head. Even though I know you aren't one."

The Grand Canyon

We moved out to the northern suburbs. I was a baby and didn't know anything about it. Our neighbors on one side were the Colemans, an old retired couple, and on the other were the Firths, who both worked for United Airlines. Our house was nice and cozy with the bedrooms upstairs, and for the first time in his life, my father lived in a place with a sweeping central staircase. Whether he found this to be neat or unusual or a luxury at all, of course he acted as though he'd always lived like that. In the finished basement, he had a wet bar, which he stocked with all his favorite liquors. My father's drinking blossomed at this time, and many nights he went to sleep down there on the couch carried over from the old house. There was also a large painting on the wall that he'd brought back from a trip he'd taken with my mother some years before I was born, to Puerto Vallarta, which had served as their second honeymoon. It was a dark painting, on wood panels, and he'd kept it in the attic of our old house wrapped in packing paper, waiting for this move up in the world to hang it. It showed a man asleep on the back of a long-eared donkey, the man wearing a shawl and sombrero, the donkey winding them on a long and lonely path through a saguaro-studded desert and toward the setting sun.

My mother was not at all happy to be in the suburbs. Ridge Lawn was an all-white town, prestigious as far as middle managers went, which my father had become, with a country club and library, a small downtown of clothing boutiques and real estate offices. And though in the summer there were block parties and children about on bicycles, there was no loud Mexican music, and the kids did not play jump rope or stickball together in the streets, but stayed on the sidewalks alone on their roller skates in front of their homes, played baseball on the park-district diamonds in their neat Little League uniforms, and my mother did not have any friends. My father began to travel for work, and he took his first golf lessons at the public driving range. Now and again on Sundays after church, he'd drive us past the ivy-covered gates of the country club, and he'd say to my mother, "You know what, Denise? Once we get a handle on the finances, I think I would like to be a member of that club."

My mother would roll her eyes and shake her head and say, "You want to be a member of that club? Why do you always care about all these things? I'll tell you what. It's never going to happen."

"Money is money, Denise."

"Money is not just money, Lawrence."

"What do you know about it?" my father would say, and in saying that, he was really saying a dozen other things to her that he'd collected inside of him, things he knew not to say to avoid a fight. Because, one by one, he had said those things to her over the years until he knew how each one hurt her:

"What do you know? In India I only knew you as a white, and to me then, that meant everything. But you are not white like I thought you were. You are a poor girl from a Detroit slum, who got an education by some odd luck. But I've since seen your family, and they are nothing here or anywhere, and just because you are white and from here does not mean you know everything about country clubs, or what lies beyond their gates, or who they will let in or who they won't. I am doing well at my company, I am treated like an equal. They have even sent me to London twice already."

And my mother did not say, "You are delusional, my poor Lawrence. You are only a token to those people. Why are you the only colored man in the company pictures, why did they put you on the cover of their brochure? And why have you been passed over for promotion twice already for white boys from East Coast colleges who started working there after you? If you didn't want to be white so badly, maybe you could see it yourself. And you do see it yourself, that's why you are un-happy and drink yourself to sleep. Country clubs don't need tokens yet, Lawrence, and they don't need you. And besides, everyone knows that this country club won't even let in the Jewish dentist." All of this was encapsulated in my mother's sigh when my father said these things to her on those Sun-day drives, and so on their marriage went, the disagreements growing inside them until they were set against each other, waiting for the odd days when one drink too many would bring them out of my father, when one mood too edgy would release them from my mother.

"You are nothing but an Indian here, a little brown play-thing to make them feel good about themselves."

"What do you know about anything good, Denise? What are you in this world but gutter trash with a diploma?"

But my father did bring my mother flowers on her birthday, blue tulips, her favorite, the color of her eyes, and she did keep his house and cook his meals.

In those first years in Ridge Lawn, the things my father most looked forward to were going to work on the double-decker Metra commuter train in the mornings, and traveling now and again to New York and London on business. The thing my mother most looked forward to was when I would sleep and she could curl into a paperback thriller on the couch in the living room with the grandfather clock my father had bought from an antique shop in Wicker Park keeping a somber and steady time. Sometimes Mrs. Firth would come over for an evening glass of wine, as well as to hold me because she and Mr. Firth did not have children, and she would regale my mother with the details of their latest trip to Hawaii on their United Airlines benefits. And sometimes Mrs. Coleman would come over to hold me like she did her few grandchildren when her sons came to visit from Davenport and Cleveland, where they had ended up.

But my mother's favorite times were Saturdays when she knew my uncle Sam would come in his car from his apartment in the city with a package of sweet *jalebi*s for her from the Indian bakery on Devon Avenue. She would put on her blue summer dress with the black-eyed Susans embroidered all over it and nurse me on the couch to make me drowsy. Then my uncle's shadow would darken the doorway, and even before he could ring the bell, she would have opened the door for him. My father was at his golf lessons at these times, and it was an arrangement they all had. My father was still too injured by the general Indian hullabaloo my uncles had brought into his life in America. So my uncle would arrive just after my father had left and spend a few hours talking about his life in the city and reminiscing about India with my mother, and when the afternoon would turn to evening and the lightning bugs would begin to rise from the front lawn in the settling dark, my uncle would finish his last beer or coffee and kiss my mother's cheek at the door. Just after he'd back his car into the street and pull away, my father would swing up in his Buick.

"Was Sam here?" my father would ask, rattling through the doorway with his golf clubs.

"You know that he was," my mother would say, nursing me, the clock's pendulum swinging.

"How is Samuel?"

"Sam is fine."

"Has he heard from Les? How is Les?"

"Les is fine as well. Apparently he's in port. Subic Bay. Did you golf well, Lawrence?"

"I certainly did."

"Put those things away and change your clothes. Dinner is waiting for you in the oven."

My uncle Sam learned to dress the way single young men dressed in the city at that time, in tight-fitting bell-bottomed slacks and wide-collared floral-print shirts. He sported a mustache again, neatly clipped, not at all like the Fu Manchu he'd once worn, and he had muttonchop sideburns. He seemed happy when he'd come to see my mother, and he smiled easily at the things she had to tell him, which were always about the quietness of her week, where Babu had traveled to for work, the chocolates from Europe he'd brought home for her that she'd eaten up already. When my uncle Sam would accept one of my father's bottles of beer that my mother offered him, he didn't guzzle it the way my father would have, but sipped it at the table while my mother looked at him with eyes that said she was glad he was there. "Did you sell many washing machines this week?" she'd ask, or "Are you still looking to move away from Division?" And he would describe all the places in the city that his life had taken him, the stingy people he'd had to deal with at work. When he would say something funny, she would laugh and touch his hand. She did not say things to him like, "I am so glad that you come to me every Saturday, Samuel," or "You don't know how much joy your visits bring to me." She simply smiled as he told her stories from his life in the city, touched his hand now and again. The colors and sounds and smells of Chicago were easy things for my mother to imagine, and more than longing to be a part of it again herself, she was proud of him, this skinny boy who had been too shy to look her in the eye in India, sitting here now with a Konkan man's mustache, smoking a cigarette casually, alone in America and happy, moving easily through all those raucous neighborhoods she missed so deeply from her fine and quiet house in Ridge Lawn.

"How is Javier?" my mother would ask.

"Always up to a scheme."

"And the Molinas and Cordovas?"

"Always more children."

"Do you still see those Puerto Rican girls of yours and Les's?"

"Their fiancés have come."

"Are you brokenhearted?"

"Those were young-people things."

"What about love? Don't you want to be in love?"

"Ah," he said, and blushed, tapped the question away with a knock of his cigarette in the ashtray.

"I have an idea, Sam. What about Lenore? How would you like me to call Lenore for you?"

My uncle could have said that his love life wasn't empty. He could have said that he didn't need my mother's help. Instead he said, "Do you think it would make me happy?"

"I think we could try it out, Sam, why not?"

That my mother was made of unusual things should be obvious in her desire to go to India, to marry an Indian. Her childhood had developed these things in her. My mother's mother was a redhead named Margaret Klein, a second-generation American of German descent, a waitress, an alcoholic. But before any of that, it was my grandfather on that side who had started my grandmother's troubles. The boy next door, he took my grandmother to the mattress in the building's basement, where the kids who did that went to do it. She was fourteen. He told her that his long-absent father was Henry Ford's chauffeur, that he lived on the beach in Florida and was rich. My grandmother believed him.

He was a grade ahead of her in high school, and by the time he left all of them behind for California six years later, my grandmother had three little girls and a senile grandmother to take care of, as well as more spite, resentment, and meanness than any other woman in the neighborhood. In the bars on the way home from work, men complimented her on her hair. She freelanced herself to those men, called them her "boyfriends."

Not one of my grandmother's daughters inherited that red hair, but they ended up hating her as vividly as that color. The three girls shared a double bed in a room with their own great-grandmother, the woman who had brought the German genes to America from a fishing village near Hamburg. She also baptized each one of her great-granddaughters Christian in the bathroom sink when their mother could not be bothered. The only good memory my mother had of Detroit was of a balding man named Barry who gave her a teddy bear with a red ribbon around its neck, and who lived with them through a winter until her mother had either suddenly woken up one day and realized that a man named Barry Weinberg was a dirty Jew, or his money had run out, or she had simply gotten tired of his nagging about her drinking. She threw his clothes out the window.

My mother's great-grandmother died when my mother was seven, and then my mother had to bathe and feed her sisters herself. She inherited her great-grandmother's bed, as well as the one secret that her great-grand had told her when she'd been small: their real last name wasn't *Klein*, which meant "little," but *Kleinschrot*, which meant "little pebble." They'd made her shorten her name when she had entered the country. Even my mother's mother didn't know that.

When my mother was thirteen, her bones ached from her growth spurt, and she had a terrible time sleeping. So she was awake when a naked man opened the door and stood in it. He was backlit. My mother knew her mother was passed out somewhere. The girls were asleep in their bed; she could hear their breathing. There was no one in this world who could save her from this man. He weaved across the room, kneeled on the bed, licked her neck, squeezed her breasts, laid heavily on her, and fell asleep. When she was certain he wouldn't wake, she inched her way out from under him. She put on her clothes, stuffed her few things in a laundry bag. Her mother was asleep on the couch, her black underwear around her ankles in the tattered room. My mother took the money in her mother's purse, spent it on a train ticket to Chicago. My mother's great-aunt on her father's side took her in. The old woman grudged her every instant of those years, and my mother's only prayer was that the old woman would not die before she could manage to get herself through school. The old woman didn't. She saw my mother all the way through a bachelor's degree in education.

My mother was a freshman at the University of Michigan in '60 when Kennedy made his speech in the middle of the night from the steps of the student union inaugurating the idea of the Peace Corps, and nearly six years later, after a brief stint as a typist at Standard Oil in Chicago, she was in India herself, wearing a white sari and teaching low-caste women how to make smokeless ovens in Chikmagalur. My grandfather, the police commissioner of that place, invited her to dinners on Sunday evenings, and he sent a telegram to his son Lawrence in Bombay saying, "Get down here, Babu. There is a white girl dining at our house." My father wooed her with walks along the stream that ran through town, and it wasn't a hard thing to woo my mother because my mother was ready for that. She loved India, wanted to tie herself to it with a family of her own.

In the spring of 1969, my father and mother came to America, to her great-aunt's, where they stayed for three weeks before buying the house on Nelson Street. My mother taught second grade at Nettlehorse Public School, while my father went on the job market. Despite all his bravado in India, his job search in America staggered on for six frightening months. Later, after he'd been at Hinton & Thompson a year, they had their honeymoon in Mexico. At Christmastime 1972, they made a trip to Detroit in their first car, a secondhand Pontiac Executive with a leaky oil pan. Her mother met them at her door.

"You're the one who left us, Denise. Even without him, do you think I would let you in?"

My mother took a last look at her mother, whom she'd never see again, to remember the lines of her aging face in case she might forget them. Then she turned my father around by his elbow. As they walked back to the car in the cold, my mother was pleased because she was done with those people, and my father quietly realized that even in marrying a white woman, he had married below his caste.

On their first date, my uncle Sam took my mother's Peace Corps friend Lenore to a basement restaurant at Lincoln and Clark: The House of India. He wore a jacket and tie, and Lenore wore a blue sari she'd brought back with her from her years of service. Between her eyebrows, she'd pasted a saffron *bindi*, which matched the color of her hair. When he'd picked her up, she had pressed her palms together, bowed her head, and said, *"Namaste."* In his car, my uncle lit a cigarette and turned on the radio. There was Chuck Berry and Jefferson Airplane and Steely Dan and the Doors as they drove through the city, and my uncle wanted Lenore to ask him, "You listen to this music?" but she didn't. They ate mutton curry with their fingers, drank three Kingfishers apiece, and Sam let her talk about India. She had been nervous there, sometimes frightened; she'd had the happiest times of her life. She had been really glad when my mother called. People lost touch so quickly over here.

"And what about right now?" Sam had asked her.

"About right now, Sam?"

"What makes you happy over here?"

Lenore turned her face away for the only time that night, caught a glimpse of herself in the mirror beside them. For an instant the *bindi* on her forehead looked silly even to her. She shook a Camel out of her cigarette purse, lit it, shrugged, and said, "What is there to talk about over here? I clerk for a tort lawyer."

Would she like to go to the beach, my uncle asked Lenore after dinner. Lenore said she would. They drove again, were quiet in the car, and then Sam pulled in among the line of darkened cars at the North Beach parking lot. There were stars out over the lake. She said, "Sometimes all I can think about is that place."

Week by week, Lenore called my mother with the details, they talked about my uncle on the phone like girls. Lenore laughed and said to my mother, "Who knows, Denise, after all that we've been through, maybe we'll even be in-laws."

Sam was exciting for a girl who knew India and could have very little of it here. He knew all the courtship rules Lenore had come to appreciate while living there, and more than that, he could confirm her memories of it, make her believe that she really had been there. Talking to him, she felt that India was still out there as vividly as her memories of it, though it felt so far away. India had teemed with boys like Sam. Falling for him now, Lenore told herself it was fate that one of them should find her here. Besides, Denise was happy.

Lenore loved my uncle's stories of India. In the car at North Beach on their dates, one of the stories my uncle told Lenore was about the time he'd managed my grandfather's coffee plantation high in Karnataka's mountains. It hadn't been much of a plantation, more of a parcel of terraced land in the forest, and all along the terraces grew Robusta coffee bushes, tended by *harijans* in rags in the rain.

The mountains had been a different place, full of gods and superstitious Hindus and spirits and night animals. During his two-year sojourn in the unfinished cinder-block house that my grandfather had had built there, my uncle walked the paths that ran through the terraces of the plantation during the harvest with a flashlight and shotgun at night, to keep bean poachers from stripping the plants. He carried the shotgun loaded, two more shells in the pocket of his shirt, and when he'd hear rustlings in the bushes, he'd slip out of his sandals and stalk the sounds in his bare feet. It was always animals: spotted cats and gazelles, a porcupine, a mongoose. One time he flicked on the light, and all around him were long-horned sambars, their eyes glinting like embers before they turned to leap away.

"Wasn't it hard to be so far away from people?"

"The *harijans* were there. But even with them, it was like being alone. Except for the harvest time, I came down to my parents' house twice a month. But the harvest time was very busy. First, the *harijans* dried the beans on the cement patios. Everything was green and red. Then they did the shelling and roasting, and the beans turned black as oil. Everything smelled of the flavor of coffee. Then the buyers' trucks would come. Once the sacks were sewn shut and loaded on the trucks, I would pay the *harijans,* and even the grandmothers would ride down out of the mountains sitting on top of those sacks. I would sit in the cab with the high castes. After me, my younger brothers went there. It could rain for three days without stopping. There was always mist in the trees. Always I was alone in that house, nothing to do but look at the forest and wonder. My brother Lawrence never went there. At our house in Chikmagalur, he was the only child allowed to drink coffee with my father. But he never saw it grow."

"Even the cities feel like dreams to me now. Even all those people."

"Those things happened long ago."

The first time my uncle made love to Lenore was at the end of July, in her studio apartment in Andersonville. She invited him up, and my uncle sat on her couch in his tie. Lenore gave my uncle a glass of red wine. Then she sat down beside him. The bed was a large thing before them in that small room. How could they talk about anything with that bed standing there? Both of them wanted this; neither knew how to make it start. Cars passed outside in the night like the sound of the waves on the lake.

Lenore breathed deeply, calmed herself, and then she stood and took a photo album down from her shelf, sat on the edge of her bed with it. She patted the place beside her. "Come and look at some pictures with me, Sam."

Together they leafed through the album's pages of Lenore's time in India, of the town in Maharashtra where she had lived. These were all pictures of people my uncle knew, or rather, of people he had never seen, though he'd seen them every day of his life in Chikmagalur. The poor Hindu and Muslim women Lenore had befriended and worked among. All of those men with their arms crossed on their chests who would never know a thing in this world.

Seeing Lenore among those people in the pictures, Sam remembered how strange it had been to see my mother whirling on her bicycle through Chikmagalur's streets. Who among them hadn't stopped to look? Even when she'd walked in her saris, in her *salwar kameez,* her height and white limbs had blotted out the whole world. How tall my mother had seemed at first. A giant white woman come among them like a god.

But looking at the pictures of Lenore now, it was not the white woman who seemed out of place, but the rest of it, the skinny women, the mustached men, the cattle with their humps lying in the road, the bearded Hindu priests in front of their temple. It was India that had become strange, and he closed the album on Lenore's knees away from that emotion.

"What was the name of this town where you lived?"

"Ahmednagar. Near Poona."

"I was never north of Goa."

"I always preferred the south."

"You have seen more of India than I have."

"And the south was my favorite part."

"The south was all I knew."

Lenore looked at my uncle, took his hand and pressed it to her face. Then she closed her eyes and kissed it. She set the album on the floor, reached and tugged the cord to turn off the lamp.

Lenore was the first white woman my uncle had ever touched in this way. Her breasts, the smoothness of her thighs, her scent, her flavor, even the way she moaned was just the same as other women. But when he'd open his eyes to see his hands on her shoulders, on her waist, he was surprised each time to see how dark his skin looked against hers. Then all these questions would rush into his head just when they didn't belong there, of race, of worth, of who he was, of who he should and shouldn't touch. It had never been this way with anyone else. Only with Lenore. In this way, my uncle came to know that secret thing that my father already knew, what it felt like to make love to a white woman.

As they lay together afterward, Lenore said, "I wanted to do this the very first night."

Sam and Lenore's affair put a lightness into my mother's step. She had her nails done and her hair curled. She dusted every inch of the house. Even the meals were elaborate now, Cornish hens with steamed asparagus, poached salmon sprinkled with capers. My father couldn't help but notice, and finally one Saturday after my uncle had left, he came home from golf and found my mother up on a chair in the kitchen, scrubbing the molding. He set his golf bag on the floor and said, "What is going on, Denise? What is all of this that is suddenly going on with you?"

"Why do you think anything in the world is suddenly going on with me, Lawrence?" my mother had said and smiled.

"You're acting like you did when we first met."

"What's wrong with that? That was a very happy time for me."

"Please don't give me one of your history lessons. Simply tell me what is going on in my house."

My mother hopped off the chair in her rubber gloves. She looked at my father in his golf shoes, his visor, his checkered pants. She said, "Have you completely forgotten how to have fun? So what about you. I called Lenore, and she and Sam have been dating. Things have been going very well for them. Who knows, maybe they are even in love."

My father looked at my mother a long moment as though trying to figure it out. Then he picked up his golf clubs and carried them downstairs. He didn't come back up again. Not for dinner and not for bed. My mother decided to ignore it, though maybe she shouldn't have. If she had gone down to the basement, she would have found my father with a drink in his hand, sitting forward on his couch and scratching his knees, looking at the painting of his lonesome rider, which is what he did when he hatched his plans.

What my father decided was this: My mother should invite Lenore and Sam over on a Saturday night, and he would grill steaks. Then they would all eat and drink wine on the back porch, which he'd recently had screened in. In doing this, my father planned on letting them all know that, firstly, he approved of his younger brother's dating Lenore, and secondly, that he'd forgiven my uncle for all the difficulties he'd caused when he'd first come to America. Though he couldn't allow himself to admit it, my father missed my uncle. Calling Sam to the house on the subject of Lenore would allow my father to address the real issue—his relationship with his younger brother—without losing any face as a firstborn son. For as far behind as my father had left India, there were still many very Indian things about him.

Sam and Lenore came in my uncle's car soon after, on a Saturday evening in late August. My uncle wore a jacket and tie, and Lenore wore a mauve dress. She'd planned on wearing a sari, of course, but my mother had told her not to. All things Indian put my father in a foul mood, especially a white woman in a sari. This was his night to show off his new American screened-in porch. The best thing was to humor him.

My mother wore a blouse and blue jeans as a statement, though she did also wear the pearls my father had given her for their anniversary. My father was dressed for golf. The first of the belly that would come and go over the years could be seen beneath his argyle sweater, and he grimaced as he grilled the meat over coals that were burning too hot. Around him, the year's last lightning bugs lifted out of the yard.

On the porch, the others sipped cold retsina, which my father had learned about from his boss, Marshall Caldwaller, a Harvard man whom he admired and emulated, and who had just come back from a sailing vacation in the Greek Isles, where everyone drank that wine. Sam felt stiff and uncomfortable around my father. After one attempt to make conversation at the grill in which my father had grinned and said out of the corner of his mouth, "What about golf, Sam? Have you ever thought about investing in a set of clubs?" Sam said, "All these American sports, Babu, hey? I don't know about any of it," and he tossed back his wine and went inside. The way my father had said it felt to my uncle as though my father had really wanted to say, "How do you like it now, little brother, fucking these white women?"

My mother's latest hobby was music, and on the turntable she brought out from inside, she played exactly one song each from her new Bob Dylan, Francis Faye, Barry Manilow, and John Lennon albums. Then she put on Simon & Garfunkel to remind Lenore of when they had smoked pot at the beach at Goa on their first R & R, how they'd taken off their tops in the moonlight to splash into the warm water of the Indian Ocean with a couple of scruffy American boys who were traveling the world after their tours in Vietnam. My mother had not slept with her boy on their towel on the beach, but she had let him grip her body with his eyes closed as he moaned over and over, "I missed you. I missed you so much." But Lenore had slept with hers. Later, on the bus back to their very first Indian posting in Hassan, where they shared a two-room functionary's house so close to the busy market that some old man or other was always prying open their shutters to peek in their windows any time of day or night, which caused them to scream and drop things, like breakfast bowls of morning *dal*, or glasses of mango *lassi*, though never their bathing towels, which is what the men were hoping, Lenore had admitted to my mother that it had been her first time with a man. How alive and free she felt away from her family, as though they, and Nebraska, and the Presbyterian Church didn't exist in the world at all. "I don't miss them," Lenore had said on the bus.

They had had other adventures, too, that first year, like the time they'd gone to see the Taj, had run out of money, and let a couple of old Tatas in *dhotis* with a big black Mercedes wine and dine them. The men had bought them Western hats in a boutique on the main street of Agra, showed them the Red Fort in their car's air-conditioned comfort, and at the last hotel bar in Delhi, where the men had conspicuously paid for rooms at the desk, my mother and Lenore had excused themselves from the table to powder their noses, and crawled out the bathroom window in those silly hats. Somehow the Tatas found out the hotel they were staying at, and they showed up in their car to shout curses at them from the street. My mother and Lenore had held each other in the dark of their room all through the tirade, but their luck held out and the proprietor did not let the Tatas in.

And then of course there was Lenore's brief affair with a married doctor from the Marathi Ministry of Health, the opal ring he'd given her that Lenore threw in the waves at Chowpatti Beach when the doctor told her his wife was pregnant again. Lenore had written my mother all about it over the months that it was happening. She made a big stink at both the Peace Corps and the ministry, and the doctor received a transfer for himself and his family to Madras. My mother had not liked that part of it, though she'd never said that to Lenore.

The giddiness of what being at my father's house meant was all over Lenore at that dinner, and while her face was flushed with the wine and the knowledge of what she'd been letting my uncle do to her in her apartment, my uncle Sam sat at the table in his tie and was quiet. They smoked cigarettes after the meal while my mother went in to check on me, and when she did, my father leaned back from the table in his chair, patted his belly, and sighed in his happiness and wine. He smiled at my uncle then as though to let him know that this house and this yard and this screened porch that kept the mosquitoes out and this table and this food that they had eaten all belonged to him. My uncle knew my father was thinking, "How about all of this, Samuel? These women? This porch? All this meat we've eaten? Could we have eaten this much meat in a month back there? What an awful place. But it's over now. We have made it out. Now we are here." My uncle Sam spun the last petal of his wine in his glass as he thought about it, and then he swallowed down what my father said.

My mother came back nursing me through her opened blouse, and she said to my uncle and Lenore, "Here's my big boy. My Francisco. He's made me so happy. And now isn't it good that you are happy, too?"

My father fell forward on his chair and folded his hands on the table. He said roughly to my uncle in Konkani, *"E puri kon achi?"* "Whose daughter is she, isn't it, Sam? Papa will be proud."

My father slept on his couch in the basement that night because my mother locked the bedroom door against him. My father didn't care. All the things he had hoped to accomplish he had, and he happily sent himself off to sleep with a few last tumblers of single malt.

Sam drove Lenore to her building, and though they listened to music all of the way, it was as though they went in silence. "Come up with me, Sammy," Lenore said to him.

"It is late. We are tired. It is better that I go."

"Will you call me?"

"Tomorrow."

"I had a nice time, you know."

She waved good-bye from the door, let herself in. When the door closed behind her, my uncle Sam began his drive home. There had been no arguments or apologies at the dinner, just as my uncle had known there wouldn't be, and still much had happened. It had all been done with glances and gestures, subtle words, the clothes, the food. Big things were always discussed this way among the Konkans. Babu had welcomed him back to the fold. But Babu also wanted him to marry this woman. That Sam hadn't gone upstairs with Lenore this night meant something, too.

In her bed as she reeled from the drinking, Lenore understood that Sam had received permission from his older brother to marry her. And in her heart of hearts, she was certain she was happy.

At home in his nothing life in his nothing apartment off Division, Sam smoked cigarettes at his window and watched a cop car pull over two Hispanics on the street. The driver staggered through the sobriety test, and while the rest of the world was asleep, my uncle witnessed the cops put the men in cuffs, press their heads down to guide them into the back of the car. No one in the world had seen this but him. And yet it existed. The cops stood together in the beams of their headlights, shared a joke that made them laugh, and one touched the other on the shoulder. No one but him had seen this either.

My uncle brushed his teeth in his tiled bathroom, spit, rinsed his mouth. Then he looked at his face in the mirror. Was he getting older? He could not see it. His face was as his face had always been, even despite its being in this place, in this small apartment in America. He undressed in his room, hung his clothes on their hangers in the closet, lay on his bed to sleep, and after a half an hour of it, he sat up and looked at the dark.

It was time, Lenore told him, that they meet her parents in Lincoln. Sam decided to let this happen, too. Lenore called my mother and told her they were going, and the next Saturday that my uncle darkened my mother's doorway, my mother ran to open it onto him.

"Can you get the time off work?"

"They have already given it to me."

"You must look them in the eyes, Sam."

"I will look them in their eyes."

"Lenore is a nice girl."

"Lenore is fine to me."

"You must be good to her and give her time with all the difficult things that will come."

"I know this, too, Denise."

"You are a long way from home, Sam."

"I feel that."

"You can be whoever you want to be here."

"I know that as well."

Lenore and Sam drove in Sam's car through the cornfields of Illinois, and it was September, and the corn stood tall in its rows as far as they could see. At the Mississippi River, they stood on the bridge and waved down a motorcyclist who snapped pictures of them with Lenore's camera without taking his helmet off. The pictures still exist, taking up a page of one of my uncle's disjointed albums from that time. The albums speak of the confusion of my uncle's heart: page after page of different sizes of prints, odds and ends, the photos all given to my uncle by other people. There's him and Les freshly shaven in my father's basement the night they arrived in America, him and Les dressed in Cubbie blue and holding up beers at Wrigley. Him and Javier at a neighborhood yard party, drunk, crossing their arms in macho poses, him in his Polk Brothers uniform and smiling with his hand on a washing machine still wrapped in the plastic. Him at the wheel of his Cutlass, a cigarette in his lips, him and my mother in my father's backyard in Ridge Lawn, the lilac bushes in bloom behind them. And then two pictures from that trip to Nebraska; my uncle and Lenore on the bridge over the Mississippi, a skinny Indian in a white collared shirt and a curvy white girl in a scarf and sunglasses, leaning against the railing like a movie star. And then the two of them turned around and leaned over the railing looking down into the water, Lenore with her left leg cocked up behind her. Years later, my uncle would touch his finger to those pictures as he'd tell me the stories behind each one of them.

"What do you think of this part of America?" Lenore had asked my uncle Sam as they drove through the wheat fields of Iowa.

"It's big."

"What do you think of all this empty space?"

"It makes me feel quiet."

Lenore made a joke as they passed through Council Bluffs that they should find a motel room and make love a last time. Because at her parents' house, they would have to sleep in separate rooms. Sam drove on, and Lenore took her heels off and put her feet up on the dashboard. She coasted her hand out the window on the wind and said, "It's been three years since I've seen them."

Visiting Lenore's parents was like visiting dead people. They were formal and old in their living room, in clothes as

drab as the curtains over the windows. Their measured conversation revealed that they had been killed by their daughter's
long absences, first by her time in India, and now even more
so by the time she'd spent away from them in Chicago. They
put Sam in Lenore's brother's room, the child they loved in
the void created by their other child, a good boy, as they said,
a manager at the gasoline distillery in Omaha. Sam folded his
clothes into the brother's empty drawers, and the house felt
as quiet around him as the people who lived in it. The son
had played baseball through college, and there were trophies
on the dresser, pictures of him on the walls with his various
teams. In them, he was a pleasant-looking young blond man.

At dinner, the parents clasped their hands before them for
the prayer, and Sam bowed his head and thought of all the
long blocks of Lincoln they'd driven through to get here, the
homes, the lawns, that the people all around them lived like
this. Lenore's father said with his eyes closed, "We thank you,
O Lord, for the safe return of our daughter once again, we
pray that we make up for time that has been lost, that we can
come again to understanding ourselves as a family. We welcome Lenore's friend Sam and hope that he feels welcome in
our home. We'd like him to know that we respect his culture
and the distance he has traveled to visit us."

Lenore wore her white sari to dinner and told stories of
the dust and noise of India as she again showed her parents
her pictures from the albums she had brought with her like
documents to plead her defense. Again and again as she explained the details, she said to my uncle, "Isn't that right,
Sam? Isn't that how it is?" To which my uncle could only say,
"That is how it is," as her parents paused in their eating at
his confirmation that the women of that foreign place really
did build their cooking fires from dried cow dung, that the

Hindus really did worship the lingam by pouring milk over sculptures of it.

"Will you come to church with us in the morning?" Lenore's father said to my uncle when Sam asked permission to go to bed, and of course my uncle said, "Yes." Lenore squeezed his hand and smiled at him from her chair. Then my uncle went upstairs and closed the door of that room. He lay on the covers of the brother's bed in his clothes, looking at those trophies. Soon, the voices downstairs, though not loud, carried the sounds of disagreement and hurt up to him.

Late in the night, neither having changed out of his clothes nor slept, my uncle Sam opened the drawers of the dresser, quietly packed his suitcase. He put on and tied his shoes and went out to his car. By dawn, he was a hundred miles west, and within three days, he was at the Grand Canyon. He did not have much money, and he slept in the backseat. He bought a cooler in Denver and lived off roast beef sandwiches. He sent my mother a postcard from Phantom Ranch, at the bottom of the canyon, which arrived at our house stamped CARRIED BY MULE; and from the redwood forest on the coast of California, he sent a postcard with a scene of those trees printed on an actual shingle of wood. The message read, "These are very tall trees. Sam." Then he disappeared into the Pacific Northwest through the winter. He did call Javier, who shouldered in my uncle's door and collected his few important things in a box. Javier also wired my uncle the money he had asked for to a Western Union in Portland. Javier dropped the box off at my parents' house. He said to my mother, "I'm saying prayers for him, Denise."

When Lenore called my mother from Lincoln, she was neither angry nor embarrassed. She asked my mother, "Why do you think he needed to do that?" and my mother said back, "You know how difficult their lives are here." Lenore returned to Chicago on the bus. A few years later, she married an actuary who had always dreamed of visiting India. Lenore invited my mother to the wedding. The timing was bad for my mother, and after that, Lenore didn't call again. Many years later, Lenore mailed those pictures from the bridge over the Mississippi to my mother in the same envelope as some shots of her three children. In her letter she wrote, "Were we ever really there?"

For the rest of our lives, my uncle Sam would let slip with comments like, "Salmon are covered in slime," or "Eagles eat at the garbage dump." But for six months, through that winter and spring, my parents neither heard from him nor had any clue what he was up to. My father traveled often to New York and London on business, and he bought an at-home green to practice his putting in the basement. He didn't mention Sam to my mother, and my mother didn't mention Sam to him.

My mother read many paperback horror novels during this time, nursed me, left my father to his work and me to my growing. She lost weight and was so often too tired to host Mrs. Firth or Mrs. Coleman when they dropped by that they stopped calling, too.

Late in the spring, the flowers and trees in bloom, my uncle Sam pulled into our driveway. It was a Wednesday afternoon, and my mother had turned thirty-two three days before. Even before my uncle could ring the bell, my mother had let him in.

Sam's hair was longer, he'd shaved off the sideburns. He looked younger than he had before. He wore a blue knit shirt under a blue down vest, and there was a quiet in him that hadn't previously been there.

"I thought I'd never see you."

"Where could I return but here?"

"I worried about you every day."

"Every day of it the only thing in my mind was you."

My mother pulled my uncle to her, and they kissed in the doorway for the very first time. My uncle pushed the door shut with his foot. Then they stopped and opened their eyes.

"You've seen the Grand Canyon."

"To the very bottom."

"You've seen those tall trees."

"I see them even now."

It was just the two of them, their grand friendship, their long and aching desire. My uncle drove away before my father came home for dinner.

Gore Road

My father and uncle's cousin Winston wanted to come to America. Sam was living in Logan Square near the Kennedy Expressway at this time, in a small rental house where he grew a garden in the back. He had an orange chair in his living room with a feel to it like sheep's wool, and when my mother would take me over for a visit, my uncle would hold me in his lap and spin us around and around in the chair until I was dizzy and laughing and glad because just what I had known would happen is exactly what did. My uncle had become a great cook in his *lungi,* his bachelorhood, and while I didn't like most Indian foods, I liked my uncle's *biriyani.* He put extra lamb chunks in the saffron rice of it just for me, which I'd pick out and eat with my fingers on the table where they'd set me with a bowl of it. Often, my mother would take me out to the garden in my bonnet to let me stumble around and lose myself in the colored rows of my uncle's blossoming plants.

My mother had put on weight and shortened her hair, but this only made her an even prettier woman than she had been. She had hips, pink in her cheeks, and the cutting of her hair had released the color of her eyes. She liked to drink beer, and smoke, and they did not worry about my father, who was always away on business. I remember seeing my mother kiss my uncle in the kitchen those times as he cooked, and I would stop eating to look at them. My mother would help herself to a beer from my uncle's fridge as though his house also belonged to her.

"Have you heard from Les?" my mother would ask as she reclined on my uncle's couch with her beer. My uncle would stop spinning me in the chair long enough to tell her, "He called the other night. He is happy and doing fine. He likes the desert. I saw it once, you know. Too hot for me, but he says it suits him."

My uncle Les had left the navy the year before and had settled in Tucson with a white girl he'd met while stationed at the naval base in San Diego. He was an HVAC repairman and seemed content with what his path had brought him. His life departed from ours in that way.

My uncle Sam took us to Cubs' games, to Saturdays at the beach on the lake. He had graduated from washing machine salesman to real estate agent, though when money was tight, he would still sell stereos out of his trunk, which his old friend Javier had taught him to do. He plied this trade among the growing Indian community on Devon Avenue, and when he'd take my mother and me for North Indian food at The Taj restaurant, sometimes the waiters he'd sold stereos to would come quickly to him and my mother and say, "Hey, Konkan D'Sai! So long we have not seen you here. Any new deals in your trunk?"

Even though I could not yet speak, my uncle began to tell me things about India, that I was a half-Indian boy even though I was white, that one day I must see the beautiful Taj Mahal as my mother had done and send him a postcard to tell him that I had seen it. He'd bounce me on his knee as he'd tell me these things. What could I do but laugh and hug him?

One night at his house, my uncle brought out a blue aerogram from his room covered in the curlicues of Kannada script, and he read it to my mother while I dozed in a sleeping bag on the living room floor. The letter was from Winston, who had only been a boy when my father and mother and uncles had left India. None of them really knew him. He had not been able to get the education that my father had, he wrote, but he had done his best in public school, and he wanted a chance to come to America. Couldn't they try to help him, as my grandfather had once helped them all with the gold?

"Do you remember this boy?" my mother asked.

"There were so many boys like this," my uncle said.

"But he must be good if he's gotten himself together to write a letter."

"Which one of them is bad?"

"One more here wouldn't hurt, would it, Sam?"

"I am not a citizen, there is nothing I can do," my uncle said and shrugged.

"Then there is nothing else we can do but let me sponsor him. Lawrence won't like it, but Lawrence doesn't have to know. I'll sponsor him over and he'll live here with you as you lived with us when you first came. We've settled it already. It will be nice to have someone here who still has the scent of India on him."

But it wasn't as easy as that, my mother and uncle soon discovered. Because Winston wasn't an immediate blood relation to my father, the government did not recognize my mother as someone who could be his sponsor. She and Sam tried everything, my mother taking the train downtown with me in the stroller while my father was at work to meet my uncle at the immigration office early in the mornings. They'd take a number like at the deli and wait in the chairs, and with them they brought all the documents they thought they'd need: bank statements, the title to my parents' house, the titles to their cars, my mother's birth certificate, letters of recommendation from her Peace Corps friends who were now lawyers and teachers all over America. The petitioners at that time were mainly Mexicans and Latin Americans, but there were also Poles and Haitians, and swelling numbers of Cambodians and Vietnamese, spilled over from the wars in Southeast Asia. My mother and my uncle made their way to the immigration officers' cubicles a half dozen times, and a half dozen times the immigration officers listened to all that they had to say and calmly handed them back the forms.

Since they were in the city anyway, my mother and uncle would eat lunch at a cheap Chinese takeaway, then walk through the windy downtown, my mother's dress rippling around her calves as she pushed my stroller through the business crowds. My uncle leaned into the wind as he smoked. One time, they went up to the observation deck of the Sears Tower and tried to pick out their neighborhoods through the haze of the city's smog, and another time they went to the Field Museum and looked at all the large animals of the world that Teddy Roosevelt had shot and had had stuffed and donated. When the weather warmed and it was May, they took rolls of bread and a package of Camembert that my mother had brought with her, and walked to the beach beside the planetarium. They unscrewed the cap from the bottle of red wine my uncle had stepped into a shop to buy, and sipped from it—the bottle wrapped in its brown paper bag. Some kids were playing hooky, the girls squealing in Spanish and splashing water at the boys from the lake's edge, the boys peeling off their shirts and jeans from their lean bodies to dive into the cold lake and wrestle with the girls like seals. Gulls coasted by on outstretched wings. Far out on the lake were the white triangles of the season's first sailboats.

My mother rolled her dress to her knees to feel the sun on her skin. She said, "Ever since I lived in Chikmagalur, I cannot help but think about the wider world. I think about myself as I lay on my bed, the world moving me on it as it turns, the planet turning about the sun, all the other planets and their moons. Sometimes I feel big in myself, but other times I feel very small. And then I wonder what any of this can possibly mean? Why I should have brought a child into this world when I don't even know the answer? But then I think about how much I love Francisco, and then I'm sure that it really does matter. I don't feel that all of the time, but most of the time I do. The spring here makes me happy. It's nice to open the windows and hear the new leaves moving in the breeze. Do you ever think about life like that, Sam?"

"I wonder why I should be here sitting and looking at this lake when I grew up in Chikmagalur and only knew the things of that place. I think, 'How could I have known all of this would become my life? How could I have arrived right here?' And I look about me and everything seems strange. Then I become confused and quiet. You have more time for it, Denise, than I do. I am always too busy with work. When I drive in the car, stand at my window at night, I think about it. But then there is work and the people I must deal with. Sometimes when I am driving, I see some trees or flowers or water and I want to do nothing but stop and look. Over here there is work and no time. In India, there was family and no space."

"Sometimes I worry about what will happen to us, Sam."

"Everyone in the world must worry that."

"I worry about what will happen to my son, and I worry about you and Lawrence and everyone. What will happen to all of us?"

"The moment must be now, Denise. We will all be fine."

"Are you sure of that?"

"How can it be any other way?"

"How is that something you can know?"

My uncle shook his head, looked out at the clouds scudding over the lake. My mother, too, was quiet. The teenagers were lying in the sand in each other's arms now, whispering to one another, their wet bodies drying in the sun. At the far end of the beach, a woman approached with a black dog that strained on its leash. It was a fine day. My mother said, "Lawrence wants to have another child."

My uncle closed his eyes. He said, "Children are the riches of the family."

"It doesn't bother you, Sam?"

"It is normal that a man should want to have children with his wife."

My uncle lit a cigarette and looked at the lake, and what else could my mother do but that same thing? She tilted her face to the sun and my uncle stroked her hair awhile, from her scalp to the nape of her neck. Then my mother cut the bread with the knife she'd brought, spread the cheese onto the bread, and they ate on the bench where they sat.

"Don't eat that, Francisco!" my mother yelled at me about the cigarette butt I'd found in the sand where she'd set me, and my uncle ran to pick me up. He fished the butt out of my mouth with his finger, brushed the sand from my bottom with his hand, carried me back to my mother on the bench, sat me on it between them. The passing joggers certainly took me as their child.

Steeped in my cousin Winston's pleas and all means of sponsoring him legally explored and dead, my mother and uncle became more creative in their thinking. One Saturday afternoon, lying together in my parents' bed, my mother petted my uncle's face to draw him back from sleep. She said, "Sam? I've had some new ideas about helping Winston."

My uncle said, "I've been thinking on that, too."

"I think you should talk to Javier. He must know all about getting people into this country. He's your friend. Call him. Explain what's going on and see what he has to say."

"I thought of that already. If Winston was to come in through Mexico, Javier said he would know who to call. But that is a hard and long way, and often they are caught. That's not the way for one young Indian boy on his own. Javier says to try Canada. The visa laws are not so strict. I am going to see the Sardar on Devon Avenue who Babu sold the gold to. All of these new Indians who have come in have not all come in on visas."

My father of course knew nothing of what was going on, not about their trips to the immigration office, their walks on the beach, their feelings for each other, or any of it. The first week of July that year, he was sent to London for a seminar on marine shipping insurance, and while there, managed to work in a day at Wimbledon. Despite the infamous labor strike that year by the ATP players, my father was able to witness the beginnings of "Borgmania," the mobbing of the young tennis star by screaming women every time he arrived for a match. He saw both Ilie Năstase and Billie Jean King dismantle their opponents with brilliant backhand volleys on Centre Court. But more than any of that, he was able to savor again the impeccable decorum of Britain, taking afternoon tea in the public clubhouse, having pleasant conversations with the ticket taker, with the girl in the uniform who waited on him, and the club official in his jacket who directed him to the "loo." They had all addressed my father as "sir." He left the All England Club at the end of the day on the Tube, under his arm a neatly tucked umbrella, which he'd brought in case of rain, as any proper British person would. My father, as my mother would later describe him to me with a smile, was like a pig in shit in England.

I don't want to portray my father as a cuckolded fool because, of the three of them, he was having the happier time. He wore his Wimbledon T-shirt at home after work, he practiced his golf game, he traded in his Buick for a slightly used Audi, red, which he polished in the driveway with the tenderness and attention Pygmalion paid to his statue. This was a period in my father's life of work and advancement and solidifying his position in America. If there would ever be a hiccup in his ascent, now wasn't it. Now and again he'd tell my mother to get dressed up, to hire a high school girl from our church to watch me for the night, and then he'd take my mother in his Audi to a company social at a fine restaurant downtown, often the Italian Village. My mother would regulate his drinking masterfully at these events by whispering to him, "Your cheeks are getting their glow, Lawrence," behind her napkin, and he'd later say to her, as he drove them home with one eye closed, "Why do you always have some comment to say to me?" But when he'd wake in the morning and realize he hadn't said a single embarrassing thing to anyone, he'd kiss my mother's cheek as she scrambled eggs in the kitchen for breakfast in her nightgown to thank her and say, "Where have you been all of my life?" He'd said that to her in India when they'd been courting, having picked it up from a movie.

My uncle was sending money back to India now and again, not as much or as steadily as my father, but he sent what he could. But what he did do that my father didn't was write to the Indians in a real way, letters to my grandparents full of details and news of this life in America. In this way, my uncle Sam became the tether to India, whereas my father often didn't put anything in the envelope but the check. "How is Babu? How is the baby Francisco?" the Indians would write to my uncle Sam. My uncle would unfold a new aerogram at his kitchen table from the sheaf of them that he kept, light a cigarette to think about it, then set his pen to telling them all the things they needed to hear: "Babu works like a *harijan*. The boy grows like a tamarisk."

My uncle's life was harder then than he would have let on to anyone. He didn't know enough people in the city to have more than the vaguest success at real estate, and the reason that he'd rented this house, which he barely could afford, was more about giving my father the illusion that he was getting on in the world than about any desire he himself had for the extra space. Trying to live up to his perception of my father's expectations was as ingrained in him as a second-born Konkan son as conquering the world was in my firstborn father.

Week by week, letters arrived from Winston, the tone of them growing more hopeless as the months passed. "What am I to do here, Uncle? Pedal a rickshaw? Push a cart? Always to wear slippers on my feet? I am young and have energy. Why would the world see me waste my youth? Just because of a vagary of birth?"

Sam kept the letters in a bundle in the drawer of the night-stand beside his bed. They were only inches from his head as he slept. Of course they infused his dreams.

Sam was no longer the naive young man he'd been when he first arrived. Any honeymoon he may have had with America had long since evolved into sipping Dunkin' Donuts coffee in the dark mornings in his car, listening to Cubs games on the radio in his nightshirt as he panfried chicken gizzards and onions on his stove for dinner. Though he'd had fun when he'd first come, at times now he felt the nation subsuming him into another of the multitude of people who did not matter to it except for the work they produced and the taxes they paid. The thing with Winston began to consume him, to take on an import that it probably really didn't have. If the boy wanted to come here, then the boy must come. Maybe then he would understand that life in America was not simply happiness. Finally, one Sunday in July, my uncle went to Devon Avenue to see the Sikh who had bought my grandmother's gold half a dozen years before, whom my father had taken him and Les to after they'd shaved off their mustaches because the Sikhs of Devon Avenue were specialists at finding new immigrants jobs.

What had once been a one-room storefront displaying a few jewelry cases, with discount basmati rice stacked in the back, had become half a block: the Singh Brothers Jewelers and Emporium. They even had their own lot off the side, where my uncle parked his car. Stepping into the store now, Sam saw two things instantly: They had white girls working the checkout lines, and Mohan Singh had gotten very fat. He sat on a stool in the corner in his sky-blue turban, cracking peanuts out of their shells from the sack he sat beside, his

wrists jangling with silver bracelets and chains as he watched
a line of young Hindus carrying twenty-five-kilo rice sacks on
their backs out to patrons' cars. Aside from the white girls, the
emporium still had the smell and bustle of India, and seeing
the fat Sikh in his turban reminded my uncle of what could be
accomplished in this country if one had the kind of determi-
nation he himself did not.

The Sikh looked him up and down as he approached,
glanced at his shoes as though taking in the brand, looked
at his face as though judging his worth as a man. Then he
cracked a peanut like warming dice in his hand, popped the
beans in his mouth. *"Mujhe tum bahut yaad aate ho,"* he said
to my uncle in Hindi, and winked. "You're looking for work
again, Konkan D'Sai, isn't it?"

"I'm not looking for work, Sardarji," my uncle said to the
Sikh, and smiled.

"And you still can't have that gold back," the Sikh said,
and wagged his finger.

"Sardar, we have long since begun to send our mother
money for new gold."

"That brother of yours, maybe he is sending money back.
But you and that smaller brother. I am sure that the two of
you are not buying gold. Your elder brother brought you two
to me like lambs to market, told me any job for you would do,
just find something. You should be glad that you were speaking English at that time or I would have had you carrying rice
sacks on your back like these useless Marathas. What is the
little one doing?"

"Married in the West to a white woman. He served in the
navy."

"Ah, that is good. It is good that you Konkans are paying
your dues to Uncle Sam. And you?"

"Real estate."

"Then you should be owning a Mercedes-Benz by now, Konkan D'Sai. Tell me, is your older brother owning a Mercedes-Benz?"

"My brother Lawrence drives an Audi."

"That is good. And you?"

"Not an Audi."

"Come and drive a taxi for me, Konkan. I'll have you in a Mercedes-Benz in a decade. Now," the Sikh said as he stood from the stool, "tell me what you want."

"Immigration," my uncle said.

"Over here? Or still over there?"

"Over there."

"How many?"

"Just one."

"Come to the office," the Sikh said and took my uncle by the elbow. "Out here is for shopping, but in there is for business."

In the simple office crowded with steel desks, the Sardar chased away the women working at them in their embroidered *salwar kameez*s, motioned to a plastic chair, and my uncle sat in it. It was a windowless room with a Chinese calendar on the wall with the girl of the month holding a parasol opened over her shoulder before a woodland scene with a red pagoda on a hillside. The desks were buried in papers and receipts, and the sound of the busy tandoori kitchen next door came through the wall. It was hot in there, despite the fans. The Sardar folded his hands on the desktop, his *kara* and other bracelets clinking on the metal of it, and he looked at my uncle a long moment as though sizing him up before dealing a hand of poker. Two young Sardars in saffron turbans and black beards came in and leaned against the wall like toughs. One was chewing *paan,* and he spit strings of the red juice into a styrofoam 7-Eleven cup.

"What do you want, and what do you have to give, Konkan?" Singh said to my uncle.

"There is a young cousin who would like to come. It is not the necessary blood, so we cannot sponsor him. We would like to know the possibilities. My brother is not involved in this. What I have to give is my real estate license."

The three Sardars conversed some moments in Punjabi, which my uncle could not follow. The sound of it was neither positive nor negative, more bored than anything, and when they were finished, the one not chewing and spitting the *paan* went out. Singh cracked his knuckles in two rippling sets. The joints of his knuckles were alive with hair.

"Money?"

"None."

"Contacts here?"

"None but me."

"Immigration is becoming difficult, Konkan D'Sai. Truly difficult. Too many are coming. Too many browns and less and less whites. Uncle Sam has noticed. Still, where else in the world do we Indians have left to go? Papers will cost more than you have, even if we could arrange them."

"I understand this, Sardarji-baba."

"We want to help you. We like you Konkans. You are a very small people in India, as are we Sikhs. But when you roar in the crowd, your roar is heard like ours is. We are the soldiers of India, you are its Jews. Both are good. Here is what you must do. Uncle Sam is granting visas all the time for engineers. America is sucking out India's brains. No matter. The engineers don't need to live like we did when we first came.

They have jobs and money, they need homes. You know real estate, you will find them homes. You will give your commission to me. You will place ten in homes and forfeit your commission."

"Seven," my uncle said.

"Spoken like a Jew Konkan. Eight and we are settled. Now, you write to this cousin, tell him to apply for a tourist visa to Canada. The laws there are behind what they are here. If he can secure the visa, then there is a way. I like you Konkans. It is strange and good that you are also here. Every piece of India should be represented here so that we can all feel at home. Agree to this, Konkan?"

"I agree, Sardarji," my uncle said.

The fat Sikh sat back and clapped his hands, and he spoke to the young Sikh spitting into the cup. Soon enough a plate of purple tandoori chicken was brought in with naan, and my uncle and Singh ate a quick meal of it to seal the deal, which was the way.

"Is it going to happen?" my mother asked my uncle as he held her.

"It is going to happen," my uncle told her.

"But you've never shown houses, Sam."

"I am going to show houses now."

"You are the best of India," my mother told him, "resourceful like no one else in this world."

My uncle wrote the necessary letters to India, and just before Christmas, my cousin Winston wrote back that a Gujarati tile merchant had transferred enough funds into his father's account to satisfy the Canadian embassy that he would go back home because of it: The Canadians had granted him a ninety-day tourist visa. The price had been expensive, the Gu-jarati had taken all the bangles off his mother's and married sister's wrists, but Winston wrote that soon enough he would be in America and working, and he would quickly buy the bangles back. Sam went and saw the Sardar, and the Sardar congratulated him and gave him an envelope. In the envelope was a piece of paper, and on the paper was a map. The map was a hand-drawn detailing of the rural roads that connected Canada with Vermont. On one of those roads was an *X*, and the Sardar had written in vernacular Hindi, "Lax border con-trol at this crossing." My uncle folded the paper into the bible in his dresser drawer and the following Saturday, he and my mother looked at it over beers in my uncle's kitchen.

"Lawrence is going to New Orleans for a conference in early February," my mother said. "He's very excited because he'll get to see Mardi Gras. You know how he likes all those things. I'll leave Francisco with the Firths, and we'll drive in your car to Vermont. Winston will come down from Mon-treal, and we'll wait in Burlington until he calls us. Then we'll follow the map and pick him up."

"I'll write to Winston with the dates and times."

"Do you think he can manage to get it right?"

"If he means to come as much as his letters say he does, then he'll be waiting at the border even before we get there."

My uncle wrote the letter and Winston wrote back that he understood. There was no quibbling in his letter that Canada was a place he'd never been, that maybe he wouldn't be able to manage the French language in Montreal. He simply wrote back, "I will be there. And, Uncle, I am very happy." Then it was for my mother and my uncle to wait quietly in anticipa-tion of their trip, to keep their excitement from my father, to think about the time they'd have alone together, as neither of them could bring themselves to mention that part of it.

My father, on the other hand, crossed off the days to Mardi Gras with red *X*s on the calendar on our fridge as though counting down the days to his election to heaven. In his excitement, he even began to say things to my mother like, "The women show their breasts for nothing more than a necklace of plastic beads," and "If I wasn't already married, Denise, perhaps I'd be about to have the most wondrous days of my life."

What could my mother do but roll her eyes? She said to my father, "Watch your drinking, Lawrence. The last thing I want to happen is to see you drunk in a jail in New Orleans."

My father said back, "I know that you only say these things because you are jealous. I'll take a lot of pictures and bring you and Francisco souvenirs. Maybe I'll even keep some of those necklaces for my own. Everyone is saying that this conference is less about work than it is about Mardi Gras. Six years without a break, imagine? Finally I get to have my reward."

My mother dropped my father off at O'Hare in the snow. He was bursting with excitement, had bought new white slacks, a cuffed red shirt, and a blue corduroy hat just for the occasion. He kissed my mother squarely and deeply at the curb, pinched her ass like he hadn't done in a very long time. My mother loved my father when he was in moods like that. Soon enough, he was gone through the sliding doors, and my mother also loved someone else.

My mother left me with the Firths on the pretense of visiting a sister, who didn't exist, in Moline. The fact was my mother had no idea where her sisters lived, and the Firths were very glad to have me because they'd never had children.

My uncle was sitting at our kitchen table in his jacket, waiting for my mother to come back. I remember crying when my mother kissed my cheek good-bye, but also that the Firths had two blue-eyed Siamese cats, and that I was soon engaged in tormenting them.

My mother and uncle had two days to themselves before they had to be at the motel in Burlington where they would wait for Winston's call from Montreal. And though they had to stay focused on driving in order to get there on time, they also had enough time to make a trip of it. They drove through Chicago in the late and gray winter morning, and the afternoon saw them across Indiana's and Ohio's bleak fields of snow. In western Pennsylvania, they turned north. My mother had brought all of her favorite eight tracks, Dylan of course, John Lennon, and Fleetwood Mac, and my uncle had brought Marvin Gaye and Al Green. They stopped once to have a late lunch at a truckers' diner on the interstate, where they each drank two bottles of Stroh's. As they drove into New York State late in the night, my uncle rested his hand on my mother's thigh, and she looked at the dark woods passing at the side of the road beyond the reach of the headlights.

In their motel outside Buffalo, finally, my uncle held my mother's body to his as the moon arced in the finest of slivers across the sky in its new light. Neither of them slept, though it didn't have anything to do with the moon.

Burlington was a historic and nice town once they reached it, the forests leading up to the city deep and green against the snow, many of the homes and college buildings from before the turn of the century, and students in scarves hurried everywhere. My mother and uncle held hands as they walked up the main street toward the high steeple of the Unitarian church. Would my mother like a candle, my uncle asked her outside the beeswax-candle shop, and though my mother nodded yes, she also said she didn't need to be bought anything. Would my uncle like a pair of fur earmuffs? My uncle said that he would, but also, that his ears weren't really all that cold. In the late afternoon they went bowling, which my mother liked to do, and for dinner they had chicken-fried steak at Denny's. My mother's cheeks grew rosy in the motel room after a couple of Michelobs from the six-pack they bought, and then Johnny Carson took his golf swing into the band to end his monologue that opened *The Tonight Show*. When my uncle opened the drapes to look out at the lot, he saw falling snow.

"Snow will always be beautiful to me, Denise. So long I wondered what it would look like, feel like. It is the one thing I will never tire of in this life," my uncle said softly as he looked at it, and my mother smiled at him from the bed and said, "And what about me?"

"About you?"

"Yes, about me, Sammy."

"You were in my dreams even before we met."

"It's wrong, you know."

"I don't know what's wrong or right in this life," he said, and pulled from his beer while standing at the window.

"Then maybe we should run away for good. Live every day in rooms like this. Leave this world and its garbage and finally be happy."

"I wonder if it seems happy to us only because we can't do that."

"But don't you ever wonder what it would be like if we could?"

"I don't torment myself with impossible things."

"Why do you tell yourself it's impossible?"

"Because you are my brother's wife. Because I love my brother, as well as you, and you are the mother of his child, who I also love."

"I made a mistake."

"It wasn't a mistake."

"I married Lawrence because I wanted to marry India. Now I've given my life up for that."

"Your marriage to Lawrence has brought you many good things."

"You know, there was once a time when I didn't know what a Konkan was."

"Konkans are now half your life."

"Once there was a time when you knew nothing of America."

"And now America is all around me."

"Come and sit by me, Sam."

"I know that I shouldn't."

"Come and sit by me, my Sam."

"It is the one thing I know simply that I should not do."

My uncle went and sat beside my mother on the bed. The people on TV were talking, but my uncle and my mother couldn't hear them. My mother took my uncle's bottle from his hand, set it beside hers on the nightstand. Then she reached over and turned out the light.

"We shouldn't."

"I know we shouldn't."

"It's bad, what we do."

"Then we are bad."

"Then they will always say of us that we were bad people."

"Let them say that, then. Do we care? Who are those other people? Let's forget there are any other people tonight and not share this with anyone."

Only the phone's ringing in the morning roused my uncle from my mother's arms.

"Uncle Sam?" Winston's voice said from the phone, "I am here. I am in Montreal. I came off the plane last night. I am at a student hostel and all of the people are speaking French. What am I to do?"

My uncle stood up from the bed in the dark room. He said into the phone, "Listen to me, Winston. You have to get this exactly right. You get into a cab and tell the driver to take you to Philipsburg. If he asks any questions, tell him you are going to visit your uncle. If he tells you a higher price, then pay it. If he runs the meter, pay him that, too. When you get to Philipsburg, you must go to the end of the town. Don't let anyone see you. At the end of the town, go into the trees. Keep the highway in your sight. But you must stay in the trees, and if any cars come along the road, hide yourself until they pass. You have to do this for four miles. Do you understand me, little cousin? Like walking in Chikmagalur from the soccer pitch to the water tank. It is not a short walk. Stay close to the highway so that you don't lose it. But don't go so far into the trees that you get lost. When you see the signs marking the border, go into the trees so that you cannot see the road. When you feel that it is safe, come to the road again. Then it isn't far to the first crossing. This will be Gore Road. Wait in the trees until you see a blue car pass twice on it. If it goes and then comes back, that will be our car."

"Are there tigers in this forest, Uncle?"

"Why are you asking me such a thing?"

"Are there animals in this forest, Uncle?"

"They've killed all the animals, Winston. Do not fear."

"I was not ready for this cold."

"So you are beginning to know about America. Enough.

Now go and buy the things you need. Buy a jacket and gloves. Don't worry now about saving money. South along the road in the trees is all. Do not talk to anyone. If you see any people, run away. We'll be waiting for you at five P.M. Today will be cold, but tonight you will be with us in America. Bring me a souvenir. Buy me some small thing so that I will know that you were in Canada."

"I am going to make it, Uncle."

"I know that you will."

"I am going to become a very great man in America."

"Then you will share that money with me."

My uncle hung up the phone. He looked at my mother. It was still dark in the room.

My mother and uncle watched television in the room to pass the day, *The Price Is Right, The Days of Our Lives,* and in the afternoon they went out for Chinese food and came back and watched *Emergency!* On the news were scenes from Cambodia, another Khmer Rouge bombing in Phnom Penh. Then they went out to my uncle's car and drove the few minutes in the settling evening to Gore Road. All around them was falling snow. They did not play music or smoke cigarettes. Nothing they had ever done had prepared them for this. Sam drove a mile along Gore Road's dark length, and then he turned the car around. My mother said, "He could freeze to death out there."

There were no other cars this night, nothing but trees in their mantles of snow, and even the tracks the car had left behind were covered by the time they turned around again. After three more passes, my uncle idled the car on the shoulder with the lights out where Winston should have already emerged. The flakes fell in a hurried flurry.

My mother said, "What do we do if he doesn't show up?"

"What can we do?" my uncle said as he gripped the steering wheel.

"We'll have to find the police."

"Not yet, Denise. First we have to wait."

There were so many things they could have talked about, but didn't. The snow fell, and the windshield wipers pushed it away. My mother could have said, "What are we really doing?" And my uncle could have said, "What about what we are doing do you think is real?" The snow fell and melted on the hot hood of the car. Then a figure hurried across the road with a suitcase.

My uncle started the car and swerved around. The door opened and closed, and Winston was in the backseat. All of them would eventually talk about this for the rest of their lives. But not yet.

"Hello, Uncle Sam! Remember me, Auntie Denise! Chikmagalur is very far away now. Uncle Sam, I have a souvenir for you!"

My mother looked over the backseat at the boy. He was wearing nothing more than a sports jacket over his shirt and tie, and she knew he was wearing Indian loafers on his feet, even though she couldn't see them. Snowflakes were melting on his shoulders, and he shivered even as he smiled. He was a thin young man with a downy mustache on his lip. She had seen Indians like him a thousand times. So another one of them was here.

My uncle drove them through the snow to Burlington, Winston regaling them with the details of his adventure.

"The taxi driver spoke nothing but French. I said to him, 'Philipsburg,' and gave him the money. Then he asked for more but I said that there wasn't any. That was very smart of me. He let me out on the side of the road and pointed this way and said, 'America.' Certainly it is something I will tell my children.

"I walked through the trees, can you believe it? I have never seen snow before yesterday, and now I have walked all through it. I could not have imagined that it would be so cold. It was like pain all over my skin. I thought that my fingers would die. The cold is such a burning thing. Montreal is so full of people and lights. If it was America, I would have been happy to stay there. I ate pizza from a stand in the street. It was the only food that I could afford. I like pizza very much. Is pizza the food that we eat here? In the hostel, there were men and women sleeping in the same rooms. Some of them came back to the room very drunk! So many white people everywhere. Everyone was very nice. Then I walked through the trees. How cold it was! I felt that I would die in it, but the idea of America kept me warm. Everywhere I saw tigers, even though I knew there weren't any. Still, I saw them, and I tell you that they are really there. When I tell my children the story, there will be tigers in it. Even if nothing better happens to me, walking through the trees was good. How alive I felt. But also afraid. How could I know that you would really be there? Now I have something to tell my children. Certainly I must be married first, but once I am, what a story I will have to tell. How I walked through the trees. How my feet made prints in the snow until even my socks were wet and frozen. Are we far from Babu's house? How I want to tell Babu my story."

My uncle glanced at my mother, and she glanced back.

"How is Babu? Why didn't he also come?"

My mother and Sam took Winston to his first American meal at the Burlington Denny's. At the table Sam shook the snow globe that Winston had brought for him from Canada, a barn and horses, a pastoral scene. Along the blue plastic of its bottom was printed the word QUEBEC. What the boy had done felt real and absurd. They ordered a steak and fries for Winston, and as they waited for it, they explained to him that Babu did not know he was here, would not be pleased to know what they had done. It was a very dangerous thing they had done in bringing him to America, and someone with a good job like Babu's could not be a part of it. If he was ever to see Babu, he must tell him that he'd gotten a visa on his own, that they'd picked him up at the airport in Chicago. Not a word about this trip. Winston ate greedily and nodded. He was so glad to be in America, and the food was better than any he'd ever had. As he threw it up later in the bathroom in the motel, my mother and uncle sat beside each other on the edge of the bed.

"At least we've had these days," my mother said.

My uncle looked at his hands and said, "These days belonged to us."

Winston came out of the bathroom with his smile, wiping his mouth on the back of his hand. "It is very fine food," he told them. "It is only that my stomach is not as ready for America as my heart."

Winston stayed at my uncle's for four months, working days as a stock boy at Dominick's and nights at Walgreens to save money, before he struck out on his own for New York City, where he found work as a waiter in an upscale Gujarati restaurant in midtown Manhattan. Within a decade, he would go into partnership on a restaurant of his own in Schenectady, and first he brought his older brother over through Gore Road, and then his two younger brothers and their wives. If we were ever to visit New York, he always wrote, then we must stay with him. But we never made it to New York. A dozen Konkans came into America through Gore Road before the Border Patrol closed it, and then they came in through a different crossing, in northeastern Maine.

But before all of that happened, my mother and uncle brought Winston back with them to Chicago. He was in the backseat of the car when my mother and uncle went to the airport to pick up my father. My father's neck was heavy with colored Mardi Gras beads, and after kissing my mother hello and rounding the car to get in, he looked in the backseat to first see my uncle, whose face was grim, and then Winston, who was beaming. All the stories my father had brought back from Mardi Gras disappeared in an instant. Winston opened his mouth as wide as my father's eyes and said, "Look at me, Babu! I am also here!"

"E Puri Kon Achi?"

My uncle Sam's deal with the Sardar cost him in the short run, but within a year he was on his way to fulfilling his commitment to the Sikh. And something greater happened because of it. Showing houses to all those people, my uncle began to become known and trusted among the Indian community of Devon Avenue, at least as far as real estate went. Between their natural distrust of the greater white world, and their growing and well-founded distrust of the Hindu and Sikh merchants now established in the city, the burgeoning class of Indian doctors and engineers newly arrived in America on their skilled workers' visas found my uncle Sam, the lone Konkan among them, to be a safe third way; someone who knew India well enough that they could do business with him in their slow and fickle manner, but who was not so much a part of their community that they were beholden to him to let him cheat them.

My uncle was not destined to grow wealthy by any means, but he would do better, and by the time I was nearly four, he had managed to buy a two-bedroom house in Norridge Park, only two and a half miles from where we lived. The Kennedy Expressway separated leafy Ridge Lawn from working-class Norridge Park just as surely as any railroad tracks separated the nice part of town from the bad. So though he was much closer to us than he had been, my uncle was still on the wrong side of the tracks as far as my father was concerned.

In the winter, my uncle would pick me up in his Cutlass. He'd given up smoking because of a long bout of pneumonia the summer before that left him feeling exhausted and distant from his own body at times, and he drove with his hands holding the bottom of the steering wheel in a casual way in his newfound health, his elbows resting on his thighs. That was my uncle's way about everything in the world, never pushing the way my father always did, at ease, enjoying the day and the ride wherever it would take him. Instead of taking me directly to his house, he would sometimes drive through Ridge Lawn's side streets. There were hundred-year-old elms in the parkways at that time—though they would all be lost to the Dutch beetle in the late eighties—as old as the town itself, stately and sacred, arching in their tallness to reach their mates' branches on the other side, like lovers holding hands. Even in winter they formed vaults over the streets like the lofty innards of an immense cathedral.

At my uncle's house, I would sit on the table where he set me and help him cook. What this meant was that I peeled the onions and garlic as best I could, and then he would chop them before browning them in a pan with curry powder. The onions made my eyes water, the smell of the curry made me sneeze, and my uncle would give me a slice of white bread to chew and calm down. Next came the coriander and meat that led up to the evening meal. Often after we'd arrive, my uncle would pull off his shoes at the door, go into his bedroom, and come out again in a checkered *lungi* wrap, the traditional dress of the Konkan male. There was always music from his tape player, Hindu and Konkan, and as he'd shave ginger on the cutting board with a razor, he'd lift a piece to his mouth now and again. He'd offer me a sliver to see if I would try it. I always did. Sometimes it would be fine in my mouth like a piece of peppermint candy, and other times not. He'd cool my mouth with a glass of milk.

My uncle always told me stories of India, and I did not know enough about anything to wonder if they were true. He had left India as a very young man, and so his stories were childhood stories, stories drawn from the times even before he had been born. My uncle wore a gold necklace with a St. Christopher medallion that hung in the hair of his chest where the V-neck of his T-shirt revealed it, and above his bed hung a plain brown cross with a dried palm frond tied around it. The week before Ash Wednesday, he, like my father, would take the frond to church to be burned, to wear it again as ashes on his forehead.

But even though there was always music and the crackling of the cooking things in the pan on the stove, my uncle's house had a quietness to it that made it feel as though we were the only people in the world. He had some assorted furniture, a television, his old orange chair that he'd used to spin me in the living room by the window, but he had no posters or paintings or ornamentation to add any distraction to that place. The white walls were the canvases on which my uncle's words painted his stories.

"Who is the father of the Konkans, Francisco?" my uncle would ask me, grinding fresh coriander for chutney in his stone mortar.

"God is."

"And after God?"

"Captain Vasco da Gama."

"Who came to India with Vasco da Gama on his ship?"

"St. Francis Xavier."

"And what are the gifts they brought us that made us the Konkan people?"

"The Catholic Church, Konkani, and they taught us how to count and read."

"Where is Captain Vasco da Gama now, my Francisco?"

"At the bottom of the sea."

"And where is St. Francis Xavier?"

"In a glass coffin in Panjim."

"What is the most important thing for a Konkan boy to learn how to say?"

"E puri kon achi."

"And what does it mean?"

" 'Whose daughter is she?' "

"You are the firstborn son of the firstborn son. Do you know what that means?"

"I always have to protect my family."

"And what is your God-given name?"

"Francisco D'Sai."

My uncle would pop a sprig of coriander into his mouth and chew it as he worked, and then he'd smile to himself and say, "One day when you are grown, you will go to India and visit our home, and we will take you in a rickshaw to one of the five beautiful rivers. They will cut a fresh coconut for you, and you will drink its milk. It is very hot in India, Francisco, you will sweat like you do when we are in the garden in the summer. But there, you will drink the coconut milk and be cooled, and you will sit on the bank of a beautiful river. Fish will be swimming in the dark water, and now and again they will leap from the water to snatch the yellow insects that flutter above it. If it rains a moment, all the trees will drip with rain. Then the sun will break through the clouds, and you will see a girl in a golden sari crossing the river on a canoe. She will be standing up because Konkan women stand up when they pay the ferryman to pole them from bank to bank. She will have white flowers woven into her hair, and she will look like the goddess Lakshmi. Then you will fall in love with her, Francisco, so much so that you will not want to see anything else in this world but her. From the very first time that you see her, she will enter your dreams. Perhaps I will be there with you, to speak Konkani to her for you. Or perhaps it will be your father. But regardless, we will be old and you will be young, and you will see this girl, and then what will you say to me, my son?"

"*E puri kon achi.*"

"That's right. 'Whose daughter is she?'"

I liked it when my uncle Sam called me "my son," and sometimes when he did, I'd say, "I am not your son, I am Lawrence D'Sai's son," even though I liked it. And my uncle would pop a carrot or celery chunk in his mouth and roll his eyes at me and say, "Come on, old man, give me a break. Are you not a Konkan like I am? In India, every old man is 'my uncle,' and every boy is 'my son.'"

"But I'm not really your son."

"No, you are not."

"So where are your sons, Uncle Sam?"

"In heaven, in the stars, looking down at me and saying, 'When are you going to get married, man, so we can come down to earth and play with our cousin Francisco?'"

"Mom wants me to have a sister."

"Whatever you get, you must lead it, just the way your father has led me. You are the firstborn son of the firstborn son of the firstborn son. Me, I'm nothing but a second, but you old man, in India they show your picture to one another and say, 'This is our Francisco. Our little Rama.'"

"Dad says there is only the Holy Ghost and Jesus and the Father."

"Ah," my uncle said and turned and wiped from the board the mound of the latest thing he'd chopped to sizzle in the pan. "Your father is right. There are only those things."

"Then why did you say 'Rama'?"

"It is only a thing we say."

"My dad doesn't say that."

"Then it is only a thing your uncle says."

When the meal was ready and set on the table with its steaming pot of curry, the bowl of new rice with the damp cloth spread over it, my mother would arrive and let herself in. I would run to her, and she would take me in her arms and kiss me. In the winter, her coat was cold from the air, and in the spring, her jacket would be wet from the rain. She'd hang her things up in the closet and shake out her hair, and she was always happy in a way that she wasn't at home. Once in a while she would swing me around in the living room and sing to me in an Indian language, before setting me down and saying, "Francisco, when did you get so big? And who told you to grow up anyway? Not me."

"Uncle Sam told me."

"Then your uncle Sam is a very bad man."

My father would be away on business, which I liked because he always came home from wherever he'd been with a treat, a T-shirt from London or a candy bar from the airport, and once he brought me a stuffed lion as big as I was, with a long tail and wearing glasses from the Harris Bank in New York, where he'd had a meeting. "I told them about you, my son. They said to me, 'Lawrence D'Sai, what is your son like?' and I said to them, 'He is as tough as a lion.' So they gave me this to give you." And the times my father was at home, he was either playing golf or closed up in his study.

We'd sit at the table, my mother, uncle, and I, and I would sit on two telephone books. Then my uncle would spoon mounds of rice onto our plates, then ladles of the curry that turned the rice red. Even the window above the sink misted over from the heat of it. The rule at my uncle's house was that we eat with our fingers, which my mother loved to do, just as she'd done in India.

"Did you have a fine afternoon, Denise, with all your men away?" my uncle would ask.

"It was quiet and wonderful."

"Did you get anything special done?"

"Nothing but reading a book. I lay on the couch and read. That's all I did from the moment you boys left. It's my favorite thing in the world. Soon enough, Francisco will learn to read as well, and then he'll know why his mother likes to be left alone with her books. What did you boys do over here?" my mother would ask, and make a face at me. I'd chew and smile and say, "My uncle Sam told me a story about a Konkan girl in a golden dress who is waiting for me in India to be my wife."

"But I thought you were going to marry me when you grow up?"

"I'm going to marry her, and then I'm going to marry you, Mom."

"*E puri kon achi?*" my uncle would say, and wink, and I'd say back, "Whose daughter is she?"

After dinner, they would make a bed for me out of a sleeping bag and a pillow on the floor of the living room, and the living room would be dark, and I would watch my mother in her chair at the table through the doorway of the lighted kitchen. My mother smoked a cigarette and drank from a golden bottle of beer, and though I could see her, I couldn't see my uncle. Often they would talk about Les and Winston, about my uncle's real estate job and his dealings with the Hindus and Sikhs, and sometimes they would talk about my father, about how hard he worked. One time my uncle said a strange thing to my mother in a quiet voice that made me remember it: "We thought we knew so much about the world, didn't we, Denise? About who we were and all the things we thought we knew about ourselves. But what did we know? What will we ever know? We thought that coming here would make everything good. Winston, Les, all of us. That we would set our feet here and life would be easy."

"But it hasn't turned out that way, has it?"

"It only gets harder."

"My heart will always long for it."

"I don't know where my heart is anymore."

"I worry about Francisco."

"He is an American boy, Denise."

"It won't always be easy for him."

"Who is it easy for? Francisco has many people who love him. Not like you had. Not like what happened to you. I also felt alone as a boy in my own way. People all around me, yes, but always it was Babu who mattered. That was a small thing. But you, to be as alone in the world as you are?"

"Everything was worth it, Sam. To get me here to this place with my son. I'm not alone anymore. I also have people who love me."

"You have people who love you very much."

"I know that it's true," my mother said, and my uncle's hand touched hers on the bottle in that lighted kitchen, which was the last image I saw of them before the heavy sleep, which I'd been fighting, rolled me into itself. I would wake up in my bed in the mornings, not remembering how I had gotten there, who had carried me out to the car, who had taken me on their shoulder, then later, up to bed.

Sundays were my father's day, and he made breakfast for us in his paisley pajamas. We had scrambled eggs and pancakes, and my father melted extra butter on my toast in the pan so it was soggy and yellow, the way I liked it. Then I'd shower with my father while my mother brushed her hair for church. I'd ask my father why his penis was big while mine was small and as the water thundered all around us, my father would laugh above his mustache and soap my body and say, "Your elephant trunk will grow as you do, my son. Then you will use it to make a son for yourself the way you are a son to me."

"How will my elephant trunk make a son?"

"First you have to find your wife, and then she will explain everything that you must do. How to make sons is the secret thing that only our wives can tell us. If you have patience and find your wife, she will tell you every important thing. What will you name your son, my Francisco?"

"I will name him 'Lion.'"

"But you are already my lion."

"Then there will be two lions."

After my father had toweled me dry, I'd sit on the cool counter beside the sink where my father would set me, and watch him shave while my mother came in, too, and put on her makeup beside him, and sprayed her hair. The sound of my father's shaving was loud like it hurt, but he'd only smile at me from where the razor had taken away a line of his white beard of soap and left behind his smooth skin.

"Who is my good son?" my father would say as he shaved in the mirror.

"I am, Dad."

"And who is our God?"

"Jesus."

"Everyone is proud of you, you know. Your grandfather, your grandmother, your uncles and aunties and every single person in India."

"Uncle Sam says a girl in a golden dress is waiting to be my wife there."

"Ah, what does your uncle Sam know? Four years in this country and where is his wife?"

"Maybe Uncle Sam's wife is waiting for him in India."

"If his wife is in India, then your uncle Sam should have stayed in India. Too much music and running around. Your uncle will grow up to be a lonely old man if he doesn't start to get his head right about what it means to be in this country."

"What does it mean to be in this country, Dad?"

"To leave India in India and be a man here."

"Isn't Uncle Sam a man here?"

"Not if he doesn't have a wife."

My father would dress himself, and I would pick his cuff links for him out of the leather box on his dresser where he kept his tie clips and watches. I always picked the black cuff links, but sometimes he'd send me back for the green. Then, when he was dressed and smart in his suit, he would help me on with mine, would knot my tie around my neck, pull it tight. As he did, I could look at him closely, at his mustache and long eyelashes, at the color of his skin, which was darker than my own. That his skin was dark was a marvel to me, the way it never was with my uncle Sam. I would look right into the pores of my father's nose. Then we would wait by the door for my mother, who always had some last thing to do in the bathroom, and then we'd go out to the car, my mother with her purse and hat. At Communion, I would be alone in the pew, the people in the church moving forward in their lines, and then my father and mother would come back, kneel in the pew on either side of me, fold their hands, and close their eyes, chewing the bread that the priest had given them.

"What does it taste like?" I'd ask my mother, and my mother would hiss at me to be quiet.

"We don't talk in church," my father would say when they were done praying, and twist my ear. Always there were people in the crowd outside at the end who would pinch my cheek and say, "Francisco is becoming handsome. Such a unique little boy," and the priest in his robe would pat my head and say to my father, "A fine boy here, Lawrence. A future altar boy if I've ever seen one. Everyone is so glad that you came today, Francisco. Everyone is so glad that your family is here."

Sometimes we would go after church to the Bailey's restaurant with the fountain in the front with the big goldfish in it, where many of the families went, and my mother would eat a salad, and my father would cut a corner of his steak off for me, and sometimes we would go instead to the gym of the school beside the church, where there would be cookies and juice, and my parents would drink coffee and talk to the other adults while the priest, in his black clothes, would go around and talk to everyone. I'd wrestle with the other kids in our Sunday clothes under the drapes of the tablecloths. But the times I liked best were when my father would say, "Let's go for a drive."

It was a long way on the highway where he wanted to go, and I would sleep and wake up with a world of green around me. This was Barrington and Inverness and Crystal Lake, where the big homes were, where he wanted us to live one day. I liked to go there because there were horses, and some of the houses looked like castles. They had creeks running through their long lawns with little bridges over them. There were never any people.

"What do you think of this one, Francisco?" my father would ask as we'd pass a house, and from the backseat in my tie, I'd say, "I like it, Dad."

Then in a different voice, my father would say to my mother, "What do you think about it, Denise?" and my mother would sigh and say, "What do you think I think about it, Lawrence?"

"That's what I'm asking you. Would you be happy living out here?"

"I was happy in the city."

"Marshall Caldwaller lives out here. He says it's a good place to raise a family."

"He's your boss and rich. Of course he would say that."

"Why is nothing good enough for you?"

"The city was good enough."

"Why are you always so miserable?"

"Why are you always running away?"

"Who is running, Denise?"

"You are."

"I am only trying to do what's best for my family."

"Your family was just fine on Nelson Street. Well, you took us away from that. It's still a sore point with me. Don't you think it's better that we not get started?"

"Nelson Street was where we began. We cannot stay at the beginning."

"There is only so far we can go, Lawrence. Being here won't change who we are. And as soon as you're here, you'll know that. Where will you go when there is nowhere left?"

"I am only trying to make my family happy."

"Your family is me and one little kid who would be happy anywhere we went."

"You don't know what nice things are."

"Don't start that with me."

"You and your people don't know."

"At least I know who I am. Why do you take us to these places? Why do you insist on doing this to me? Even if we could afford to live here, why would we have to? Can't we say no sometimes? Why do we always have to win? You're sad, Lawrence. You of all of us don't know how to be happy. What do you think when you bring us here? That someone will see you in your fine car, which isn't even new by the way, and stop us and say, 'Hey, what is a guy like you doing not living out here? Come on and buy a big house. You are one of us. We've heard the Ridge Lawn Country Club hasn't let you in after two years of trying, but we're different. You won't have any problems here. You definitely need to live here. Come on and hang out with the gang.'"

"I don't understand you."

"You're never going to."

"You should have stayed in India."

"I think so, too. But do you know what? Without me, you wouldn't be here."

"I'd have found a way."

"You'd be a bank clerk in Bombay with two pairs of shoes to your name."

"You have no idea what I would be."

Then we'd drive home in silence, and I knew better than to say anything.

My mother came up to my room one Saturday in the summer when I knew it was time to put on my shoes because Uncle Sam was coming to get me. When I brought my shoes to my mother from the closet, she set them aside and lifted me onto her lap on my bed. She pulled up her shirt and put my hand on her belly. She said, "You grew inside here, Francisco, do you know that?"

"I know that, Mom," I said.

She petted my hair. "What do you feel now?"

"Your tummy."

"Do you know what's growing in Mommy's tummy now?"

"No."

"A baby, Francisco. Your little sister is growing inside me. In a few months, you'll be able to feel her kick. What do you think of that, my little boy?"

"I'm happy."

My uncle Sam did not come to pick me up that Saturday, or any more Saturdays after that. My father was home more, and my mother stopped smoking. My father read his newspaper in his armchair in the living room while I played with Lincoln Logs at his feet. My mother slept upstairs. The grandfather clock kept time in the quiet room. When I'd tell my father that I wanted to see Mom, he'd lower his paper and put his finger to his lips and say, "Both Mommy and the baby are sleeping. We must not disturb them so the baby can grow big and strong. We want our sister to grow up to be beautiful, don't we? It is time for us to be big men and leave them alone."

My mother became a foreign thing, always sick, drawn and distant and short with me when she was there. At first, she was very thin, and then she got bigger and bigger. My father came to inhabit the house in a way that he never had, and I think that it was in this way that I first came to know my father.

When he wasn't reading his paper, he was at his desk in his study, looking at papers in his hunched way. The study was the one room of the house whose door was almost always closed, and even the few nights that it was open, I was afraid to go in there. But now that my mother was sick with the baby and my father was home, that's where he always was. I would stand at the doorway and watch him work. For a long time, he would stare quietly at a paper, licking his finger to turn a page, and at other times he had a pen in his hand and was writing, the sound of it in the quiet room like he was making cuts in the top of his desk.

"Dad," I said to him one evening, the word leaving me as soon as I'd thought it, when I hadn't really wanted to say anything at all. He turned in his chair and looked at me in his way that let me know he was angry, and then that left his face.

"Come here to me, my son. Come and sit on my lap."

I went to him and he lifted me to his lap. He kissed my head as he held me close to him. Then he said, "Sometimes your father forgets what is important to him in this world.

"Do you know who we are, Francisco? Who of all these people in the vast world just you and I are?"

"Who, Dad?"

"We are firstborn Konkan sons. Do you know what this means?"

"No."

"I am the firstborn son of my father, just as my father was the firstborn son of his father. You are the firstborn son of me.

The pressures become more and more difficult for us as the generations pass."

"My uncle Sam is the second-born son."

"That is good, Francisco. Yes, your uncle Sam is the second son, and his life is very much easier than our lives are, than your life will be. We have more responsibilities as first-born Konkan sons than anyone else in the world. Do you know what these responsibilities are?"

"No, Dad."

My father petted my hair again, held me close to him as he never had. From the bottom drawer of his desk, he took out a picture. It was black and white with a thick white border all around it. The people in it were all Indians, and I recognized the stern face of my grandfather. Beside him was a small woman with a dot on her head, and I knew she was my grandmother. All about them on either side were children. They were standing in front of the gate of a house with many plants and trees in its yard. There was a dog that looked yellow, even in black and white, sitting on its haunches at the edge of the picture.

"Do you know who these people are, Francisco?"

"It is Grandfather and you."

"Do you know which one I am?"

"This one. The tallest one in the white shirt."

"And which one is Sam?"

"This one on the side."

"These are all my sisters and brothers, Francisco. There are many of them, aren't there? There would be more, but some died as babies. Still there are many, seven in all. Now Samuel and Lesley and I are in America," he said, and touched his finger to each one of their faces. "The rest are in India. These are the servant girls. This one is the boy who cleaned my father's shoes. All of these people need food to eat, clothes to wear, medicines when they are sick. And do you know who must give them these things?"

"Grandpa."

"And when your grandfather dies, who will it be?"

"I don't know."

"It will be me, Francisco. I am the firstborn son of the firstborn son. Taking care of all of these people is my responsibility. Sam and Les can run and play as much as they like, but I must work. I must see that all of these people are safe and happy, just as I must see that you and your mother and your sister to come are safe and happy. That is why I am always away. That is why I am always working when I am home. Does your uncle Sam work at his desk like I do, Francisco?"

"No, Dad."

"No. Your uncle Sam can run and play. And I am happy for him. I want him to enjoy and do those things. That is what my responsibility is. To let my brothers and sisters run and play even though I cannot. And you are the firstborn son, so when you are big and I am old, that will become your responsibility. To work so that your sisters and brothers and cousins can run and play. You and I are the same. We are the only ones. We are special. The others will always come to us and call us 'Babu,' and we must not let them down. Will you promise me not to let them down, Francisco?"

"I promise, Dad."

My father shifted me onto his knee, put the photo away, closed the drawer. It was quiet and dark in his office, the only light the small one over his desk, and the house was quiet around us. My father said, "I am going to tell you a story. Do you want to hear this story, my son?"

"Yes, Dad."

"When I was your age, India was not yet India, but still a colony of Britain, the jewel in the king of England's crown. We were all subjects of the king of England. It is the same as if the Firths came to our house and told us everything we could and couldn't do, how to spend our money, what jobs we could have, who could go to school, who could not. It would not be nice to be told these things, would it?

"In our town, Chikmagalur, the British officers had a club, and in their club they had all the nice things, the nice food, the nice clothes, the servants in uniforms to bring them all those things. They made the servants wear white gloves, because they said that the servants' hands were not clean. But the servants' hands were my hands, were your hands, Francisco. Many people did not like the Britishers because they behaved this way, but to other people, the Britishers were good.

"The Britishers made laws so everyone wasn't running around like dogs in the street. The Britishers built trains so we could move around, gave us electricity and running water so that we could live like proper people. Despite all of these good things, many people began to fight the Britishers. They put bombs on the trains and broke all the laws. The Britishers needed help to stop these bad people, so that they could go on making India a modern place. Our family was very poor before the Britishers came because we are Konkans and Catholic, and the Hindu people all around us did not like that we would not follow their ways. So your grandfather went to the Britishers' club in his best shirt while they were at dinner, and he clicked his heels together and said, 'Thank you for bringing law to India so we don't have to live like dogs. Thank you for making us modern in every way.' And the Britishers saw that your grandfather was a good and strong man and they said to him, 'Santan D'Sai, you must be one of our captains,' and they gave your grandfather a uniform and sent him to police school in Bombay, and then he became the police commissioner of Chikmagalur.

"Well, there was a great forest around our town, and in the forest were sandalwood trees. The sandalwood tree has the best scent of all the trees of the world, and it is very precious. The Britishers made laws so that the Hindus would not cut down all of the trees, as they otherwise would have done to make money selling the wood. The Hindus did not like that at all. They began to go into the forest and cut the sandalwood trees at night, just because the Britishers had told them that they couldn't. When the Britishers noticed what was happening, they called Grandfather to them at their club. Grandfather was in his uniform, and he clicked his heels together and saluted them like this. He said, 'Yes, sirs. What can I do for you, sirs?' The British officers stood up from their tables and they said, 'Santan D'Sai, you must stop the Hindus from cutting the sandalwood trees. If you do not stop them, there will be no more sandalwood trees left in the forests of your people.'

"'Yes, sirs, I will take care of it, sirs,' your grandfather said, and saluted them at their tables. Then he gathered his police officers at their station and made a plan. They would march into the forest and hide themselves among the sandalwood trees. And when the sandalwood poachers would come to cut them down, they would shoot them.

"I was a boy your age at this time, Francisco, and I loved my father very much. Sometimes he was very harsh with us. When we were bad, he would take his belt down from its hook in his closet and strap us with it, but your grandfather was also very fair. When we were good, he would bring us *jamun* fruit from the market, which we all loved as a treat and it would stain our teeth purple.

"So Grandfather put on his heavy belt and hung his gun off the side. All of the others were still babies, except for me and your uncle Sam. But I was your age, and your grandmother said to me, 'Lawrence, you must kiss your father good-bye tonight before he goes on his mission into the forest.' I did not know what this meant, but still I kissed Grandfather, and then Grandfather went in his uniform with his police officers that night and hid in the trees. The forest in India is very frightening at night, Francisco, there are tigers and leopards in it. There are leeches in it that will suck the blood from your ankles if you are not careful. But Grandfather was very brave, and he hid in the sandalwood trees with his men. Most of them were also Konkans. But your grandfather was the very bravest one. The moon came and went, and then it was very dark. They could not even see their hands. Everyone was listening and waiting, thinking about their families asleep in their homes. And then they saw lamplights in the trees and heard the sawing and grunting of men at work in the trees.

"The sandalwood poachers were there, and Grandfather and his police officers began to shoot at them. The sandalwood poachers shot back. On and on went the shooting until all of the poachers were dead. But when the shooting finished and the other police officers put their lamps on your grandfather, they could see he had been shot as well.

"'Santan D'Sai, you have caught a bullet!' the other officers told him, and Grandfather said, 'But I feel as fit as a tiger.' Then they approached him with their lamps, and even he could see the blood spilling out of the side of his shirt. Then he sat down on the dirt and said, 'Take me to my family.'

"The police officers carried Grandfather back into Chik-magalur, and they laid him on our family's table. Then they sent a servant boy to fetch the Konkan surgeon. They lit lamps all over the room. The other children were asleep, but I was not. We did not have electricity then, only those lamps, and I could see Father's face sweating and twisting in the lamplight. Moths came and beat themselves against the lamps. Their shadows fluttered all over the walls. I knew my father would die, and I could neither think nor breathe. All that I could do was stand to the side and watch as he writhed on the table. All of our dinners we ate there. Now I knew that Grandfather would die there. Then the surgeon came with his bag, and he yelled at Grandmother to boil water, and he cut Grandfather's uniform from his chest with his scissors. The wound was wet on Grandfather's side and all the men in the room were quiet when they saw it. The surgeon put his metal tools into the wound, and every time he did, my father screamed. 'It's good that he is screaming,' someone said to me, but I was afraid to lose my father. Then the surgeon washed his hands in the water that my mother brought because he was going to cut into my father's side. My father called to me from the table and I went to him. His face was covered with sweat. He reached and held my face in his hand. Do you know what he said to me, Francisco?"

"No, Dad."

"Your grandfather petted my face and he said, 'Lawrence, if I die, you must not cry. You are the firstborn son of the firstborn Konkan son. For five hundred years, we have lived among these Hindus. We will not start crying now. You must be brave, or I will not be proud of you. And more than anything, my son, I want to be proud of you. Everyone will depend on you when I am gone. Do you understand me, son? These Hindus may have killed me tonight, but they have not killed my son. Will you let me live in you as all of our fathers have lived in me?'

"'I promise, Father,' I told him. That was when I understood what it meant to be a firstborn son."

"Did Grandfather die?"

"You know that he is still alive, Francisco. The surgeon cut his side and took the bullet out. When Grandfather was well, they gave it to him and he threw it to the pigs in the yard. He still has the scar, right here on his belly. But he is old, and now it is my time to be the firstborn son. Do you understand me, Francisco?"

"Yes, Dad."

"We must always protect the people we love."

Then my father opened the bottom drawer of his desk, and in it were a ball, and a wooden elephant, and a carved box with a knife in it. The knife was made of ivory, and my grandfather had given it to him when he'd first gone away to school in Mangalore, to open the letters my grandfather would send to him with news of the family. There were not many things from India in our house, but in the bottom drawer of my father's desk were the few things that he had kept: the cricket ball from the tournament in Chikmagalur in which he'd bowled and taken six wickets, the carved elephant he'd been given by the beloved servant who had cared for him when he was a boy, the sandalwood box that my grandmother had kept her gold earrings in, the ivory knife with its scene of rajas riding on elephants in a tiger hunt. From that night on, I always wanted to open that drawer and touch those things, but I knew my father's temper, and I never did.

One time when my mother was very fat with my sister and my father was away at golf, my uncle Sam came over to tell me stories about my wife in India while he put me to bed. But first, I lay coloring a clown's face on the living room floor while my uncle and mother sat on the couch and talked about what my sister's name would be.

My mother said, "How about Beatrice? That's my great-aunt's name, the one who took me in after I ran away from home."

"Do you really want to give her a name from your family?"

"What about your mother? She was nice to me the year after I finished with the Peace Corps and lived in your home."

"My mother didn't trust at first that a white woman would make a good wife for a Konkan. We had our ideas about white women then."

"I know that."

"She also wasn't very happy about that gold."

"Well she's happy about it now. Tell me another name, Sam. I want you to have a say in it."

"It is not my place to have a say."

"Sam, no matter what, I know that you will be more of a father to her than Lawrence could ever be, just as you've been to Francisco."

"Lawrence will always be her only father."

"I want you to tell me a name."

My uncle was quiet on the couch a long time, his legs folded, the grandfather clock keeping time. The shadows on the walls were tall things now, but neither my uncle nor my mother went to turn on a light. My uncle said, "The only name I can think of is Sabitha."

"Who was Sabitha?"

"No one. A girl I played with. I was a small boy, she was a neighbor's daughter. We played in the gutter with the pigs. Later, her family moved to Mangalore, and I never saw her again. I don't even know what her father did, or their last name. When I opened that sweetmeats shop in Chikmagalur, I called it *Sabitha*. Workmen painted that name above the shutters for me with blue paint. Those were the best times for me. Two good years after you and Babu left. Everyone came and played carom in my shop and listened to my music. Then my father told me I must come here, and that was the end of it."

"Sabitha is a pretty name."

"She was a pretty girl. A friend. A child of my youth. Every time I saw her I felt happy. That was before everything became about men and women. We were children and we did not think about those things. It was playing only. Playing in the gutter with pigs."

Listening to them, to the mention of my grandfather, the things my father had told me in his study came into my head, and I said to them as I colored, "Grandfather is a firstborn son, like Dad and I are. Uncle Sam can run and play, but Grandfather had to shoot the sandalwood poachers."

My mother looked at me like she'd forgotten I was there. She made a face and said, "What do you know about it, Francisco?"

"Grandfather was brave and killed the bad men. Dad told me so."

"Did your father tell you what happened to the sandalwood after your grandfather killed those men?"

"No," I said, and looked at her.

"He and his police officers sold it themselves. They didn't tell the British. They sold coffee and silver and gems, everything they could get their hands on. How else do you think he could afford to buy your grandmother all of her gold? Your father has a very selective memory, Francisco. He chooses what parts of stories to remember. Remember that when he tells you things. Your grandfather cheated the Hindus and the British both. And he was smart to do it. When the British left, they didn't leave him with anything, they didn't even tell him, 'Thank you.' And the Hindus remembered all the bad things your grandfather had done to them. They came to the house and wanted to burn it down. They wanted your father and your uncles and everyone to live on the street. But your grandfather gave them back their gems, and they let him start again as a clerk. But they took away his badge and his gun. Ask your father about that someday."

"Don't do these things, Denise."

"I don't want Francisco to turn out as screwed up as them, Sam."

"Francisco is too young for these things."

"Not if Lawrence has already started him in on it."

"Your life here is because of all of those things, too."

"You don't think I think about that?" my mother said.

My uncle carried me up to bed. He tucked me in, and lay beside me on the covers. He petted my hair and sang *"E puri kon achi"* in his soft voice. Then he told me a story while I closed my eyes. He said, "One time, Francisco, the Hindus came to our house after the British left, and we watched them from the windows with our mother because we were scared. Some Hindus had done bad things to the people who had helped the British. Gandhi told them that they must not do bad things, but some of them were very angry and they did not listen to him. They killed people. They hung the children from the trees. When the Hindus came to our house, my father went out in his *lungi* and met them at the gate.

"'Santan D'Sai, where are your Britishers now?' they yelled. 'All the time that they were here, you were very bad to us. Now we have come to make you remember what you did.'

"Grandfather folded his arms. Though the Hindus were very many, he was not afraid. He had never been afraid of Hindus, so why should he be now? That is what your grandfather is like. He said to them, 'My family is inside. Whatever we have is between only us. I never touched the slightest hair on your children's heads. Whatever you must do, then do it to me here before my children's eyes. But you will not come into my home and touch my children so long as I am alive.'

"The Hindus began to quarrel. Some of them wanted to shoot your grandfather right then. I know that if your grandfather had shown them any fear, they would have killed him. That is what people are like, Francisco. But Grandfather was not afraid of them, and so they became confused. Some of the Hindus said, 'These Konkans have been helping the Europeans steal from us ever since the very first Portuguese. We have had enough of these Konkans. Especially this one. No matter who is watching, this Konkan should die right here.' But others among them said, 'If we kill him, then we will be as bad as the British have been to us.'

"We all watched from the window, Francisco. We were all very frightened for our father. What had we known until then but that we were Konkans and the Hindus were Hindus? We did not know any of these things they were saying. Even now, I don't know what is true. But what we did know was that we loved our father. We began to pray to the Virgin Mary that the Hindus would go away.

"They spit on Grandfather, they spit betel-nut juice on his *lungi* so that it was stained red, and he would never wear it again. But they did not kill him. They gathered our pigs, the pigs of all the Konkans of Chikmagalur, and drove them into the forest, where the tigers would eat them. Konkans have always been allowed to keep pigs, Francisco, but after the British left, the Hindus came and drove them away to teach us a lesson because they said we had been mean to them."

"Were we mean to the Hindus, Uncle Sam?"

"Everyone is mean to everyone, Francisco. But everyone also loves everyone, even though they don't know it. The British had not been good to the Hindus, and the Konkans had helped them do it. But the Hindus had been mean to the Konkans before the British came, so when the British asked us to be their officers, what choice did we have? The Hindus made our lives very hard for a time after the Britishers left. I was very young, four, five, the age that you are now. We used to have all the fine things. But then we were hungry.

"One day, your grandfather was begging rice for us from the Hindus all up and down the streets. He did not have his uniform anymore, and he went about in his *lungi* like any pushcart driver. Grandfather came to the house of a Hindu whom he had once beaten with his baton and put in jail. Who knows why? Maybe the Hindu had been a bad man, maybe not. He said to Grandfather from his gate, 'Oh, Santan D'Sai, how does it feel now?' 'It does not feel good,' your grandfather told him, 'but my wife and children are hungry, and they do not deserve to be hungry when it was I who did the things.' The Hindu said, 'But the things you did made your family fat while my wife and children were skinny,' and Grandfather said, 'Everything belongs to you now. I only want to feed my children.'

"That Hindu had been beaten by Grandfather's own hand. Why should he have given Grandfather anything? But he gave Grandfather a sack of rice, and we were able to eat. Then the terrible anger of those times began to pass. And the Konkans were still there. Do you know what I am trying to tell you, Francisco?"

"No, Uncle."

"We must always be good, no matter what has happened to us. And we must remember that it is easy to become bad."

"Am I good or bad, Uncle Sam?"

"You are good, Francisco."

"And Grandfather?"

"He only wanted to feed his family."

"Like a firstborn son."

"That's right."

"Like Dad is."

"That's exactly right, old man."

My mother gave birth to my sister in the dead of winter, just after the first of the year. The world was white with snow. My uncle Les had come from Tucson to stay with us for the holidays, and he gave me a rattlesnake's rattle to keep in the drawer of my nightstand for good luck, like he said the red Indians in Arizona did. He was there when my father drove my mother to the hospital to have the baby. After the baby had come and she and my mother were resting, my father took me and my uncles to the Victoria Station restaurant in Niles that was made out of old train cars. We had a room of a car to ourselves, and my father and uncles drank whiskeys and ate steaks and ribs. The waitress brought the ribs on metal platters to the table, and they were long and curved things, covered in so much barbecue sauce that she tied a plastic bib around my neck so I wouldn't get sauce on my shirt. I still did.

My uncle Sam sat beside me and was very quiet, while my uncle Les and my father were very loud. They kept standing up together to sing that song I knew, *"E puri kon achi!"* "Whose daughter is she?" My uncle Sam sat in his chair and didn't sing. "What's the matter with you, Samuel?" my uncle

Les said to him. "It's time to celebrate. *E puri kon achi! E puri kon achi!*"

My father held my uncle Les around the shoulders and said, "All of Samuel's mistakes are keeping him in that chair. He regrets not marrying now. He regrets not having kids. Come on, Samuel, stand up with us and let it go. *E puri kon achi!* There is a new Konkan daughter in the world. It is time to sing!"

My uncle Sam wiped his mouth on his red napkin. He went and stood with his brothers, and they draped their arms over each other's shoulders as they sang the song. Soon, even my uncle began to sing and smile. The three of them kicked up their feet, and their drinks sloshed out of their glasses.

"E pu-ri, e pu-ri, e puuur-ee! E pu-ri kon ah-chi?"

My sister was named Elizabeth Sabitha D'Sai. Elizabeth after the queen of England so that she would have an American name. And my mother insisted on Sabitha to remember India by, the name of my uncle Sam's sweetmeats shop, the happiest time of his life. "Whose daughter is she?" my father and uncles sang. The waitress ignored their singing as she brought them drinks long into the night.

PART 2

The Konkans

My uncle Sam took long drives through Chicago that spring after the snow had melted and the first crocuses had pushed up from the thaw in their blues and yellows in the city's window boxes: meandering and meaningless journeys up and down Lake Shore Drive, along the Kennedy out to O'Hare, to the South Side, where he didn't belong and didn't care that he didn't, and even beyond the lights of the city and onto the straight and dark highways of the Illinois prairie, where he belonged even less. Last year's corn stubble stretched out on either side as far as the eye could see. Perhaps it was the wandering spirit of the Konkans rising up in him, but perhaps it was something else. He liked to sit in his car in the gravel lot at the O'Hare fence where lovers went at night to watch the planes thunder up from the tarmac like ponderous birds, he liked to turn off his car on the shoulders of rural highways and look at water towers standing up against the fading light of evening like monuments surrounded by the electric susurrus of crickets. Whatever his brothers were doing in their places in

America, whatever the rest of his blood was doing in the dirt roads of the Konkan Coast, there was my uncle Sam in his car, the stars above him and full of meaning, at thirty, trying to listen to the world from his place in it.

No longer did he sing and dance the way he had when he arrived here, no longer did he get himself involved in adventures with pigs and journeys to pick up Konkans who appeared out of the woods at that obscure intersection in northern Vermont, and he became absent again from our house. My mother called him now and again, but she had changed, too. The labor had exhausted her, as did the nursing of my sister.

It was during this time that my mother woke up one morning while the rest of us slept. It was night still, really, and the windows were open onto the new spring, and what woke my mother at a time when she was otherwise hard to wake was the smell of the lilac bushes flowering in our yard. The syrupy thickness came to her like a scent from India. All those smells that India had been: the fish stink from the morning market, the roasting almonds, the dung of the field buffalo, the perspiration of herself and all those people under the tropical sun in the humidity of the monsoon. And the flowers, of course, too many to ever hope to name, the jacaranda and hydrangeas and bougainvillea and frangipani, the blossoms of the orange and lemon trees along the streets of the town, the hibiscus. The lush scent of those lilacs in our yard woke my mother into the person she had been in India, a white girl on a one-speed iron bicycle riding through all those milling men to teach poor women in the Hindu and Muslim shantytowns how to build smokeless ovens.

What had she really taught those women, my mother wondered in the dark room, what had she taken away from them?

India, nearly a decade removed, somehow felt like a grand thing that she had heard about happening to someone else. Here now, she ran her fingers along the wall to the hallway, to the bathroom, closed the door, turned on the light, and a bleary, bloated woman looked back at her from the mirror.

How could this be her face? How could she be this person? In her mind, she saw herself as someone else: that girl on that bicycle doing all of those brave things. It would be better in the day, but right now this face made her hate herself. Why had she ever lost faith in that girl? Why had she ever given that girl up? That she deserved the memories she had, that she'd ever been arrogant enough to think that she deserved any happiness in this world could not be justified by this ugly face. This ugly face deserved what it got, and there would be no more happiness for it—only fleeting moments with its children in its task of getting them raised. The thought of what she'd done with my uncle was a nasty thing, as nasty as this face was with its bloated lines, the arrogant act of someone who had thought she was prettier than everyone else, when in fact she was not. My mother turned out the light, laid herself again in bed beside my father, who snored loudly from the drinking that had put him to sleep. My mother lay there until the yellow dawn crept down the walls of the room. My father's alarm clock came to life with the voices of the news of the world, and my sister, in her bassinet, lifted her arms to mewl and grope at the morning.

"Did you sleep?" my father said as he rubbed his eyes.

"Yes, Lawrence, I slept a bit."

"Did Elizabeth cry?"

"You know that she did."

"I didn't hear anything."

"She didn't cry long."

"I'll dress and feed Francisco."

"I would appreciate that."

My mother was as full of stories as my uncle was. There was a story she loved to tell about herself, a story from when I was a baby. She would tell this story when she drank, at off moments at a table of people, to friends she'd have in later life, to women from the neighborhood, to me, when the wheel of conversation swung to her and she knew she was expected to reveal herself.

My mother's eyes would light up as she'd remember, she'd smile, she'd lift her hands from her lap to illustrate the story's movements. My mother had long fingers that would have been good for playing piano, had life given her the chance to do that. But life didn't, and so those fingers conducted her minuets of the spoken word instead.

The story went like this: In those early years in America, on Nelson Street, when there was no money and she lived in a house purchased with smuggled gold with her husband who was still more Indian than American, though he wouldn't have admitted it, where she would soon have a baby in the bassinet, and two wild boys from India living in her basement, my mother rode her bicycle. It was a three-speed Schwinn cruiser, green with sparkles in the paint, with a basket and bell that my father had bought for her because he was ashamed that they couldn't afford a car. And even once they could afford a car, my mother still went everywhere on that bike.

In the fall and spring, she rode her bicycle to the Nettlehorse Public School, where she taught second grade, with her books, lesson plan, and lunch in a bag in the basket. And on weekends, and all summer long, she rode up and down Belmont, through the DePaul campus, even along the lake, to see the people going about their lives in this American world, which she still didn't feel a part of, though life had already made its decision about that.

She'd ride her bike to see the Mexican men in their wicker hats pushing their carts with the bells on the handles and selling shaved ice corner to corner, the girls in braids skipping rope, the hustle of traffic, the trees, the young people of those days on the sidewalks holding hands in their long hair and sunglasses and looking in the windows of the music stores and incense shops. She liked to ride to the totem pole at Belmont Harbor and look at the carved animals squatting on top of one another, she liked to ride to the Lincoln Park Zoo and toss bread to the ducks in the rookery. After I was born and old enough to sit in the yellow plastic seat that my uncle Sam had bought and attached to the back of the bike, my mother would pedal through the streets in her jeans and T-shirt with the same abandon she had before, and she had more time to do it now because she wasn't a teacher any longer.

One summer day, me asleep behind her in my bonnet, she rode us past Wrigley Field. The crowds in their blue hats and Cubs shirts were leaving the stadium through the turnstiles, and the game had certainly been another loss despite the slugging heroics of Billy Williams. The crowd's revelry didn't admit this defeat, of course, as Cub fans never will.

But it was hot, and she stopped at the Baskin-Robbins ice-cream shop, took me into her arms from the seat, and leaned the bicycle against the window. She should have locked it up, that was always a part of the story, but she was happy and loved the world and her place in it, no matter how she felt in her continuing culture shock, and she didn't unwind the lock from around the neck of the seat. She ordered a scoop of

Pralines 'n Cream, her favorite, in a cake cone, and she sat at a table with me on her lap in my doughiness. Then she went to work at licking that ice cream.

Through the window, she watched as a white kid in a white T-shirt, his hair greased back in the style of poor white kids of that day, with pimples like a purple rash blooming across his cheeks, looked at her bike a long moment as he passed it. Even though she knew right then that he would steal it, the surety of that fact put a lethargy into my mother that kept her in her seat. Who can know for certain? Maybe she even wanted it to happen. He came back into the window, straddled the bike, stood up on the pedals, and pistoned away. For my mother, it was like watching a film. But she also knew that it wasn't a film. So she did what she would have done in India or anywhere. She handed me and the cone across the counter to the man in his hat, and dashed out the door in her sneakers to chase the thief.

In India, my mother had had to learn to deal with many things: with being a white woman in a place where white women spread their legs in the dreams of the poor and long-colonized brown men, where men would lick her neck on crowded buses, would get drunk and peer in the windows of her house as they fondled themselves in the folds of their *lungi* wraps. It had toughened her without making her hate, because my mother had the ability to see the world from outside the reference of her culture and body. White women were held up to those men as the most desirous, the most sexually beautiful women in the world, as well as the most forbidden under the reign of the British. But also in India, seeing herself through Indian eyes, my mother had come to a private acknowledgment of her own physical beauty. India was where she began to love herself.

The rigors of being a white woman in India, coupled with the nightmares of her childhood, made my mother strict in setting her boundaries in the world. She threw her elbows into ribs to make the neck lickers yelp, she slammed shutters on the fingers of the men who had hoped to jack off to her bathing.

My mother ran and ran down those city blocks. The boy on her bicycle did not know that she was running after him, and though her every fiber wanted to shout *Thief! Thief!* she knew from her time in India not to trust crowds, that a shout for help among unknown people would do little more than turn the people into gawkers, that they would gather and obstruct her way, that they would let the boy know in doing so that he was being pursued. She ran as if fleeing a fire, which maybe in fact she was, and a half a block ahead of her, the boy on her bicycle stopped at the intersection to let the traffic pass. He shook a cigarette out from the pack he kept rolled in the sleeve of his T-shirt. Just as he was about to touch the flame of his lighter to the cigarette in his lips, my mother left her feet, her hair unfurling behind her like a cape, and she tackled him. The bike clattered to the curb, the cigarettes scattered like matches, pigeons burst up from the sidewalk, and her body carried his into the street. Taxicabs blared their horns as they swerved away from their heads.

For a moment, my mother held the boy under her on the pavement like a lover. If anything else in the world was happening at that time, my mother didn't know it. She looked into the boy's startled eyes, and with a broad smile she said to him, "That's my bicycle."

"Lady," the boy said beneath her, "you are one crazy bitch." Then he scampered up from underneath her and ran away.

My mother pushed the bicycle back the six blocks to the ice-cream shop. Her elbows were scraped and bleeding, and the people who had stopped to watch looked at her with faces so creased it was as though she was the one who had committed the crime. My mother smiled despite them, because my mother at that moment was proud of herself.

At the ice-cream shop, the man in his hat was spooning me vanilla ice cream from a dish as I sat beside the cash register. People were standing up at every single one of the tables, ice cream melting in their hands. My mother looked at them as though to say, *Say something to me. I dare you.* None of them did. I looked at my mother, she grinned at me, and I turned to the man and opened my mouth for more ice cream. My mother wiped her hair from her sweating brow, tucked it behind her ears. She said to the ice-cream man, "May I have my son back?"

"Here you go."

"What about my cone?"

"I'll get you a new one."

"I got my bike."

"You certainly did."

"Did my boy behave himself?"

"He didn't make a peep."

"He's my kid. My kid and my bike. Just try and let someone take something from me. I like this feeling."

The idea of ice cream had passed, and my mother put me in the seat and rode us home. As she did, the reality of leaving me with strangers so she could chase a bicycle thief down the street began to settle into her. First she felt ashamed and frightened, and then she felt proud again. All the way home, these emotions alternated in her like the light and shadow of the trees she rode under. At home, she swabbed her abrasions with Mercurochrome in the bathroom, sipped the beer that my uncle Sam came upstairs to offer her. Then she lit a cigarette at the kitchen table and let the last of the emotions of the bicycle thief leave her with the smoke.

"A bicycle is not worth a son," my uncle Sam said to her, though he was smiling.

"I know that, Sam."

"Even these cuts aren't worth it."

"It wasn't about the bicycle."

"I won't tell Lawrence."

"Why would you think you had to?"

"You must have frightened that thief badly."

"He'll never forget it."

But life quickly happened, and my mother saw her face in the mirror in the middle of the night in her suburban home in Ridge Lawn, and the tired and thickening woman in it was not her, and the memories of the things she'd done in this life did not seem to be so purely good anymore.

For his part, my uncle Sam had been living in America as though he really wasn't in it. After my sister's birth, he was more alone than he had ever felt, and there were many nights when he drove in his car through this strange, green land looking at it as a visitor would, standing later at his darkened kitchen window and contemplating the growing plants of his garden as he let this loneliness settle into him. He did not cry or lament or bemoan his fate over beers into the ears of fellow drinkers at the bars, he did not bare his soul to the priest in the confessional at church. He knew that no one else in the world suffered from his particular brand of shame, and though he was a second son and free from the weight of familial responsibility, he was still beholden enough in his Konkan self to not feel that the role of exile was something he deserved. Yes, he knew that his love for my mother was a wrong thing, and the isolation it left him in after my sister's birth could not be any other way. He worked and went on drives and let the leaves brown and fall, and then the snow blanketed everything. Snow had long since become his favorite thing about America.

Once, my uncle Sam had never seen snow, could only imagine what it must be like from the occasional ice cubes in his sweet tea in India, and in the months before he'd come over, he'd roll the cubes on his tongue until his tongue hurt. Then he'd spit the smoothed cubes into his hand and hold them up to the light like diamonds. This was on the stoop of his sweetmeats shop in Chikmagalur, where the young Konkan men his age came to smoke and drink tea and play carom at the boards he had for meager wagers they made with the few rupees their fathers allowed them.

Really, the Sabitha sweetmeats shop was a small storefront in a long line of small storefronts off the central market, where merchants sold brooms and buckets and batteries and cheap colored kickballs and kites from Japan. But when the other vendors would gather in their wares from the sidewalk to close and go home to their families in the evenings, Sam would arrive from sleeping in late at my grandfather's house, roll up Sabitha's steel shutter like a garage door, turn on the lights, set a record on the turntable, place the sweetmeats on metal trays in the glass display, and if there had been an ice truck going through the town from Mangalore, the seller would make my uncle's shop the last of his stops, would chip a steel tub full of shards from a block with his pick. These frosted shards would begin to melt immediately, until soon they were all smooth and floating in the rising pool of water. My uncle would sit in a plastic chair on the stoop of his shop, cross his legs in the Indian way, smoke a cigarette, and the evening would settle down on Chikmagalur. It was a town on the road to other places, the bicycle-rickshaw drivers hurrying past with women in saris in the seats behind them, the policemen in their brown uniforms puttering out on their motorcycles to change the guard at the highway's posts, the retired pandits in their peaked Congress hats taking their last restorative walks with their hands clasped behind their backs in the meditative way of Gandhi. The muezzin would cry from the mosque tower in the distant Muslim quarter, the cattle would return from grazing in the fields in lines and settle down for the night in the emptying market, the servant girls would hurry to their masters' homes from the washing stones at the stream, laundry folded in tall white stacks on their heads. Everywhere people were eating their evening meals in their homes by lamplight, around communal pots, with their fingers, rice for all of them, curry and chapatis as well for the wealthy, and while their fathers sat down in their chairs to listen to the BBC over tea or rum or brandy after the food was eaten, the young Konkan men in their starched shirts and wristwatches, some of which even worked, would come in groups of two and three out of the night to the light of my uncle's shop like apparitions, to sit and smoke at the tables, to talk the politics of the day, which as Konkans was always against them, to bring out the carom disks from their felt bags and shoot them like marbles on the boards with their calloused index fingers. Sometimes a young woman or two would stop by on the way to evening visits among the families, to peer into the shop from the street and see if their favorite one was there, to say then to my uncle, "Is that all that you boys do? Drink tea and smoke cigarettes and play your silly games and talk and talk and talk?"

My uncle would stand up and say back, "Don't you know that all we talk about is you?" and take off his sandal as though to slap them with it, the dirtiest insult that there was. Then the girls would dash off as though they really were afraid, reach the edge of the light the shop cast out into the street, and turn to smile and laugh. "Samuel Erasmus D'Sai, do you think we are afraid of a boy as skinny and boastful as you?"

The night bugs swirled around the outside light in a battering swarm, and my uncle would drop his sandal and toe it back on, and everyone in the shop would laugh and laugh. It was the dance of young Konkan men and women going back five hundred years. Because the fact was, none of those young people had any control over whom they would eventually marry.

Occasionally some Muslim errand boy or other would come to buy a parcel of sweetmeats for a marriage or birth or funeral celebration in their quarter, but mostly not. The Sabitha shop didn't really make any money, it was simply the young Konkan men's social club of Chikmagalur, run by my uncle, who didn't have anything better to do. It was financed at a loss by my grandfather. Despite the hierarchy of first and second sons that they had all bound themselves to for better or worse, my uncle Sam was still a son to my grandfather. Having given the family's gold to Babu for his move to America, and having spent money on educating my father in his youth, my grandfather found it in himself to dip again into the remains of the horde of money and gems he'd hidden in coffee cans, in mattresses, and the bottoms of potted plants all around the house, to let my uncle have something of his own. It didn't cost much of anything to have a simple shop like that in India then, and even so, my uncle felt grateful to his father for it because, as a second son, he didn't have a right to anything.

My uncle was everything to those Indians that my father wasn't. For one, he was present among them. All the years that my father was away in the Catholic schools in Mangalore on the coast, in his nice clothes and shoes that he'd wear on his visits home, my uncle was in his boy's *lungi,* keeping an eye on my grandfather's pigs as he played in the streets with the Hindu and Muslim kids. And then, those years when my father was working at Standard Chartered Bank in Bombay, my uncle was alone in the mountains, tending to my grandfather's coffee plantation. And finally, those first years that my father was gone for good in America with my mother, my uncle was on the steps of his sweetmeats shop in his handed-down slacks and sandals, under the light of the doorway.

My uncle had an easy laugh and spoke the Konkan language like an ersatz scholar. He knew all the stories of the Konkan migration, the terrible drought that had left the people with nothing, how they came down from the Deccan Plateau to meet the Portuguese on the shore when they arrived after their own long journey, how the Konkans, before their reduction, had been Brahmins. He knew the story of how the last of the starved Konkans had stood on the beach in their tattered white dhotis as the sails of Vasco da Gama's ship grew on the horizon. How da Gama in his steel helmet had arrived like a god from the sea, had waded through the surf half dead from the voyage, and planted his sword in the sand to claim the Konkan Coast for Portugal. How St. Francis Xavier in his black vestments had commanded everyone to kneel before his staff as the sky turned bloodred, how he had baptized the Konkans in the name of the Savior, each and every one. How they had stood up again as a new people, singular in the vast throng of India, the Indian Konkans of the Catholic Church. And though they liked all of these stories that my uncle told them, the young Konkan men of Chikmagalur admired him even more because he knew how to joke and play.

For a short time after my parents had left for America, my uncle flirted with a peasant girl named Lira. My uncle's breaking of caste to pursue her could have been simply something that was fated to happen, but maybe it was because of how my mother's time in Chikmagalur had changed him. My mother had arrived there with her long white limbs, with the bicycle that she alone among the women there bunched her *salwar kameez* around her knees to mount and ride, to live alone in her small house beside the market, to treat *harijans* as equals, to marry my father, and to throw all of the old assumptions into disarray.

Lira was dark for a Konkan, pretty, with a rope of braided hair down her back that tossed like a horse's tail from the rhythm of her gait. She was the last daughter of a desperately poor cobbler named Saldanha, and every evening this Saldanha sent Lira to beg rice in the wealthy Konkan neighborhood called the Christian Colony, where my grandfather lived. As she'd pass my uncle's sweetmeats shop on her nightly errand, she would walk through the edge of the light with her eyes downcast, just close enough to break from the shadows and be noticed. She wore a threadbare red sari, two glass bangles on her left arm, and even though she was poor, she somehow managed to always wear a string of white flowers in her hair, as the single young women of that place did for beauty. She would glance at my uncle, her eyes as dewy as those of the *gopi*s who had inspired the Hindu poets to write their fevered cantos. My uncle would draw on his cigarette as he noticed Lira, follow her hippy passage with hooded eyes. As soon as she was gone into the night, the young men playing carom inside would wag their fingers at him, smile, and say, "If she comes any closer, she will melt all the ice. She will boil all the tea. Do something about it, eh Samuel? *E puri kon achi?* Whose daughter is she anyway?"

"Saldanha's," my uncle would say, and stub out his cigarette.

"Saldanha the spice merchant, or Saldanha the cobbler?"

"Which Saldanha would have a daughter like that in this life, you stupid *bangadees*?" my uncle would say back in disgust, and the young men would groan and tap their shooting disks on the boards in misery and say, "The cobbler." They knew, as my uncle did, that none of their fathers would ever consent to a match so poor. The cobbler Saldanha would never be able to pay the dowry for Lira that their fathers would expect, especially after the marriages of his older daughters had already impoverished him. There would be nothing left for this last daughter but to be sent away.

What all of those young men knew, including my uncle, as they played their second- and third- and fourth-son board games in the Sabitha shop, was that despite her beauty, and maybe even more so because of it, Lira was destined for Bombay, to serve as a waiting girl to a rich Konkan's family. Once there, sooner or later she would be pregnant with her master's child, and a marriage would quickly be arranged to one of the laborers on his rubber or coffee plantation, some long-serving and loyal Konkan with a missing eye or other deformity. Time and time again, the prettiest girls were born poor. It was the way these things happened. The young men in my uncle's shop also knew that their own marriages would be arranged soon to the plain third daughters of their fathers' social friends.

My uncle could have smoked and accepted the fact that this girl who cast eyes at him could never be his, but he was full of life, and my mother's marriage to my father had put new ideas in him. Yes, the world had made it so nothing would ever really belong to him, but the world also couldn't take away the fact that this girl looked at him the way she did. The Hindus had their festival of the cobra, and for three days the streets were full of fakirs playing flutes for money to the snakes that rose up from their baskets in their hoods. Then the town was quiet again. Lira stepped into the light of his shop in her bangles and sari, looked at him and went on, and this time, my uncle stubbed out his cigarette, stood up from his chair, and went down the steps to follow her. In an instant, every game of carom in that shop stopped as the young men lifted their eyebrows at each other. Then they clamored from their chairs to peek out the door after him.

In the darkness, Lira followed a path along the stream beyond the edge of town, and there were stars on the water where it eddied and pooled. The stream began in the mountains, joined the great rivers to eventually find its end at the sea, but here, this water belonged just to this place. The quiet silhouettes of the *harijan* frog-fishermen were benign shadows on the distant bank, and ducks slept in pairs in the roots of the tamarisks with their bills tucked under their wings. Lira walked on the powder of the trail in her bare feet. Twice she glanced back.

Under a mango tree, my uncle touched Lira's shoulder. She was smaller than she looked, thinner. Was she even trembling? In a soft voice, my uncle said, "Why do you look at me the way you do?"

"I don't know why, Samuel. I only know that I do it."

"My father, my family, nothing would allow this."

"Then why did you stand and follow me?"

"I closed my eyes to think of you as you passed, and when I opened them, I was here."

In the few times they had together under the mango tree on the stream's sandy bank, my uncle would never see her body properly. All of it was rushed and dangerous, both of them feeling that slick pleasure for the very first time. Back at the sweetmeats shop, the young men would clap their hands on my uncle's back, rub his head, and he'd shake them off and blush. Yes, it was about that, but it was also about something more. My uncle lived in dread those weeks that his father would find out, as well as with his desire to do that with that girl.

In less than a month, Lira was sent to Bombay. Sometimes after that, my uncle would lie in his bed at my grandfather's house and smoke a cigarette and imagine Lira in her red sari frying chapatis for him over coals in the cinder-block house that he knew would have been his life with her. Could he have loved that life? Every day he waited for his father to come in and tell him who he would marry. Two years went by in this way. Then my grandfather came into the room and told him he must go to America.

My grandfather had planned on the immigration of his sons to America through my mother all the time she had been in Chikmagalur. Though he saw her spending her time among the poorest of the Hindus and Muslims, still she was white and he knew that one day she must go home. My grandfather decided that she would take his son Lawrence with her, and in taking him, open the door to all of them.

What my grandfather did was this: He invited my mother over to the house for meals on Sundays, and though she couldn't have known it, he made everyone dress in their best clothes, and paid the servants to fetch choice cuts from the Konkan pig butcher at the edge of town, which was like procuring contraband moonshine in India ever since the Hindus had come into power. The first time that my mother came to the house, my uncle Sam was the one who led the conversation, because he had been through middle school at the Catholic mission in Chikmagalur, and his English was the best, though he couldn't bring himself to look at her. The first Sunday, my mother had picked the coveted chunks of *obbe* fat out of the curry and set them aside in a pile on her plate.

"Ask her why she doesn't eat the meat," my grandfather said to my uncle Sam, and my uncle said to her as he looked at his hands, "Ms. Denise, my father would like to know why the meat doesn't please you."

"I work with Muslims. Even though I am in your home, I must not disrespect their customs."

"But we are not Muslims. We are Konkans and we eat this meat."

"I do not work with Konkans. And since everyone here knows every little thing that I do, it is best for me to be careful. It wouldn't be good for my work if my Muslim friends heard that I was eating pork in your house."

My uncle Sam translated all of this to my grandfather, and my grandfather grunted and said in Konkani, "Everything in this world worth anything requires more work than men at first understand. Let her refuse our pork tonight. One day, she will cook pork for us herself." Of course my uncle didn't translate this to my mother.

After she had left that night on her bicycle, my grandfather made two changes in his plan. The first was, he told the servants to prepare vegetarian meals on the nights that my mother would eat with them, and the second was that he telegrammed my father, in Bombay: *Come home this instant,*

Babu. Something of great import is going on here. Your family needs you now.

My father telegrammed back, *No time off from work allowed, save for a death in the family.*

My grandfather telegrammed back: *Then I have died.*

My father stepped off the bus and into the dusty street outside the market the next Saturday, and some chickens ran past him, a nearby buffalo mulled its cud, and he was right back in the thick of all that he hated most. There was dust on his shoes by the time he reached my grandfather's house with his satchel, and in the central room, the old man himself was in his *lungi* plucking the wet feathers from the evening's chicken.

"What is it that you've called me from Bombay to set my feet in this foul dust storm of a town to do?"

My grandfather was chewing *paan,* and he spit a long red rope of juice into the pot where he was also tossing clumps of white chicken feathers. He looked my father up and down in his fine clothes. Then he said, "You've turned into something, have you not, my Babu?"

"I've become something more than I was here."

"Then come and show us what you can do, my son. There is a white woman in this town, teaching something or other to the *harijans.* She comes to dinner on Sundays. Let's see if my money has been well spent on you. Let's see if all that proper English I bought you can turn this white woman's face toward us."

My father began it with my mother like this: My mother was teaching the poor Hindu and Muslim women of the shantytowns how to build smokeless ovens, riding her bicycle through Chikmagalur in the mornings to their quarters, spending all of her days with them. Since always, these women had cooked as most Indian women did, in low-roofed kitchen shanties over dung fires that filled the rooms with smoke, and led to black lung and cancer by the age of forty. Teaching them how to build the domed covering out of clay that would vent the smoke out of the wall was what my mother had heeded Kennedy's call to do.

When she'd first signed on with the Peace Corps, she was sent to the University of Wisconsin–Milwaukee, where she and the seventy-five others in her training group logged eight hundred hours of classroom work in Indian cultural and language studies. Then they were sent for two weeks to the Stockbridge-Munsee Indian Reservation in northern Wisconsin, where they lived in canvas tents. The Peace Corps had constructed a mock Indian village there, replete with shanties and stocked with educated Indian functionaries they had hired and flown over from Delhi to play the role of the poor and underserved.

Acting the part of people they didn't even condescend to speak to in life, those high-caste Indian educators needed help from the American trainees, some of whom enjoyed camping, to light the mock hearth fires, to pull water from the well, and they were glad when the day was done so they could retreat to their nearby hotel rooms, turn up the thermostats, and watch American television. The trainees were altruistic college grads, mostly hippies, and the men were avoiding a potential draft. It was cold in Wisconsin that fall, it rained every day. The Mohicans who lived there looked on as they drove by in their pickup trucks. My mother learned how to count to twenty in Kannada, and how to build smokeless ovens out of clay. The other trainees learned these things as well, but they also spent much of those two field weeks fucking each other in the tents, smoking pot, and gossiping. My mother wasn't interested in any of that. She even took the calisthenics part of the training seriously.

Finally, in Washington, where the group was shipped for their last three days in America, they were given vaccinations at the Peace Corps medical office, were lucky enough to be sworn in at the headquarters by the director, Sargent Shriver himself, and put on a plane to Madras. My mother stepped out of that plane and into the light of India when she was twenty-three years old. Volunteers would begin to quit that very first week; some of the men decided, their shirts plastered to their fevered bodies, that even Vietnam must be a better place than this. But my mother took off the sweater that had kept her warm on the plane, gave it to the happy porter at the bottom of the steps, let the airline women in their uniforms slip yellow welcome garlands around her neck, and pressed her hands together to return their greeting, *Namaste.* Then she began to fall in love.

All of the things she loved about India—the flowers in the women's hair, the call of the fishmonger in the mornings as he pushed his cart through the streets, the fuss and hullabaloo that went along with every simple transaction in the market for the day's salt and rice—she recounted to my father when he'd escort her home from dinner at my grandfather's house. Though my father didn't tell her so, those were all of the very same things that made him hate that place.

"How can you not find it backward, Ms. Denise, to haggle all day over one rupee here, one rupee there, that determining the price of a sack of rice should have the same import as buying and selling a car for these people?"

"For some of these people, Lawrence, one rupee here or there is as important as buying a car. Not everyone is as privileged as you are."

"All the noise, the crowd, the filth?"

"The kaleidoscope of life."

"Illness all around?"

"The healing festivals and spirituality."

"The lunatic babble of languages?"

"The songs and dances."

"The corruption and lack of opportunity?"

My mother hesitated at a rain puddle in the path, took my father's hand, and in her sari she hopped over it to him. "I know that not everything is perfect here, Lawrence. But don't you think that will change with time?"

"Not before your short visit here is over, I don't think, Ms. Denise. Not even before the end of our lives. I feel here that I'll never get to discover who I am. What my capabilities are and what I can do. Here, I am another unfulfilled face. But as you say, there are many interesting things about it. I am glad you are having a wonderful time before you will return to your own country."

"That is also true," my mother had said quietly.

My father confused my mother, made her worry about her idea of India in a way she hadn't before. What did he think of the work she and the Peace Corps were doing in India? she would ask him. What could even a thousand naive young Americans accomplish in a place that housed six hundred million people? my father would grin and say. But wasn't the world changed one life at a time? my mother would argue. Again my father would grin. "Then why not change mine?"

Though my mother couldn't have known it then, my father had given up his job in Bombay to be here, to sit in the enclosed garden of her house and have tea with her twice a week. He would often arrive with an umbrella opened above him just at the end of a heavy rain. He'd have to bang on my mother's door to be heard above the din, and she'd let him in, out of the downpour. They began to move about each other with ease without even noticing it, my father shaking the umbrella dry out the door, my mother lighting the kerosene stove in her kitchen to put on water for tea. It would be too loud from the rain to talk to each other, and sometimes they'd stand at the window together and look out at all the sullen people in the market huddled under the metal sheeting of their lean-to stalls. One time, they'd watched a gang of white cows trot into the market to find shelter from the rain. The cows had rolled their eyes in confusion when the people beat them back with sticks, had lowed like children crying in the rain, and my mother and father had looked at each other and smiled.

Perhaps my father timed his arrivals. After the rain, the air was cool and fresh, the world felt open and new, and he'd have brought a packet of almond cookies with him that they'd eat with their tea. My mother had placed purple daturas in old pickling jars about the patio, and they were surrounded by the lush leaves and color. The water would drip around them from the corrugated roof to the puddles on the patio, and then the still puddles would reflect the blue of the opening sky. My mother and father sat in her slat-backed chairs to look at this.

"For as much as you love India, Denise, you also like to spend your time in here."

"I get tired of all the staring. Any normal person would."

"It's the same for you here as a movie star, isn't it?"

"They have mansions and bodyguards, Lawrence. What do I have but my patio? And now I have you."

"Why are you quiet today, Denise?"

My mother looked out at the patio. The noise of the market was like a waking thing. Somewhere someone shouted. An oxcart driver cracked his whip, and the hooves and wheels began with a start. "I don't know why I'm quiet today, Lawrence. I snapped at you. I'm sorry. Let's talk about something else."

"Let's talk about that thing," my father said, and looked at her. "Whatever it is that is troubling you. Tell it to me, Denise. And all of my things, I will tell to you."

My mother said, "One of my women asked for money to buy clay for a stove. They are supposed to save and buy it on their own. I gave her the money. She bought glass bangles with it."

"That's only one of them, Denise."

"It hurt me. It made me feel foolish. It made me feel like nothing can be done. Even after all of this time here, what she did makes me feel like I don't want to help anyone."

Speaking English with my father was a respite, talking about the greater world with someone who knew there *was* one let my mother rest her mind. She didn't like my father's tailored clothes, his disdain for all things Indian, but she found that she didn't hate those things about him either. He was easy to be with, well mannered, polite. Whether he was stepping around her to open a door, or looking the other way in the market as she stopped to touch hands with a *harijan* friend, he was always exactly who he was. My mother liked my father's attempt at a mustache.

The monsoon rains muddied the town; men whipped buffalo at the plow in the rice paddies on the terraced hills. My mother and father began to talk about other things now, at other times, later at night, in the kitchen, where moths cast large shadows on the bare walls as they battered themselves against the lantern. Did my father feel pressure from his family to do something with his life? An unbearable pressure at all times, my father said. And what about her family? Did they support her in this endeavor of hers in India?

My mother looked down at the tumbler of rum and lychee juice in her hand, at the jokers and aces on the table from the game of three card they'd been playing as they talked. In her quiet voice, my mother said, "I'm not like you, Lawrence, with family all around me. In fact, I'm very envious of what you have. I see all the noise in your house, all the people. Even though your father is stern with you, when I visit your house, all I see is love."

"Your family is smaller, is it? Mother, father, sister, brother? That is how families are in America."

"It's more than that. My family is so small, it's as though I don't have any family at all. My mother abandoned me when I was young, and I had to live with my aunt. I have two sisters. I haven't seen them in twelve years, and I doubt I'll ever see them again. So I see your family, and I see everything I never had."

"And I see your independence here, Denise, your ability to move about, to think, to do what you want. I imagine the sort of freedom from family that you must have for yourself at home. To live as I desire. To work at my chosen career. That is all I want from this world."

"Do you want a family, Lawrence?"

"'Family is the door to happiness.'"

"And do you want to love your wife?"

"'The wife is the path to family.'"

My mother touched my father's hand. She said, "I want to stay in India."

My father looked at her hand on his and his heart leaped into his throat. Still, he was my father. He said, "Then we will stay."

That Sunday morning, my father brought my mother white garlands, which she wove into her hair, and then they walked through the town to let everyone know what had happened, my father in his suit, my mother on his arm in her white silk sari. My mother wore a sandalwood *bindi* on her forehead for beauty, and the sari came all the way down and covered her feet, making her look smaller than she really was. Her right arm, which my father held, was white and bare. She looked like a porcelain doll beside him, and in the market as they approached, the bicycle-rickshaw drivers waiting in their lines sat up and rang their bells, the chai vendors clapped the lids on their steel pots, and the people rushed out of the market to line the road and look at them. The white woman was so beautiful! Like Lakshmi herself. The young women ran into the market, came back, and scattered flower petals before my mother's feet. The older women covered their mouths with their hands as they smiled. My mother glanced at them, blushed, composed herself again. My father looked straight ahead.

At the Catholic church on the hill, the young men slouching and smoking cigarettes outside hopped up and opened the doors for them, and the church was full of the well-dressed Konkans of Chikmagalur, the men in the pews on the left in suits, the women and children in the pews on the right in tidy outfits and dark saris. Every single one of those five hundred faces turned to look at my mother and father as they stood framed in the doorway of the church, and when they did, their mouths dropped open. In the front pew, my grandfather waited just long enough for everyone to get a good, long look, and then he stamped his cane, cleared his throat, and the Konkans shut their mouths and turned their faces back to the altar. All through the Mass, children glanced at my mother where she stood alone among them, and my mother tried unsuccessfully not to sweat. Then my father led her on his arm to my grandfather's house, where my grandfather told the servants to put pork in the curry for *dukrajemas*. For the very first time since she'd been visiting them, my mother rinsed her fingers in the washing bowl, and she ate the food of the Konkans.

My mother and father were married in Velha Goa, the Konkan capital's old quarter, three months later. My mother was at the end of her service, and would have had no choice but to go home anyway. They chose to travel to Goa for the wedding because it had hotels on the beach that my mother's Peace Corps friends could enjoy themselves in, as well as to get away from Chikmagalur, which had turned into a tiresome carnival, strangers coming to my mother's house to throw flowers on her doorstep and sing benedictions, so shocked and pleased were they all that a boy from their town, even though a Konkan, would be marrying a white woman. This commotion had also ended my mother's work there.

Velha Goa was where the Portuguese had erected some of their oldest cathedrals, and my mother and father were married in the Church of Our Lady of the Rosary, built in 1549 on the quarter's highest hill. On the right side of the small church stood tall and white Peace Corps volunteers in a hodgepodge of borrowed dresses and slacks, and across from them were my grandfather and all his family in suits and saris, including my uncle Sam. It was hot, and the Americans fanned themselves with their missals. The Indians didn't move. My father wore a raw-silk Nehru jacket that was too big for him in the shoulders, and my mother wore a box hat and veil, and a simple white dress that revealed her calves. The dress she'd had tailored in Mangalore, the hat she'd bought in a European clothing store while in Bombay. Though the Konkans did not really have that tradition, a Peace Corps volunteer named Steve Stewart, who had been my mother's friend in training, stood in as my father's best man, and my mother's maid of honor was Lenore. There was a short reception and buffet at the King Manuel I Hotel in Panjim, to which my grandfather paid to have my parents driven in a black Mercedes limousine, and then the Indians boarded their buses for home, and my parents went with my mother's Peace Corps friends to party on the beach. Still ringing in my father's ears were my grandfather's words as they had left the church: "So we gave up a dowry, Babu. That is okay. But don't let them say of me, 'What a fool that Santan was, who paid for the wedding of his firstborn son.'"

My mother lived in my grandfather's house for one year as my father's wife, and as the months dragged on, my grandfather instructed my grandmother to scold and nag her in the kitchen until even my mother was ready to go home. And once she was, it wasn't a hard thing to complete the immigration papers, because my father had long since sent for them and filled his half of them out.

"You've known all this time, haven't you?" my mother said to him as she sat in exhaustion on their bed. My father said back, "Neither one of us will ever be real Indians." My father's visa came a few weeks later. My mother cried quietly as she folded her saris into her suitcase. In the lining of the suitcase was my grandmother's gold.

At the bus stand in Chikmagalur, my grandmother embraced my mother with her arms, now bare. She said, "You have made me so happy, Denise. You have made me proud of my son."

They had not been on speaking terms in weeks, ever since my grandmother had accused my mother of stealing her favorite paring knife, which of course my mother hadn't. So my mother made a face at my grandmother and said, "Eugenia, how can you say that to me now?"

My grandmother rubbed my mother's hands and said, "Simply because I am now allowed."

My mother and father waved farewell to everyone from the windows of the bus. Then they settled into their seats for the long ride to Bombay. In two days they would be in Chicago. My mother would never see India again.

The Second Son

All these years later in America, my father began to worry about my uncle Sam in a real way. So many of my father's dreams had come true; getting here in the first place, and beyond that, advancing and doing well. He had two fine children, a home in the suburbs, an Audi, an improving golf game. As he'd sip his evening tumblers of scotch in the basement and look at his painting of the lonely rider slumped over his donkey in the desert, he'd tell himself that he was happy. While he still usually passed out down there, now that my sister was in her bassinet beside my parents' bed, he'd go upstairs after his first sleep had worn off, to sleep again beside my mother in the early hours of the morning. Then the alarm clock would sound with its voices, its busy traffic reports, and he'd get up to wash and dress himself for work, commute into the city on the train, labor in his office, and come back home to do it all again.

It was summer, and my mother was always asleep at these times because raising her kids wore her out, but she'd wake

when my father would get in bed beside her with his cold
body, chilled from the night in the basement. Most nights
she would sigh at this, turn on her side away from him, and
the times when my father had a headache, he would lie with
his hands behind his head, looking up at the darkened ceiling. What did he think about at those times? His hopes and
dreams, surely, as people do in the night. But also, what was
this vague unease he felt?

"Are you awake, Denise?" my father said one of these early
mornings.

"I'm awake, Lawrence."

"Do you remember when we were first married and living
in my father's house in Chikmagalur?"

"I remember it."

"Do you remember how late we'd sleep in together? How
we'd hear the whole house wake up around us? How we'd lie
there even when we could hear them talking about us, wondering if we were sick? How my mother would quiet them,
telling them that we were newly married, and that the newly
married are always tired?"

"Your mother was nice to me in the beginning."

"It was nice to lie so long in bed, wasn't it?"

"Yes, Lawrence. It was nice."

"It was also a long time ago."

"It was."

"Did Elizabeth wake much while I was downstairs?"

"Every three hours. You know that."

"We were happy when Francisco was a baby, too."

"It was our very first time."

"I'll dress and feed him in the morning."

"That would help me."

"Our daughter Elizabeth is very beautiful, isn't she?"

"We've been lucky people."

"Francisco has been a good boy about it, hasn't he?"

"Francisco is a good boy."

"You don't talk to me anymore like you did in Chikmagalur."

"You don't talk to me that way either."

"Life has gone on, hasn't it, Denise?"

"Life has happened to both of us."

"We have a happy life."

"We have wonderful children."

"Denise," my father said in the dark.

"What is it, Lawrence?"

"I'm worried about Sam."

"About Sam?"

"I'm worried that he's unhappy."

"Sam's fine, Lawrence. Sam's just the way he's always been."

"That's not what I mean."

"Then what do you mean?"

"Sam will be thirty-one this year."

"So we'll throw him a party."

"He'll be thirty-one, and he's not married. It's not normal for a Konkan man to pass thirty without being married, let alone to be thirty-one. All that Sam has done here is run and play. I worry that he will always do only that."

My mother turned to look at my father in the dark. She could see the shape of his body. She had been his wife nine years now. Many times in those years, she had loved him. For how tired she always felt since my sister's birth, she did not feel tired now. She said, "Why in the world are you suddenly worried about Sam?"

"It's not normal for a Konkan man to be alone the way he is."

"Since when has he been a normal Konkan man? All of that ended when he got off that plane. And then you made him shave off that mustache. Why did you make them do that, Lawrence? That must have been so humiliating for them. All of us are here because you wanted to come. You know as well as anyone that when people come here, they can't be who they were before."

"Sam should be married."

"Sam should be left alone."

"I'm worried that he's not happy."

"Since when have you worried about Sam's being happy?"

"I have always worried about my brother's happiness."

"You have always told yourself that you worried about his happiness, just as you tell yourself that you worry about all of them. But when was the last time you wrote a letter to India? And why is it that we've never visited? You know what's really going on. And it's your worry about those things that's tearing you up. Your work. Your career. Where you live. Your car. And now it's the country club more than anything."

"What do you know about it?"

"I know everything that goes on in this house."

"Sam's situation is unseemly."

"There it is. There we are. I knew we'd get to the truth if we only tried."

"I should have left you in India with all the other trash."

"How would you have gotten here?"

"I would have found my way."

"And who would you take to your wretched company parties?"

"There are other women in this country."

"Then why don't you go and find one?"

"If you tempt me, then I will."

"Then I've tempted you."

"Then I will."

"Be my guest."

"What's happened to you?"

"What's happened to you?"

Then my sister began to cry.

If the opportunity for other women had ever presented itself to my father, he had not had that in him. For one, he wasn't brave enough to face what that would bring to his house. He knew my mother would leave him, and sooner or later the news would make it to India, where they would devour it the way they did all gossip. Then he would have failed in his duties as a firstborn son, and even here in America, he would know nothing but shame. And for two, in the fingerprint that was my father's sexual identity, my mother was the only one in the world he would ever be able to meet in intimacy. My mother had been his first and only. His imagination could not move beyond that.

If, in fact, my father were to fail to succeed at the American way of life, there would be nowhere in the world he could go to escape the regret he knew would follow him. So he dealt with my mother's resentment against him the way he dealt with everything that did not fit the plan: He ignored it. And when his anger against her rose up in him again in the evenings, with the children asleep and the house quiet around him, he'd sit in the basement by his painting and imagine that he was the man on the donkey's back riding through the desert of his life. As he'd drink, he'd feel the nobility of his hard calling rise up, and toward the end of another session, his cheeks warm and red, his vision spinning, at that moment when he'd understand that he'd numbed himself enough to shut his eyes and sleep, he'd feel ecstatically proud of himself, that life had turned out good despite all, that he was lucky indeed to have achieved so much: his job, this house, his children, even his lawn with the oak trees on it. In Chikmagalur, as a boy, he'd put himself to bed dreaming of being welcomed into the Britishers' club, the white men standing up in their red jackets and waxed mustaches to hurrah and clap for him. No, America was not Britain. But America was the most powerful country in the world. So my father felt, in those last euphoric moments, that every choice he'd made to get here had been the right one, that what he'd do tomorrow would be just what he'd done today. He'd lay himself on his couch, puff out a few quick breaths, curl his knees up to his chest, and sleep. Some four or five hours later, he'd blink his eyes awake, sober again, his head pounding, and the times he was sick with it, he'd say aloud in that basement, "Why do I do it? Why do I always do it?" He'd walk up the two flights of stairs in the dark, past his antique grandfather clock with its pendulum swinging away ever more bits of this life, and he wouldn't think any one of those self-congratulatory thoughts he had before in the drinking, would even feel remorse for having thought them. There was so much more to do. He hadn't achieved anything yet. Then his new hobbyhorse would come into his head and as he'd lay himself down beside my mother, he'd say to himself, *It is time for my brother Samuel to marry.*

My uncle's time on my grandfather's coffee plantation had informed him about himself more than anything else in his youth. What a miserable time that had been. The plantation wasn't large by any means, was something the great Hindu planters of the mountains might have given to their third-born sons, but it was what my grandfather had managed to scrape out for himself in the time that he had served the British.

The plantation measured sixty acres along the steep slope of a mountain on the road to Kemmangundi, and my grandfather had hired a crew of *harijans* to throw up a two-room cinder-block house on the level hilltop for the times he'd thought he'd spend there. If the British hadn't left, my grandfather would have built a proper coffee planter's house for himself with a portico and deck, an orchard of citrus and breadfruit, he would have enlarged the holdings until it was an estate, and one day he would have retired up there. But then the British left. My grandfather hid the titles to the land through those terrible years at the end of the Raj, and the plantation was the least of his worries.

In 1952, when his troubles had passed and he was rein-stated as a police officer as part of the reconciliations begun by Nehru, who saw early on that the fledgling India needed trained men, my grandfather rode his old Triumph motorcycle up into the mountains to see what had become of the place. He expected to find everything fallen into neglect, the embankments of the terraces collapsed by the rains, weeds risen up between the coffee bushes, the forest taking back what belonged to it. Instead, he found it even more neatly tended than when he'd left, row after tidy row of trimmed bushes on the sharp-looking steps of the terraces, beans sprouting on the branches in clusters, weeds drying in the sunlight in piles. Somebody had come to love this land in a way no one had loved it before. In fact, the only thing in disrepair on the whole of the plantation was the long-shuttered house. My grandfather unlocked the door, made a hand broom from a string and some sticks, and went to work sweeping out the rat shit.

The *harijans* came to him that night, fifty thin men in their rags in the yard. Even if it had been five thousand men like that, my grandfather would not have been afraid. They raised their fists and shouted their arguments, and for a long time my grandfather let them. Then he pointed his finger at them, all of them at once, as he stood on that raised porch with his gun on his hip and his lantern in his hand. He said, "The master has come back!

"All of this is now over. You've enjoyed yourselves in my absence. I won't begrudge you that. I also won't demand compensation for the harvests that you've stolen from me." He stood on that porch until every last one of those men receded into the trees. After that, his titles were recognized by the new Indian Coffee Board, and he sent up different cousins to manage the bean picking and sale at harvest time. When my uncle Sam turned eighteen, my grandfather sent him.

The house was full of spiders and rats when my uncle Sam arrived, and his first days were busy with chasing them out. Then he unfolded his clothes on the simple shelves in the room with the hammock where he'd sleep. As children, he and Les had often imagined their father's mansion in the coffee mountains, its high, gabled roof, the great double doors. And though on the bus ride up, my uncle had known to expect much less than that, the first sight of this cattle shed of a house had sunk him. The porters tossed his bags from their heads onto its porch, and then they ran back along the path to the bus to leave him there. There was nothing he could do but unlock the metal door, closed eight months, since last year's harvest, and let light into the house again.

There was nowhere to shit but in the bushes; he couldn't light the lantern at night because insects would swarm in. There was one table, one chair, a knife, a spoon, a pot for cooking rice, a two-burner stove on the table, a plain wooden cross on the wall of each room, and a well in the back with a hand pump. It was a place to be alone and hear the forest sounds. In time, my uncle would come to appreciate the sealed cement floor, which was easy to keep clean, the view down the mountain's slope from the bedroom window, bathing behind the house with cold well water. But not yet. On the lee side of the mountain was the *harijan* village, where the workers lived out of sight with their families. In the mornings, those men would appear in the mist among the coffee plants in their rags, slashing down weeds, pruning the bushes with hand knives, and my uncle would rise from his hammock in the back room to make himself tea on the burner before going out in his boots to see that the work was done.

It rained every day in the mountains, at night my uncle felt alone for the first time in his life. What a strange thing it was to be alone, to have no people about him as he'd always had, to have no sound from the radio, to not have one single thing around him but the forest and its might. The great Hindu plantations had elephants for the heavy work of clearing the forest, to lift the fallen trees to the roadside with their trunks once the men had sawed them down. The men buried the trees too big for even the elephants to lift in smoldering pits and turned them into charcoal.

My uncle knew nothing about growing coffee, didn't pretend that he did. The *harijans* had nothing to say to him as they went about their work, and even leaning against the trunk of a great tree and watching them during the day, he existed only unto himself. The *harijans* knew what they were doing, they didn't need him. So my uncle went for long walks in his rubber boots along those steep paths and roads, reflecting all the time on himself, and now and again he would come upon sights in the forest: scarlet birds with orange bills on every branch of a teak tree, a tumbling creek lined with a carpet of emerald ferns, a gang of Hindu mahouts in their turbans working young elephants through virgin forest. He'd watch as the Hindus whistled and clucked, tapped the elephants' knees with their sticks, and the elephants would flap their ears and rip young trees from the ground. Sometimes an elephant would trumpet and rear, and a mahout would stroke its face like a loved thing to calm it. The elephants flicked at flies with their tails, pushed down trees with their gleaming tusks. Then they would kneel to pick the trees up, lumber up out of the ravine with the vegetation clutched in their trunks. Sometimes a train of four or five of them would come swinging down a road, mahouts perched on their necks, and my uncle would step aside to let them all pass. The elephants wore chains around their feet like anklets, and the long lashes over their eyes were like women's. Who wouldn't love to look at elephants? And what was it about elephants that could make one feel so sad?

My uncle followed all of those red trails that ran through that dark forest, and once he found an old stone shrine with three rusted swords cemented into it, and another time he came upon a dead tree whose lower branches were so covered with black bangles that they looked as if they were wrapped in glass. No one was about, and a wind came and made the bangles rustle like chimes. What did these Hindu things mean? Why were the Hindus so different from him? My uncle looked about, into the forest, behind him on the path, and then he slipped one of the bangles off a branch, put it into his pocket.

All the way back to the plantation, he felt regret about what he'd done, and he woke up in the night wracked with sweats and fever. In the morning, he hurried up the mountain to find that holy place, and he put the bangle on its branch again. By the time he was back at the house, he was well.

Once, on a whim he walked into the workers' village, and it had been noisy with the sound of children playing rag ball, women hollering about this and that as they cooked, the blue smoke of their fires seeping up through the planks of the roofs to join the forest mist. Everyone fell still and silent as soon as the first child saw him. What could he do but walk past all those staring eyes? They were poor people who lived in the rain. My uncle understood that they knew who he was, and he hadn't liked that. He didn't go back there again.

When the beans came ripe on the bushes in their greens and reds, my uncle would walk through the terraces at night with my grandfather's shotgun, ready to shoot poachers. But he knew in his heart that he wouldn't be able to shoot anyone. Once, he shined his light on six sambars, their horns curving up like bows, and they'd let him look at them a moment before they'd leaped away.

Those two wet years in the mountains passed slowly, the longest time of my uncle's life. But he learned to love the mists and trees, the echoes of the birds, all that shadow and green. His heart was in his town, Chikmagalur, and he counted down the days between each visit. But this thing in the mountains also belonged to him.

Strange things happened up there among those superstitious Hindus. One night, there was a moaning at the door. My uncle lit the lantern and went to it. An old woman lay on his stoop in a tattered sari, and in the shine of his lantern he could see figures running away. The old woman looked like a wet rag, a scrap of something, all long bones and angles, bird-like, not human at all. My uncle carried her into the house and set her on the chair.

"What is it, mother?" my uncle said, shining the lantern on her face. Her face beneath her sari was as weathered as a nectarine pit.

"My master's son, I have worked for your father all of these years. Now it is my time to die. I have asked them to bring me here so that you could see my death. So long I have worked for your well-being. Look at me now at the end of mine."

My uncle made tea, gave it to her. After the tea, she vomited rice onto the floor. My uncle wiped her face with a cloth and helped her sip water.

"Your father took this land from us," the old woman said. "We had small plots here. He came the first time with papers from the British. His officers all had guns. They took our harvest because your father had those papers. My husband walked down the mountains to Mysore. The district governor said the papers meant that the land belonged to your father. If we wanted to stay on the land, we must work the land for him. When the British left, we had our land again. Then your father came back. He had new papers, from the new government. My husband walked down to Bangalore. The new government told my husband the very same thing."

My uncle didn't say anything.

"If my husband had had a gun, I would have told my husband to shoot your father. Every day that you have been here, I have wished that a serpent would bite you. My husband died here, and now I will die in your house."

My uncle took two aspirin from the bottle he'd brought with him, helped the woman swallow them with tea. This meant that he held her chin while he poured the tea into her mouth.

"Is it modern medicine, my master's son?"

"It is modern medicine, mother," my uncle said.

My uncle carried her into the second room, unfurled his *lungis* to make a bed for her. All through the night he sat over her as she moaned. In the morning, the old woman walked home to the village.

In the days that followed, no one came to say anything to my uncle, to inform him about the woman's well-being, or any of it. As quickly as someone had entered his life, my uncle was alone again. There was nothing around him on the mountain but the rain and the mist, the hoots of the night birds as they hunted in the dark.

My uncle Sam's absence from our house after the birth of my sister became an emptiness that my mother let herself feel. And though my father also never saw him, still he knew my uncle was nearby in the city, single, unsettled according to my father's understanding of that, alive and doing something, though my father did not know what. What in the world was his brother really doing?

What my uncle Sam was really doing was going on his drives. And often, these drives would lead my uncle to Ridge Lawn, to Aldine Avenue, where we lived. He'd drive slowly down the street once, twice, as though to make sure that our dark house was still there, that we were asleep, that this part of his life was a real thing. Maybe he did this to see that we, his brother and sister-in-law, his nephew and niece, were safe in the night. Maybe he did this for another reason. Though we were not in his life, we were always on my uncle's mind. Often, he would smoke at his kitchen window in the night before bed, a vice he had lapsed back into, look at the sprouting plants of his garden, and he would think, *This is what it is. This is the life that belongs to me.*

My father called my uncle to invite him to my sister's christening. And more than that, he called because he wanted to talk to his brother. This was early one Saturday morning, when my father knew that my uncle would be home. In all their years together in America, my father had not once called my uncle on the telephone, and so this was a singular moment for both of them. My father called my uncle from his study, and as he did, my father took out the picture from the drawer of the family in Chikmagalur when they'd been kids.

"Samuel?"

"Yes, Babu?"

"My daughter's baptism is next Saturday."

"Saturdays are busy for me, Babu. They are the best days for showing real estate."

"Regardless of that, it is best that you come."

"Then I will be there."

"How is work, brother?"

"Work is fine."

"Are you healthy, happy?"

"I am fine, my Babu."

"Have you written to Father lately?"

"Every Sunday after church."

"How is Father?"

"Father is aging."

"He's very proud of us, you know."

"He tells me in every letter."

"Samuel?"

"Yes, Babu?"

"I have been meaning to see you about something. There is something that has been troubling me that we must discuss."

"Is it something about the children?"

"The children are happy and fine. It is about something else. It is about you specifically, my brother."

"Babu, I am happy and fine."

"Nonetheless, we must discuss. We will see you Saturday. You will have lunch with us after."

"Yes, Babu."

My uncle Sam did and did not want to go to my sister's baptism, just as he did and did not want to turn past our house on every single one of those drives. The night before the christening, my uncle could not sleep, and he got up in the middle of it and wrapped his checkered *lungi* about his legs. In his kitchen, with his fingers he mixed rice flour and water in a plastic bowl until it was a soupy dough, and poured dollops of it onto the crackling griddle. When the bubbles rose up through these rice pancakes, he flipped them with a sliver of wood he'd knocked off a two-by-four in his garage with a screwdriver and hammer just for this purpose, a piece of wood as thin as a playing card. Then he sprinkled the *dossa* pancakes one by one with sugar as he ate them at the table with tea, his favorite treat as a boy in Chikmagalur, which he could now make for himself when he needed it. Later, he turned out the light, lit a cigarette at the window, and looked at his plants in their first shoots: corn, squash, green beans, zucchini, things he had not known before he'd come here but had grown to like eating. Then he looked up at the stars. There were few stars to see because of the brightness of the city.

Did he feel happy or unhappy in America? my uncle asked himself as he smoked. He'd often felt both happy and unhappy. Then what was this feeling now? Tonight he felt that he simply was. Yes, he wanted to go to the baptism to see my sister, to see my mother and father and all of us, but no, he did not want to go to the baptism because he also didn't want to see any of us. Our faces spun through my uncle's mind, my smile as I'd leap at him to be carried, the suck and yawn of my sister's mouth, my mother's long look at him in the darkened rooms of their affair, my father's commanding mustache and jaw. How would he be able to go through this life always wondering about all of this?

My uncle lay on his bed in his room, which had nothing more on its walls than the wooden cross with the palm frond tied around it because he had not been successful in America the way my father had. The way he lived in America meant he would go on having bare walls like this. My mother's face crept into his mind in all of those looks that she had given him, and again she was opening the door for him when he'd first come back from Portland, again she was reaching to turn out the light on them in that motel room in Vermont, again she was shutting the drapes in Babu's bedroom and dropping her robe from her shoulders for him. How could they have done those things? Her body came to him, her breasts with their dark nipples, her long and opalescent thighs. Why had she done those things to him? Her waist, her lips, how dark his hands seemed against her skin as he held her wrists above her head. Had she loved him?

My uncle turned in his bed, clutched his pillow to himself. He pounded his running legs through streets of Chikmagalur as a boy again in his memory to put the thoughts of my mother away, again he chased the pigs that rooted in the gutters, again he scaled the trunk of a mango tree to toss down the fruit. Sunday washing. His mother stood the children in buckets one by one, soaped their bodies, scoured their ears with a rough rag so hard that they cried out. Then it was head to toe with the towel and on to the next one. Putting on the Sunday clothes. Following their father in a line out of the house in their suits and dresses, my grandmother at the end with her maroon sari and parasol. They were different from the Hindus, they were better. My grandfather in his uniform, my grandfather putting on his belt. The white men in their red jackets. The trumpets, the blue and red and white flag. The crowd of them. The crossed lines of that flag. The Hindus worshipped false gods. "Take it to hell with you," my grandfather said to the laundry washer, throwing the shirt in the man's face because the shirt still had a stain on it. The heads of the Hindu gods in the temples: the elephant Ganesha, the monkey Hanuman, Lord Vishnu with his arms: the cudgel, the conch, the lotus, the shield, his knee lifted to dance. The cobras. The five gifts of the cow, even the piss. The flowers. Krishna in his chariot. Da Gama on his ship. Arjuna with his bow. Xavier with his cross. The pictures of children talking in the books. The raising of the Indian flag. "What is that round thing, Babu?" "Ashoka's Wheel." "Who is Ashoka?" "The Hindus' king." The hunched and pinching nuns. Babu crying on the bus. Babu stepping off the bus again. Babu in his fine clothes. Babu at the head of the table. The white woman on her bicycle. The white woman picking out the *obbe*. Babu and the white woman. Babu helping the white woman over a puddle. The white woman laughing. Babu laughing. "She is beautiful," said Lira, under the tree. "You are beautiful." "I have not felt like this." "I have not ever felt it." *"E puri kon achi?"* All those servants. His parents. Had anyone really loved him? The white girl. Who had heard of such a thing? On a bicycle. Her white knees. Her hair. The golden strands of her

hair. Lesley Wenceslaus had one. "Give it to me." The golden
thread in the sunlight. The white girl in a blue sari. In a white
sari. In a saffron sari. Touching all the *harijans*. Touching the
harijan children. The white woman's blue eyes. The white
woman's eyes looking at him. "I won't eat the pork." Ms.
Denise. Ms. Denise in a white sari in the rain. Ms. Denise with
her hair wet. Mrs. Denise D'Sai. Lawrence's wife. Lawrence
and his wife waving from the bus. They had all looked at one
another at the station. What had anyone to say? The first aerogram. Babu is in America. The plane on the tarmac. "But how
does it fly, Samuel?" "With the engines." "But where are the
engines?" "The round things under the wing, Lesley, can't you
see?" "I thought those were the horns." The cold like pain.
Babu is fat. The cold that burns the fingers. The lights of the
cold city. "Why have you grown those ridiculous mustaches?"
"Where in the world are we?" Ms. Denise opening the door in
jeans, in a white blouse, smiling at him. Lawrence's wife. "You
don't have to call me that anymore, Samuel. We're in America.
And we're also all grown up." "Call him Sam." "His name is
Samuel. Samuel Erasmus, as a matter of fact." "Call him Sam
for god's sake, please, Denise. He'll never make it here with
that ridiculous name." A whisper, a squeeze of the hand. The
color of her hand on his skin. "He gets so crazy about fitting
in. Forget about it. I'm glad you are here. I've needed a break
from him."

My uncle Sam shaved in the morning, put on the same white
collared shirt and black tie that he wore to show houses, picked
up a bouquet of carnations at the Dominick's supermarket on
Cumberland, and went to my parents' church in Ridge Lawn.
He arrived late and watched from the doorway as the priest
poured the holy water over my sister's forehead at the altar.

This woke my sister, who let up a cry from my mother's arms, and my mother smiled and hushed her as my father dabbed her forehead dry with the white cloth. My uncle came and stood beside me in the pew where my parents had left me.

"Uncle Sam!"

"*Shh,*" he said, touching his finger to his lips. Then he petted my hair. "Afterward, give these flowers to your mother."

The priest said, "And so we welcome Elizabeth D'Sai to the family of our Lord, and into the community of our church. Amen." Everybody in the church said, "Amen," and then it was the next baby's turn, and my sister was baptized like that.

After the service, the priest shook my father's hand, and people came to peer at the baby in my mother's arms. My mother was in a hat and veil, and people told her how nice she looked. Then the crowd went to their cars and there was no one left but us, my parents on the steps of the church with my sister, my uncle below them with me, holding my hand.

"Come and look at her," my mother said and came down the steps in her heels. "Isn't she pretty?" she said and cooed at my sister. "The prettiest girl in the world."

"Like her mother," my uncle said.

My mother looked at him and said, "That's nice of you, Sam."

We walked my uncle to his car. My father jingled his keys and was happy. He said, "Coming to lunch with us today, Sammy?"

"I have to show some houses, Babu. We'll talk another time. Very important Patels straight from Gujarat. You know how it is: 'Cheapest price only, thank you very much.' Today is for you to enjoy. Let me go and deal with these people."

"The Patels are coming every day," my father said to no one.

"Uncle Sam, I want to go with you."

My uncle pulled his hand from mine. "You should be with your family today, Francisco."

"Aren't you also our family?"

"One more Konkan," my father said, and smiled.

"Yes, one more, Babu," my uncle said.

"I will call you soon to talk, Samuel."

"I'll be waiting for your call."

Then my uncle Sam put on his sunglasses, got in his car, and drove away. My sister stirred and my mother quieted her by putting her finger in her mouth. What could I do but throw the flowers on the ground and stomp on them?

My father cuffed my ear. He said, "Why did you do that, Francisco?"

"Because I wanted my uncle Sam."

My father picked me and the flowers up. I wrapped my arms around his neck, lay my head on his shoulder. I went on crying for a time as we started back to our car, and then that left me. I watched the lot and the trees beyond it tilt with my father's stride.

"Are you finished?"

"Yes, Dad."

"You must control yourself."

"I know."

"You must never act like that."

"I won't."

"You must always behave like a firstborn son."

Before my father ever had a chance to call, my uncle Sam called my mother. He called the following Saturday afternoon, when he knew she'd be there. My father was again at his golf lessons, this time at the Billy Caldwell public links just over the border in the city. His game had improved quite a bit, and despite the costs and distractions of the new baby, he was as determined as he'd ever been that he would one day be invited to join the Ridge Lawn Country Club.

"Denise," my uncle said into the phone in a quiet voice, "what is Babu on about?"

"Don't worry about that, Sam. It's one of his silly things. Lawrence thinks that it's time you got married."

"He's worried that I marry?"

"That's all it is."

My uncle looked out the window at his garden. The eggplants were unfurling themselves on the ground, the zucchini were reaching out with their vines. He said, "How are the children?"

"The children are fine. Francisco would like to see you more. Elizabeth does what babies do."

"And what do you think about it, Denise?"

"About what, Sam?"

"About my getting married."

My mother was quiet a long time. She sat at her kitchen table and watched through the window as the beautiful clouds scudded across the blue sky. Her mouth felt tight on her face. Then she let that go. She said, "I want you to be happy in this life, Sam. I've always understood that you would marry someone."

My uncle Sam was quiet. A flock of birds, starlings, came into his pear tree. In the glass of the window, he could see his own watery reflection looking back at him as he looked out at the world. "I should see Francisco more," he said, and my mother said, "Yes," and my uncle said, "I only wanted to know what Babu wanted."

————

Among the Konkans of India, the most important event on the calendar is marriage, any marriage, and the most important of these is the marriage of a firstborn son. Traditionally, three days before the wedding, the bride and groom are isolated from each other, which is not a hard thing to accomplish since marriage among the Konkans is arranged, and if the bride and groom know each other at all beforehand, they are lucky. The boy will certainly have seen the girl a number of times during the dances she is required to do in her father's compound, to show the boy's family her knowledge of the ancient things, as well as her body, and even if after the dancing the boy doesn't care for the look of her, he'll have to argue with all of his heart for his father to break what the matchmakers and astrological signs have determined should be made one. If the girl doesn't like the look of the boy, too bad. Her mother will say to her, "Stop feeling sorry for yourself! Do you think I thought your father was Dharmendra when I married him?"

But three days before the wedding, the bride is sent to the women's quarters of her father's house, and there, the women of the family, in their finest saris, begin to decorate the bride like the gift she will be to her husband and his family. All of the women involved in this process have long since been married themselves, and however their own marriages have turned out, they will be jealous and happy for the girl, cooing at her with doe eyes, regaling her with stories about how nervous they had been on their wedding nights, how nervous their poor husbands had been, telling the girl that no matter what happens when she is finally alone with her husband, she must not laugh or avert her eyes or do any of those things that might be her impulse, but she must hold her trembling husband to her as though he were Rama himself. Otherwise, nothing might ever get done. Men trembled like that on their wedding nights. The women tell the girl that she must set all thoughts of herself aside to reassure her scared and shivering husband, who will be her guide and partner through this life.

First, they bathe the bride in the family's bathtub or bathing yard, each one of their hands taking a turn to scrub the girl's body, her breasts especially, all of her sacred places. Then she is washed in milk, and then rinsed in spring water to take away the smell of the milk. Her skin is supple then, and the women anoint her with ghee, wash her again, and then rub her whole body with coconut oil. Poor families do this symbolically with dabs of these fine things on the girl's forehead, but the rich do the whole thing. When the bride's hair is dry and combed, her grandmother, or the next oldest woman if the grandmother is dead, pulls tightly on her hair and braids it. The bride's hair glows with the coconut oil, and it won't be touched again by anyone but her husband. Then the women paint designs on her hands and feet with henna, the same filigreed designs of the flowering of life that the Hindus paint on their brides' hands, though the Konkans would never admit that this is a Hindu tradition. As the bride sits still on her stool, letting the henna dry and set into her skin, she is dusted all over with herbal scents and sandalwood powder. All of this takes place in her confinement room, usually her mother's bedroom, the room lit with votive candles set all around her feet. The women burn incense sticks and oils in the corners, offerings to the Virgin Mary. The shutters are closed against any man's eye, and the room grows thick and heady with these scents. Next, they dress her in her silk undergarments, and begin to drape her with jewelry. The jewelry is borrowed from someone rich in the family, silver anklets with dozens of tiny bells hanging off them like chimes, a silver hip chain with bells on it as well, a filigreed nose stud, delicate earrings of goldlike fans, necklaces and bangles, and finally a gold *bindi*. Then they wrap the girl in her red satin bridal sari, and sweetmeats are brought and fed to her by her mother's hand, though not too many, so that her belly won't burst out of the tightly wrapped sari's folds. The girl waits two days like this, each and every one of the women telling her how envious they are.

In the confinement room of his father's house, the groom is attended in much the same manner by the married men of his family, though not his father, who sits in his preferred chair like a throne in the living room, receiving bowed visitors and their gifts of folded cash and liquor bottles, which pile up at his feet. The groom's fingernails and toenails are trimmed, any calluses he might have on his hands or the soles of his feet pared away and sanded smooth, something especially important for the Konkans, who regard themselves first and foremost as merchants, who don't have calluses as do the Hindu laborers who work for them, until he is as smooth for his bride as a god. His hair and mustache are clipped, and though he bathes himself alone, he is then anointed with coconut oil. The men dress him in his best white satin suit in the casual Hindu style, white satin sandals slipped over his feet like ballet slippers. Then he is carried on his chair out to the wedding courtyard, usually the courtyard of his father's house, where lights of many colors have been strung up to form a ceiling, or if the family is poor, candles are placed on the courtyard's walls.

All during this time, the married men of his family have been telling him about sex, about how he must approach his bride with care, handle her as he would a flower, but how he must also be like a bee and enter that flower, and how to take the bloodied marital sheets from the bed once he has, and present them to his father. His father will then hang them on a nail beside the door to the house so that everyone can see that the marriage cannot now be revoked. And if the groom has earned himself a reputation for philandering among the servant girls of his father's house in his youth as some of them have, the men of his family remind him not to mount the poor girl like a buffalo, but to give her a chance to let her heartbeat slow, and meet her in that place women call love. Because if he is rough with her that first time, the girl will know everything he has done, and then she will nag him about it for the rest of his life, which, all the men agree, is a hell of a thing to put up with.

The Konkan wedding is more for the groom's family than anyone else, the dowry the most important part of it. Weddings were known among the Konkans at the time my parents were married as the "three keys," because the best matches earned for the young man three keys from his bride's father: the key to a house, the key to a shop, and the key to a car or motorcycle. The wedding itself was a festival: nonstop drinking and singing, gluttonous eating of *dukrajemas* pork curry, lamb-and-pea–stuffed samosas, and the men of the groom's family would form lines and sing *"E puri kon achi,"* kicking their legs with such violence that an observer couldn't be sure if this was a celebration or the protest of a travesty. So many were unhappy in their marriages that a case for the latter could be made. Weddings were like that in India.

After the conclusion of the Catholic ceremony at the church, all of the Konkans of the area would toss flowers onto the ground for the bride and groom to walk on as they left, toss rice on the couple's heads, and follow the newlyweds in a raucous procession all the way to the young man's father's house. A meal would be eaten, and then the couple would retreat to the marital bed prepared for them, until the groom would emerge with the bloodied sheets to the ululations of the women of his family. Sometimes this took less than an hour, but sometimes it took days. The most nervous of husbands knew how to scratch the insides of their nostrils to make their noses bleed. The best marital sheets had two or three drops of blood on them, nothing more. The ones that set off knowing glances among the married women were the ones that were heavily stained. Once the sheets were hung, the two fathers would embrace publicly in the groom's father's living room, exchange outrageous gifts of money and liquor to seal the new covenant between their families, which didn't really cost them anything as the gifts were at once symbolic and exactly the same. Everyone would touch the stained sheets hanging beside the door for luck: newly married women for the fertility held within them, young men in their hopes of good matches, old women for added wisdom, and old men for one last moment of virility.

And while everyone loved every instant of the drawn-out Konkan weddings, the best part for the younger brothers of the groom was the *roase,* the ceremony that happened before any of the others, the ritual that opened the three wedding days. On the first day of the wedding weekend, the groom, in his best Western suit, would leave what would soon be his confinement room and sit on a chair in the courtyard, where the lights were only just beginning to be strung up. His younger brothers would come with their own chairs in their best clothes, and sit beside him. Cousins of marital age were invited into this ceremony as well. It was something like the gathering of Rama's supporters before they wheeled out on their chariots to battle the *rakshasa*s and reclaim his wife, Sita. Everyone would congratulate the groom, and they'd pass around a bottle of cashew fenny, the liquor of the Konkans. As soon as everyone was drunk and giggling, the married men of the family, and especially the women, would come out from the house with eggs and flour, and then they'd pelt the young men in the chairs with the eggs, dump flour over their heads, until the youths were white with it. The *roase* was an informal and ridiculous event. For as much as they loved the ceremony, none of the Konkans knew any longer what it could possibly mean. And neither does history.

My father had a *roase* at his father's house in Chikmagalur three days before his wedding, and my uncle Sam sat beside him on one side, and my uncle Les sat on the other. Instead of being in seclusion in her mother's house while her groom and his brothers were being doused in eggs and flour in their finest clothes, my mother was sitting anxiously in a chair across from the country director's desk at the Peace Corps headquarters in Bombay. The director was a balding functionary from Washington, and with his fingers folded, he was giving my mother a lecture. Did she understand the economic impulse of people in matters like this? My mother looked down at her hands and said that she did. Was she sure it was really about love? My mother bit her lip and said, "Yes."

"Why don't you at least wait until your service is over, Denise? You might feel differently when you see everyone from your training group going home."

"Two months isn't a long time. I've already begun to wrap up my major projects."

"You know better than anyone that they'll expect different things out of you as a wife."

"I'm marrying a Konkan. He's not the kind of Indian you're thinking about."

"Everyone in the world has their own idea of marriage. I hope you haven't lost sight of who you are in your time in India."

"I know who I am."

"I know that you do, Denise."

"So you've decided not to pull me out?"

"I won't do that to you. Congratulations. Funny thing, this Peace Corps. So many things are coming out of it that weren't in the original plan. I've signed off on six marriages this year alone. Weddings may be its only real purpose."

While my father was laughing and washing the eggs and flour off with buckets of water with his brothers in my grandfather's courtyard, my mother was on the night bus to Goa. Above her on the rack was a box with a hat and veil that she'd bought while in Bombay, and underneath the bus in the carriage was her suitcase with her wedding dress in it. Twenty other Peace Corps volunteers from her training group were on the bus with her, and it was certainly among the rare times in Indian history that a local bus traveling through the countryside was carrying mostly whites. The volunteers had brought rum with them, and as they drank and sang to the Hindi music that the driver played all through the night, my mother rested her head against the window and looked out at the darkness. There wasn't even a single light to see in the night along the highway. Even though she knew the road was lined with villages, she could see nothing but fleeting glimpses of men sitting by lanterns and smoking cigarettes as the bus passed.

India was her life now. Lawrence would be her life. And she was happy about it. Lawrence treated her with a respect she'd never known in an American man. True, she hadn't known many American men. But once in a while. To pay her way through high school when she'd lived with her great-aunt, she'd worked at the Baby Ruth candy-bar factory in Chicago. Men from there had come out with her group of conveyor-line friends to bowl at the local alley. Every one of them had told her she was beautiful. Then when they were drunk, they would say it to all the other girls, too. And always there was that man in her room. These Indian men with their false bluster, their real innocence, were not like the men at home. She had learned that she could trust these men. She trusted one of them so much, in two days she would marry him.

All around her on the bus, the Americans were drinking and telling stories of what they had seen in India. Wasn't it good that one of them was going to marry someone here? they asked each other. It was good beyond belief. Maybe they all should marry here? They all certainly should. Too bad they weren't as brave as Denise. If they were, then maybe they really would change the world. And then once, and softly, someone behind my mother had said, "But isn't it mad? Isn't it also a lunatic thing?"

"Come on, Denise. Why so glum? Have a drink and participate," Lenore had said, and leaned over the back of her seat. My mother looked out the window and said, "I'm all right. Don't worry about me. I'm supposed to be like this, Lenore. I'm getting married."

In Chikmagalur that night, my grandfather sat in his chair in his suit with none of the gifts at his feet that would have been expected of the family of a firstborn's Konkan bride, because my mother was not a Konkan bride. The mood was somber in the house. The visitors did not know how to act, everyone glanced at each other in the absence of gifts. Was this truly worth it? What could this strange sort of wedding mean? My grandfather sat through that night the way he'd sat through all of it. Not a single instant of it touched him. So what if the floor around his feet was bare on the eve of his firstborn's marriage? To hell with the absence of gifts. His son Babu was marrying a white woman. And though the servants whispered about it in the kitchen, even this did not disturb my grandfather. My mother would take my father to America. The three keys he'd given up for his son would soon turn into a hundred keys in that rich place.

Everyone from Chikmagalur set out for Goa in the morning. Once in the heartland of the Konkans, the women of my father's family went to my mother's hotel room, and as my grandmother looked on from her chair in the corner, they decorated my mother's hands and feet with henna, braided her hair. The Peace Corps people came in and out to watch and take pictures. There was no washing of my mother in milk or any of that. Not one of the women of my father's family even imagined talking to my mother about sex.

At the church, my father's best man was a white man he'd never met. After the first nuptial night, no bloodied sheets were hung anywhere. While my parents spent their honeymoon eating shrimp curry on the beach at Goa, my grandfather walked about Chikmagalur with his cane. Even though his son hadn't received a key to anything yet, my grandfather knew what his son had accomplished. So did everyone else in that town. The Konkans had married a white woman.

When my parents came back from Goa to live in his house, my grandfather told my grandmother to make my mother's life so miserable that she would want to leave. After a year of cooking on a stool in the kitchen, of pounding my father's clothes on the washing stones of the stream so that even the Muslims snickered as they watched, my mother finally did.

Whatever my father thought he was getting in marrying an American girl, in America my father realized that he'd gotten my mother. She nagged him, she had her own ideas about how their life should be. And then she sponsored over his brothers.

The night that he'd invited my uncle over to tell him that he had to marry, my father dressed up in a suit. He told my mother to get dressed up as well, and because all the arguing they'd done that week had worn her out, she did.

"So you're going to get your wish, Lawrence," my mother said as she put in her earrings. "What is the next thing going to be?"

My father said back, "The next thing that is going to be is that all of us are going to be happy."

The table was set on the porch, my sister was asleep in her crib. Even I was in my bed in my room, not asleep, though I knew I wasn't allowed not to be. My father had grilled steaks, had turned potatoes in foil over the hot coals all through the evening. The letter he'd written to my grandfather telling him it was time that Sam married a Konkan girl was stamped and sealed on his desk. My mother drank wine too quickly in her dress on the couch, which she did now sometimes. The only thing missing was my uncle.

My uncle's headlights swept through the living room, and my father set down his newspaper to meet him at the door. My mother stayed on the couch. My father opened the door, and under the light of the entry, there was my uncle Sam, a bouquet of blue tulips in his hand, a young black woman on his arm.

Kissing on the Moon

The Konkans of south India are only two shades removed from the color of the girl my uncle brought to that dinner. For the better part of two millennia, the taller, lighter Aryan North Indians have been encroaching on the southern Dravidians' lands. Somehow, the dark Indian peoples have hung on, the Konkans among them. Five hundred years after Vasco da Gama's men trudged through the surf to spill their seed into the women of the palm-fringed Konkan Coast, the white blood has become nothing more among them than a murmur here and there, the odd child born with green eyes, tea-colored skin draping every ninth or tenth cousin. The rest come into this world as dark as the last act of evening before night.

The Konkans as a people are no more or less guilty of racism, sexism, classism, or any of it, than any other people in the world. They adhere to the general declension of the merit of the skin colors that the world has long agreed upon, with white being the best and black the worst, and whether she is clad in a burka or a bikini, a woman will always be judged by Konkan men firstly on her looks.

But the Konkans' prejudices and hates have evolved over the centuries to fit their unique needs as a small Catholic people in a sea of Muslims and Hindus. Their history of colonization leaves them favorably disposed to Europeans, and that white people are better than they are they accept instinctually. Otherwise, how could those white people have come all that way and done all those things that they did? White women are the most desirable and forbidden in the world, and white men wield power and intelligence. At least until the borders of the Slavic peoples are reached, and then it becomes easy again to think of oneself as better than those drunk and bearded Russians, those manual-laborer Poles. Generally, the Konkans delineate the value of Europeans along the same south-to-north hierarchy as everyone else does, with the dark-haired Italians and Spanish not quite as good as the French, and the French not as good as the Germans, with the British the best of all, and the English by far the best of Britain, especially in and around the "home counties." The blond-haired Scandinavians are more akin to a different, and better, species of human, but they are not superior to the English, because the English conquered the whole world. The Irish don't matter of course. Gypsies are of course garbage. The Konkans have mixed opinions about Jews. While they admire and identify with them, take pride in their own status as the "Jews of India," when the going gets tough, the Konkans are not above some friendly Jew baiting. Where the Konkans finally differ from other people is in regard to the Portuguese. While most dismiss the "Pork & Cheese" to the rank of the greasy Greeks, Konkans still think abnormally well of that long-diminished sailing superpower, which brought the rootstock of their culture to them in its little caravels.

But the people the Konkans hate, and not with Mickey Mouse Basque-to-Castilian bile, but with full-on Armenian-to-Turk acid, is Muslims, and more specifically, Bangladeshis, Pakistanis, and Indian Mohammedans. Why couldn't they have shut the fuck up before Partition? How could they have turned their backs on India? Thank you for the Taj Mahal, but why do you insist on fucking up our neighborhoods, with your fucking green houses and that goddamned wailing five times a day? And why do you cover up your women? We know it's because they only have that one long eyebrow. And the mustache. And the beard. So you converted to Islam to escape being *harijans*. Guess what? A *harijan* is still a *harijan*. Go fuck yourselves for fucking up our India, you fucking Muslim fucks.

Hindus, surprisingly, are rather admired by the Konkans. Though the Konkans know that the Hindus are all going to burn in hell in the end, still, who can't help but like all that music and dancing? Hindus invented the sari *and* the *bindi*. Bollywood films are quite pleasing to watch. Hindus are generally a kind and gentle people, rather harmless. They believe in a god who is a monkey. Of course they got mad about all that stuff during the Raj. But who could blame them really? And look at how well they held their temper afterward. Thank you for making them do that, Mahatma Gandhi.

But this admiration is extended to the higher castes only. Once we descend into the ranks of the craftsmen, and then down to the manual laborers, Konkans can only muster tolerance, and as far as *harijans* are concerned, we've left the realm of *Homo sapien sapien*. Impoverished Konkans, too, are hard to take. You're a Konkan, man, how did you let yourself get poor like that? Sikhs are good, different. Their turbans are quite stylish. Do they really have to wear that special underwear? Wouldn't it be nice if they started killing Muslims again? And what about those crazy Parsi Tatas? Feeding their dead to vultures, taking their sisters to bed? Is that what it takes to make all that wealth?

To wrap up the world, Konkans don't know where to rank slant-eyed Asians, and black people aren't humans. But neither race can work up any real hatred out of the Konkans either. Simply put, Asians are irrelevant, blacks are not human. Blacks do look like monkeys, though, and that's a funny thing.

My uncle Sam knew all of these things when he decided to bring Jacqueline Reynolds with him to that dinner where he knew my father was going to tell him he had to marry. And he also knew my father's particular biases and dislikes. While my father didn't truly hate anyone but himself, he didn't like Mexicans because he was taken for one by white people, and this shocked him every time, because my father thought of himself as white. He disliked the Hindus in this country who still practiced traditional ways. He especially disliked Patels from Gujarat, who had immigrated in droves to the Chicago area at the same time that he did. They bought all the 7-Elevens, liquor stores, and Super 8 Motels, and they didn't assimilate well because there were enough of them that they didn't have to. The Patels thought that yelling at patrons and not speaking English while chewing on veg samosas with a Ganesha poster on the wall was good customer service, and so the white people started their camel-jockey, sand-nigger, and dot-head jokes and lumped my father in with them, causing my father to hate the Patels. As far as black people went, my father couldn't care less. He'd never had to deal with them.

Until my uncle brought over Jacqueline. And even then it wasn't about the girl.

The dinner was as tense and awful as my uncle had promised Jacqueline it would be, and after they left and my parents were alone together, my mother took out her earrings in the bedroom and said to my father as he sat on the edge of the bed looking at his fingers curled with rage, "Start breathing, Lawrence. You're going to give yourself a heart attack. That was neither very nice nor very smart of Sam. But why didn't either one of us have the imagination to think that he might have already had a girlfriend?"

Jacqueline had free passes through her school all summer, and so her and my uncle's first date had been to the planetarium, on the pier past the beach where my uncle used to meet my mother those days when they'd been planning on how to get Winston into this country. They had sipped Cokes through straws and looked at a diagram of the solar system.

"Saturn has all those rings," Jacqueline had said. "And Jupiter's nice too with that red storm."

My uncle had said, "I prefer this bluest one."

"Did you know about the planets when you were in India?"

"We could even see them in the night sky."

My uncle Sam had met her at the DMV on Elston, where he'd gone to renew his license late one afternoon. He took his ticket, sat down beside her. There were other open seats among the crowded benches, but that's where my uncle chose to sit. On his other side was an old Mexican man in a straw hat holding his ticket on his knee. My uncle crossed his legs in the Indian style, which, even after four years in this country, was still his natural way. The girl was dressed in a navy blue skirt, a cream blouse, and her hair was pulled back tight in a ponytail. She held a purse on her lap that matched the color of her skirt. She was well put together and pretty.

"Here or there," my uncle said to her under his breath, "government is always the slowest thing."

"We get what we pay for," she said back.

My uncle looked at the clock on the wall, at the faces of the people, at a child sleeping on the floor beneath his mother's seat. There were dog-eared magazines scattered on the short table. People here and there were leafing through them. My uncle leaned toward the girl and said, "I admire your ring."

"My mother gave it to me."

"What is the stone?"

"Citrine. From southern Africa."

"It's very pretty."

"Thank you."

"It looks nice with your outfit."

"Thank you very much."

My uncle looked away from her then, out the window across from them at the sky above the lot. Three pigeons wheeled down into the lot and were lost between the cars. Some children came running out of the pizza parlor with balloons tied to their wrists.

"Where is your 'here'?" the girl said quietly.

"My here?" asked my uncle Sam.

"When you came in. You said, 'Here or there.' Where is your here?"

"Norridge Park."

"That's nice. And your 'there'?"

"India."

"India as in Gandhi?"

"That very same India."

She smiled and straightened up. She said, "You have to excuse me. I get nervous about these things. I know I don't have to. It's not like I don't know what I'm doing. But I start to think about it and my heart beats fast. They put you in the chair, and all I can think is that I'm going to miss every question and they're going to take my license away."

"Everyone gets nervous about these things," my uncle Sam told her.

"Not everyone. There are some people who can do these things in their sleep."

"That isn't me."

The old man's number was called, and when he didn't seem to notice, my uncle touched his shoulder and said, *"Compadre, es suyo."*

"Gracias. No sé los números en inglés después de diez."

"How many languages do you speak?" the girl asked.

My uncle Sam counted them out on his fingers. "Hindi, Kannada, English. A little Spanish, and Konkani is my mother tongue." He'd needed all the fingers on his hand.

"After a glass of wine, I can do a Southern drawl." She laughed and touched his wrist.

My uncle passed his test with ease as he knew he would, smiled for the picture, and then held his new license in his hands a minute, wondering if the face of the man in the photo could be his. Everyone knew that DMV photos were unflattering, but he found his particularly bad. Was his nose really that broad? Could his chin really have that bulb on it? He put the warm plastic in its place in his wallet.

Outside in the lot, the clouds were scudding across the spring sky. The girl was there, smoking a thin cigarette.

"It was as easy as that, wasn't it?"

"I told you that it would be."

"My name is Jacqueline," she said and held out her hand.

"My name is Sam."

"I've always been fascinated by Hinduism."

"Then I'm very sorry to tell you that I'm not that kind of Indian."

My uncle went on dates with women, usually set up by his friend Javier, Puerto Rican girls from the old neighborhood, a girl from El Salvador named Maria. But never had he felt more than the vaguest of interest in any of them. None of those relationships had amounted to much but dinner some-where, shooting pool in some bar, maybe some necking in the car at the beach, and some of the girls would tell him to call again. My uncle would drop them off at their homes, and wouldn't. Javier once got frustrated with him and said into the phone, "That Maria liked you, Sam. And there was noth-ing wrong with that Maria. What are you saving yourself for? If you aren't even going to try, then you should leave these girls alone, get on a plane, and marry a girl in India."

For their second date, my uncle Sam and Jacqueline went to Club Alabam on Rush Street for jazz. There was a cover to get in, and the man at the door patted my uncle down for a gun. Jacqueline wore a black dress and my uncle Sam wore a jacket and tie. They stood at the bar because it was crowded, and nearly everyone in there was black except for two dark-haired white women who sat at a table in their cocktail dresses near the stage, smoking cigarettes and looking bored, and then there was a long bebop saxophone solo, and Jacqueline sipped her whiskey and Coke through a straw, looked at my uncle out the corner of her eye, and cocked her hips in a way that told him she was having fun. When the music turned to rhythm later, they got up from their table and danced.

My uncle called Jacqueline at her apartment two weeks later. He was sorry he hadn't been in touch. Things had picked up at work and he'd been busy. He knew that she understood. Would she come to a dinner at his brother's house? It was never any fun over there, and he wouldn't mind some company for it. An hour or two with his brother and his wife. They could do something afterward.

At the dinner, my mother had hurried to set a fourth place, and the more she drank, the more she revealed herself. Did Jacqueline like teaching? Jacqueline didn't mind it. My mother had liked teaching, too, the four years that she'd had to do that. Jacqueline was only in her third year. Had she started carrying over lesson plans from year to year yet? Jacqueline nodded yes. My mother had made new ones every time. Where had Jacqueline done her degree? Jacqueline had gone to UIC at night.

"You could do worse than UIC," my mother had said, the candlelight in her eyes.

Jacqueline had nodded as she'd looked at her wine. "It's not the University of Michigan."

My mother regretted each of those words as soon as they left her mouth. Still, she couldn't help it, and the shock of just how jealous she actually felt was like discovering a new continent. Of course, my father hadn't said anything at all.

"I'm sorry about them," my uncle had said to her in the car, and Jacqueline had said back, "They aren't awful people."

Then Jacqueline told him, "You know what, Sam? I was pretty excited about this. I was looking forward to seeing the inside of their house. But there wasn't one Indian thing anywhere. I have more Indian things at my place than they do."

My uncle said as he drove, "Didn't I tell you that we aren't those kinds of Indians?"

The dinner had tired my uncle out, and when he dropped her off at her place on Forty-third, Jacqueline leaned in the window of the passenger's side and said to him, "You can call me if you like. There's you and them, and I can tell the difference." Then she let herself into her building.

At home, my uncle thought about the girl. Why had he done that to her? Why had he used her to make Babu mad? And why had the thought of Denise made him want to do that? Now he would be in trouble with Babu. Now he would be in trouble with both of them. But that was all right, too, wasn't it? Now was the time for them to hurt each other.

My father composed a letter to my grandfather. This took all day Sunday in his study, and Monday in his office. No matter that he hadn't often written to them, he was Babu, and they understood that he would write when it was necessary. Now was a time when it was necessary. My father burned with anger. He crumpled the papers to start again. Even work didn't matter for a change, after what Samuel had done.

In the final letter, my father detailed all of my uncle Sam's transgressions against the family. Sam was running around with loose women. Sam had turned his back on his brother and all the values the Konkans held dear. What would become of Sam if nothing was done? And then who would be the next one to be disobedient? When he had finished the letter, my father read it to my mother on the couch. My mother nodded when he finished reading. Despite herself, she said, "All of that sounds fine to me, Lawrence."

———

My uncle took Jacqueline to The Taj restaurant on Devon Avenue the next Friday to make up for the uncomfortable dinner. They ate korma and vindaloo and naan with their fingers, and my uncle Sam drank a Kingfisher beer, and Jacqueline laughed because of the mess she made of herself with the food. The waiter in his cummerbund and red turban was attentive and serious, and he pretended not to notice her inarticulate eating, which made it even better. All around them on the walls were Mughal portraitures of men playing sitars for women in saris seated on cushions, and even when they left, the hostess in her elaborate silk sari pressed her palms together and said, *"Namaste."*

The next weekend, they went to the planetarium again, because it was raining and also Jacqueline had those passes from Dirksen Elementary School, where she taught. Downtown was the halfway point for both of them. And so what if they'd already done the planetarium? They'd had their first date there, it was free, and they had both liked it. In India, my grandfather was reading the letter my father had written.

Jacqueline and my uncle sat in the dark theater in the plush, reclining seats and watched the star show that the strange machine projected on the domed ceiling. There were shooting stars and supernovas, quasars and the Crab Nebula. Part of the show connected the dots to reveal the outlines of all the constellations of the zodiac. On their way out of the theater, they looked in the hall at a lighted chart of the expanding universe, at the case of dimpled rocks that Neil Armstrong had brought back from the moon.

"Can you wrap your mind around the idea of it?" Jacqueline asked my uncle as they looked at a diagram of the gravitational pull of a black hole.

My uncle looked at the diagram a long time. He said, "I know enough to know I'll never know the first thing about any of it."

"What if somebody gave you the chance to go up to the moon?"

"I would stand on the moon and look around. Then I'd say, 'Now what?'"

"I like it here, too, Sam. I like the way the world feels around me. That's why I get scared. I don't ever want to not be able to feel it."

Along the way were booths with electronic scales in them, dark, like phone boxes, the names of the planets on placards above them. They took turns weighing themselves on Jupiter, on Venus. On Jupiter, Sam weighed 375 pounds. "Time to diet," he said, and grinned over his shoulder, patting his flat stomach. On Venus, Jacqueline weighed 112 pounds. She smiled and said, "Excuse me, can I get some assistance, please? I think I'd like to take this scale home with me." Then my uncle stepped into the booth that weighed him on the moon.

"How much do you weigh on the moon, Sammy?" Jacqueline said behind him.

"Twenty-five pounds," my uncle said, and laughed.

Jacqueline stepped into the booth, put her arms around my uncle's waist. "And how much now?"

And so they had their first kiss, kissing on the moon.

Somewhere in the world, my uncle knew as he smoked in the night at his window, my father, my mother, my sister, and I were existing in our bodies, our hearts beating, our lungs drawing in breath, the children that my sister and I were, growing, my parents aging as he was, the universe expanding around all of us. Somewhere in the world, the Konkans of India were growing and aging as well. Did he like this girl? In fact, he did. Did he want to spend his life isolated from his family? My uncle didn't know.

He and Jacqueline went to the Jazz Festival in Grant Park, to ChicagoFest later, when she was on summer vacation. They went to Sox games at Comiskey, and twice they went to Marriott's Great America in Gurnee to ride the roller coasters and eat cotton candy in those thick crowds.

Jacqueline lived on the second floor of a two-story brownstone, which she shared with an orange tomcat named Steve, and a goldfish in a cognac snifter on the windowsill of her kitchen named Anthony, whose scales glinted like metal when the sun shone through the glass. She was a nice girl, modern, image conscious, interested in things. She had a short case with books stacked on its shelves, JFK, Malcolm X, black-and-white photographs she'd taken around the city in simple frames she'd made herself and hung on the walls. There was a shot of three black men leaning against the wall of a liquor store in their hats, a shot of a garbage truck dripping beside a fire hydrant, a shot of a pigeon standing by a squirrel eating a nut on the grass in a park. There was a big framed poster of an Egyptian woman beside an obelisk, and all the words on the poster were in French. There was a beaded bag from India hanging on the doorknob of her bathroom. Jacqueline tried to get my uncle to smoke pot and dance with her in her kitchen to the Commodores, but the pot made my uncle slow and gloomy, so she opened a bottle of Spumante for them instead.

Her apartment smelled like incense, was warm in a good way even in the depth of night. And it wasn't about the apartment at all, but about her, who she was, who she'd decided to be in the world. She didn't have much money; she didn't care. There were occasional gunshots in the neighborhood; she ironed her clothes and had her nails done. Her car would break down now and again; she'd buy a newspaper and take the bus. Jacqueline wanted to know about India; she dated my uncle.

All the weekends of that summer, the night breezes lifted the gauze curtains of Jacqueline's bedroom like veils, like mists in a dream. She would lead my uncle by the hand from the spaghetti dinner they'd made together in the kitchen, from the empty bottle of wine, and light a candle on her dresser, where a framed picture of her family stood. Her family were black people; they pressed their faces together and smiled in the sun. Jacqueline would smile at him as they unbuttoned their jeans, took them off, pulled their shirts off over their heads, and my uncle would slide the straps of her bra off her shoulders after she'd unhooked it. Then Jacqueline would fold herself back onto the bed as she looked at him, and my uncle would stand a moment to look at the length and color of her body against those white sheets.

"Do you think I'm pretty, Sam?"

"Yes, Jackie. Do you think I am handsome?"

"Very much."

Biting was fun, wasn't it? But not too hard. And what was that sensitive spot in the middle of her belly? Earlobes could be as nice to suck as nipples. And wasn't it nice to go to sleep all tangled up with somebody?

In the exhausted late night, the candle snuffed out, the city around them as asleep as it would ever be, Jacqueline would say to my uncle as he held her, "Tell me about India, Sam. Some little thing. Make it a story. Make me see it like I'm already there."

My uncle petted her hair, tucked it back behind her ear. "There are peacocks in a town on the railway to Delhi called Gwalior. The peacocks live on the slopes of the yellow hill that the stone castle stands on. They gather in the banyan trees and glide up and down the slopes like kites of blue. The castle is abandoned since ancient times, but even now when you see it, you can imagine how it once was, the banners of the king waving from the ramparts."

"I see trees everywhere."

"The people who had once lived there are said to have been giants, each man seven feet tall. They built thermal baths in the caverns beneath their castle which are still steaming, even today. When the Mughals came to conquer them, those giant men put on their bronze helmets and rained arrows down from the ramparts so that they killed even Tipu Sultan's royal elephant. Then the Mughals brought their great army down from Delhi and laid siege to the Gwalior castle until every last one of those people was dead."

"No, Sammy. Not stories like that. Pretty stories. That's what I want to hear about India."

"India is not all pretty stories, Jackie."

"Let India be pretty stories tonight."

"Near my home, in the Kingdom of Mysore, there is a series of gardens in the form of mazes. A great Arab architect came to India on a camel on the Silk Road many centuries ago to design them. The gardens are still there, and when electric lights were invented, the maharaja of Mysore had the hedges and flowering trees of the maze strung with lights. Tens of thousands of lights. At night, the maharaja would turn them on for his maharini, and she would look at them from the latticed windows of the harem. Then the British lords came to Mysore in carriages with their army, and they found the gardens to be so beautiful, they decided not to take the maharaja's kingdom from him. In return, the Maharaja of Mysore invited the British women to walk in the garden with their parasols. Now the maharaja's grandson has opened the gardens to everyone. If we have the fee, we can get lost in the maze of lights as though wandering in the stars."

"And the elephants of the coffee mountains?"

"The elephants have long lashes over their eyes that are even more beautiful than women's."

"Were you ever in love there with some girl?"

"Not really."

"Tell me that you were."

"Then I was."

"What did she look like, Sam?"

"She wore a golden sari and golden sandals on her feet. Her hair was pulled into a tight braid that hung down her back. Her hair shone as though it was oiled. Her mother wove a strand of white flowers to hang all through her hair."

"Did she dance for you?"

"On the bank of the stream."

"Were the stars around her shoulders?"

"Every single one."

"You make me feel good."

"I've put you under an Indian spell."

"Do you remember our first kiss, Sammy?"

"We kissed on the moon."

"I'd like to kiss you in a sari at the Taj Mahal."

"Then we'll see it for the first time together, kiss on its steps as Shah Jahan and Mumtaz never could."

"I'd have never guessed an Indian."

"An Indian on the moon."

———

There was Jacqueline the girl who cocked her hip in a smoky bar and looked at him, Jacqueline who was always nice, Jacqueline's body in the candlelight on those white sheets. But there were also those letters that had begun to arrive from India. What in God's name did he think he was doing? the letters asked. Did he intend to bring every single one of them to their knees with shame?

What this meant to my uncle as he smoked at his window weeknights when Jacqueline wasn't there to make him think of nothing but her was that he thought of his faraway father, how his disobedience was surely tearing the old man up, that the Konkans were shaking their heads in apoplexy, that my father was livid. *Has Babu ever done one thing to bring me any happiness? Who gives a fuck about this man Babu?* my uncle would say to himself at the window. But he also knew in his heart of hearts that his Babu would always be his Babu.

Every Sunday night, away from Jacqueline, my uncle would resolve to end it with her. And then the week would go on with its busy days of work, the fatigue at night, and his desire for Jacqueline would rise in him again. Friday night when she'd buzz him in, he'd run up the steps like a sprinter.

The reality of the Konkans was that most of them were poor, illiterate, traditional people as stuck and burdened in their insular ways as the Hindus and Muslims they lived among. The stereotype of the Konkans as the "Jews of India" came from the small but visible percentage of them who had amassed wealth as traders, speculators, usurers, and when the opportunity presented itself, as collaborators. There were castes among them, not as formalized as the Hindus', but just as rigid. My grandfather's family were upper-class Konkans, not wealthy, but in relation to the tall poverty of India, rich enough. They had always managed to educate at least one son, so that he'd be able to take advantage of things when the moment came. My grandfather had been given enough education to pass the British oral and written tests for police officers, and he'd managed to educate his son Lawrence enough in turn that he was able to woo my mother. Most Konkans lived in small huts with no lights, and they always would. They told stories to their children of Vasco da Gama and his ship, St. Francis Xavier and his cross, over hearth fires of charcoal if they were lucky, cattle dung if they were not. They spun these tales—in the fishing villages of the coast, in the labor camps of Karnataka's coffee mountains—instead of the stories of Krishna and Arjuna that their Hindu neighbors told next door.

Why couldn't my uncle Sam disappear into America the way my uncle Les had, the way Winston and all the others who had stepped out of the trees in Vermont the past years had? No, he was not a firstborn son. But he was also not a third. Maybe it was the second brother's curse to have none of the privileges of the first son, as well as none of the freedoms of the third. But maybe, too, and this is what troubled my uncle most, all of this had nothing to do with any of that. Maybe it was simply about him: Samuel Erasmus D'Sai.

So every time he drove to Jacqueline's, it was with the intention of breaking up. And every time, he didn't. "You make me happy," she'd say to him, her body beside his as spent as his would be, deep in the night. What could he do but close his eyes, hold her, wonder what would happen, and take the happiness she offered him?

One night late in the summer when my mother was nursing my sister, when my father sat in his basement with his scotch and his desire to achieve something in this place called

America, my uncle lay in bed at the opposite end of Chicago with a young woman he called Jackie. They were both nude in the dark. She said to him in her softest voice, "Tell me a story from India."

My uncle held aside her hair to kiss her neck. "I have told you stories from India until you can even see the grains of sand on the beach as da Gama planted his sword in it. You tell me about where you come from. Tell me who she is, this person that I'm holding."

She was quiet a minute as she thought. Then she said, "I like to read. I like teaching the kids. I like living down here. My parents are in Gary, my grandparents in the Carolinas. I don't know much beyond that. There isn't much for me to know."

"Why do you live here when you can live somewhere else?"

"I know it's not safe down here. But I don't want to live up north. You know how they open the fire hydrants here? You know who does that? Somebody's dad. He probably works for the city himself. Has the big wrench in his car. The water spraying everywhere, all the kids dancing in it. Then the cops come and everybody runs away. The kids, their parents, the cousins, the aunties. Just the old women stay on their stoops to watch the cops get all wet as they try to shut the thing off. It's a lot of fun. We get to do that down here, Sam. They don't get to have fun like that up there."

"If we were in India, we would not be allowed to be together."

"I guessed that."

"India is not the way you wish it to be."

"I know that, too. I'm still allowed to have my dreams. About India. About any of it. You're not white. But you're not black either. If I was ever to take you to Gary, don't you know that my parents would be uneasy about it? They're proud of what I've done. But they're also from another time. I think about these things as much as you do. What is it like for me to be with you? What is it like for you to be with me?"

"Wouldn't it be nice to be on the moon?" my uncle said.

"But we're not. We're right here. I'm scared, Sam. I'm scared about what you are going to do to me."

The weeks passed, the letters came. They were covered in stamps with slogans in Hindi about the triumph of mechanized agriculture, about the might of Indian heavy industry. Some of the letters were written in the crabbed and angry curlicues of Kannada script, some came in crabbed and angry printed English. All of them had so much to say. They were from my grandfather, yes, but they were also from every uncle and cousin that my uncle had ever met. The letters all said the same thing in the end: He has been allowed to play in America long enough, a suitable girl has been found by the matchmaker, everyone is now waiting for him to come back to India and claim her, why would he demoralize everyone in this way? Everyone up and down the Konkan Coast, from Mangalore to Panjim. Even in Mysore, they are pulling out their hair. Would Samuel Erasmus be the one to disgrace the Chikmagalurian D'Sais? Would Samuel Erasmus really resist his father's wishes?

And as for my mother? What was she thinking about at this time? Of all the things she could have done or said, she rocked my sister to sleep on her knees, and did nothing.

My uncle took Jacqueline to the planetarium, and they kissed a long time on the moon. He said to her, "I have had fun all summer long. You have given me the best time I will ever know in this life."

"You can have much more than that, Sam," she said in her quietest voice. "Right here, right now, this is how we change the world."

My uncle flew to Bombay one week later, on September the sixth of that year. On the eleventh he was married. He took his bride to Mysore for their honeymoon and walked through the lights of the Brindavan Gardens. They stayed in India three more weeks, waiting for her visa to clear. Then they flew to Chicago, and my mother and father picked them up at O'Hare.

My uncle Sam brought back all sorts of gifts from the family in India. There were carved sandalwood boxes with sambars reclining on them in their horns, silver oil lamps fili- greed along their bases like lace, a cricket ball from one of my father's old teammates on the Britishers' Chikmagalur Boys' Cricket Club, and silver bangles for my mother. Both Sam and his bride smelled like India in the car, and they were quiet and tired. My uncle sat up front beside my father, and his bride, Asha, sat in the back in her bridal sari with me on her lap. My sister was in her car seat in the middle, and my mother looked out her window at the city as it passed.

"So many lights," Asha said, and my mother said, "This is only the very beginning of them."

"It is very cold as well."

"This is only the beginning of that, too."

My uncle called Jacqueline's apartment now and again in the evenings, while Asha in her sari fried onions in the pan in the kitchen for curry. He would sit in his old orange chair in his living room and sip a tumbler of scotch as he listened to the line ring. My father had given him a bottle of it to celebrate his marriage.

The one time Jacqueline answered the phone, she said to my uncle, "I don't have anything more to say to you, Sam."

"I know that," my uncle said back.

My uncle had brought back a pair of gold earrings from India, lotus blossoms, the Hindu symbol for purity. He'd left them in an envelope in her mailbox. "Did you get my gift?" he asked her.

"I'm wearing them."

"I hope you wear them every day."

"I will for a while."

"And then?"

"And then I won't."

"I'm sorry that I hurt you."

"You didn't hurt me." There was a long pause on the phone. Then she said, "You are going to hurt from this longer than I ever will. It's true that I didn't know what kind of Indian you were. But what hurts me most is to know what kind of man."

The Country Club

My father was perhaps the most enslaved person on earth. He wasn't so much a person as an engine, tinkered with before he could even babble to be the firstborn son of a firstborn son, and it so happened to be that he was born to a family of a tribe of people who after five centuries of tried-and-true methodology understood like faith that their best chance for success in this world was to put their energies, resources, and cultural imperatives into one male child—though they also had as many other children as they could—and this one male child in my grandfather's family happened to be my father.

What this meant in practical terms was that my father was always given the choicest cut of meat when there was meat in the curry, the best closed-toe shoes to be found on the Konkan Coast while the others wore sandals, the best English-style clothing to dress his body in, and beyond all else, the best education.

Education for the Konkans of India rested solely in the hands of the celibate god-servants of their religion: priests and nuns. My father's education also meant that he was exiled from the family, sent to boarding schools in Mangalore from the age of eight. So while he did learn the proper declensions of Latin verbs and the ins and outs of British English grammar, he did not know the first thing about chasing pigs in the gutters of his hometown, as my uncle Sam did. He learned that white was best, and all the rewards of meat and luxuries made him dependent on having them, and he learned to hate the India of the gutter, which he did not know, except to know that the nice things in life weren't in it. So when the telegram about the white girl came from my grandfather and found him at Standard Chartered Bank in Bombay, he returned to Chikmagalur and wooed her just as he was supposed to.

Imagine, my father was once a baby? My mother? My uncle? Winston and Jacqueline and Les and everyone else of this world? Before language, before culture, sucking on their mothers' teats with their eyes closed, not knowing any of what was waiting to happen to them.

So my father left India with my mother, and though she carried India to America in her in a way that began to harden her heart, my father's heart softened, a bud about to bloom. It only took the flight to Chicago to release him. He worked every day with whites, he wore a suit. Often, there were parties to attend where he laughed and told jokes, ingratiated himself, and cemented his position. He'd drag along my mother, who didn't want to go, and in her Western dresses and long hair, she was as beautiful as my father needed her to be. The men he worked with would call him "Laurie" the Monday mornings afterward as they recounted some funny thing someone had said, how embarrassingly drunk someone or his wife had been at the party. On top of all of that, my father worked harder than all of them.

For the first two years after our move to Ridge Lawn, my father took golfing lessons at the public driving range to straighten his swing, at the Billy Caldwell and Chick Evans public links over the border in Chicago, under the tutelage of the course professionals. He applied himself to this study with the locomotive energy he reserved for his most important endeavors, and with those clubs in his hands, it was almost as if he were guarding wickets again in his whites for the British. "From the stumps of the back foot, he hammers it all the way to the wall for a four, what a shot, my friends!," clap, clap, clap, had now become in his mind, "A booming drive splitting the middle of the fairway, look at that thing go, he's made his life much easier with that approach, ladies and gentlemen," clap, clap, clap.

When he could chip a shot from a sand bunker so that the dimpled ball of legend would drop from the sky and stick on the green like a chunk of lead, when he could crouch with his putter in his hands like a surgical tool while the cumulus clouds, which he never noticed, passed in their rafts through the blue of the sky and sink the ball from six feet out with a firm and measured putt, he came home and told my mother that he was ready to apply for an invitation to the Ridge Lawn Country Club.

All of those Saturdays that he practiced in preparation for this, my mother had been putting me down for my afternoon nap and taking my uncle into her arms in her languorous way, living India again through him, not hating my father, but not loving him either. Three times, once each of those following years in the spring, the country club's prospective-member preliminary-inspection committee came to our house with their clipboards and sundresses and wicker hats, and three times my father had my mother dress herself in her best clothes to offer the women tea and finger sandwiches on a silver platter. There were five of them, the wives of the club's board of directors, Margaret, Maggie, Sylvia, Bea, and Francine, and the first year my mother got their names all confused because it was the first time, and the second year she got them right, and the third year she mixed them all up again on purpose. Each time after they left, my mother closed the door, rolled her eyes, tousled out her sprayed hair, and said to my father, "I did my best, Lawrence. Please don't take it out on me. They won't let in the Jewish dentist. I can't begin to imagine what they think of us," and my father, watching from the window as the long sedans pulled away, would say back, "Why did you tell them the clock is a copy? Why didn't you have honey this time for Bea? I don't know that you've ever been a real wife to me. A real wife would understand and do these things."

The letters always came in cream-colored envelopes embossed with a picture of the country club's main building on the back fold. It was ivy covered and English looking, seeming from the outside like a fortress that could not be breached, and maybe it seemed that same way if you were in it. And three times, my father swallowed a double tumbler of scotch in his basement, drew deep breaths, then carried the letter up to his study. The light umbrellaed down from his green shaded lamp, making the room seem smaller than it was and the moment all that more important. He opened the letter with the ivory knife that his father had presented to him in a velvet box on his acceptance to St. Aloysius Catholic Men's College in Mangalore. The letter was the same all three times. It began, *It is with sincere regret that we must inform you* . . . Then my father would walk down to his basement as though in a dream and drink until he threw up.

There was a rage in my father that threatened to destroy the whole world, but also a restraint in him when it came to his wife and children that made him bear that rage down onto himself. Whether the drinking hurt or helped, I don't know, but it helped him manage. When he'd wake up on the basement bathroom's floor and return to the world above him in the morning, my mother would cook him a big breakfast of bacon and eggs, strong black coffee. Once the food began to work in him to mute the stunning hangover, my father would look at his empty plate and say blankly, "They said no."

"I'm sorry for you," my mother would say, and refill his coffee.

My sister was born, my uncle Sam was married. All of those things that my father had felt sure would make him happy hadn't, and the next thing now was the country club. *Three years in a row!*

The first two years he had understood. But now he played golf well. Now he drove an Audi and was making respectable money. The house was too small, the furniture too simple. Now was the time for a new decision. They would move. They would find a house in a more desirable neighborhood of Ridge Lawn. They would fill it with fine things. They would invite the ladies from the country club. My mother had given up protesting my father's decisions ever since my sister had been born. He told her this new one and she simply nodded. So my father found a four-bedroom house in Ridge Lawn's prestigious Southwest Woods neighborhood and secured a loan from the First National Bank.

The immensity of America stunned my uncle's wife, just the way it should have. Asha was twenty, a girl really, and all she had ever known before coming here was saris and helping her mother cook. Whatever her dreams of her married life had been, they were based only on her life in India, and while she had been raised to serve her future husband, whom my uncle Sam turned out to be, she had not been raised to imagine the bare walls of his house, the isolation of their life among all these white people, the cars, the buildings, the strange love shows on TV. My uncle Sam didn't help her with any of this. Though he crawled on top of her at night to grunt and moan and say other women's names before rolling off of her to sleep, he also did not do any of those other things she had imagined that her husband who lived in America would: He did not take her for a fine meal in a restaurant where her gold bangles would shine in the light for all to see, he did not bow before her on the bed and say, "You are my sacred one. The pathway to my children." He didn't in fact have much at all to say to her, and he left her alone at home during the day to show houses for his work like leaving behind a pet.

My mother visited often, nearly every day at first, and though soon it became less so, she was still a presence in my uncle's house. The jealousy my mother had felt when my uncle brought Jacqueline to dinner was gone. Now my mother insinuated herself into my uncle's life as Asha's savior and confidante, a sudden best friend when Asha had no other choice. My mother told herself that all this was really true, that she was happy because Sam was now happy, that she was Asha's friend.

"You should take her to a show, Sam. You should take her to see Navy Pier and the lakefront," my mother would say, the girl beside her on the couch in her blue sari and *bindi* like a peacock while my mother wore what she always did, a blouse and blue jeans. I had books to color down on the carpet, and my sister had the curtains to try and tug down.

"That is what I say to Samuel! That is exactly what I tell him each and every day," Asha would say in her shrill voice. As he cooked, my uncle would drift in and out of the kitchen to listen to them talk. Even Asha's cooking had grown to irritate him.

"This girl is here now, so what? Has she changed my life? There are bills to pay and I must pay them. What does she do to help? Who has the money for shows, the time to go into the city?"

"Take her somewhere, Sam. Help her get used to life here. She's a young woman. You should feel lucky. Do fun things with her. Take her to a disco. Show her how to dress."

"That is what I say to him every day, Denise-auntie. Every day I say these things to him."

My uncle would duck his head in the doorway, blinking from the sizzle of the onions in the pan he held. "How can she dress other than she does, Denise? I bought clothing for her. I bought her a pair of Calvin Klein jeans. Do you think that she wears them?"

"I have never worn pants before, Auntie," Asha said in her quiet voice, and she looked at her hands. Even her hands seemed dirty to her here, the marital henna lingering on them in brown smudges.

My mother petted Asha's hands. She said, "We'll do it together. Step by step, we will figure it out. Have faith. It was hard for Sam when he first came. He might not admit it now, but in fact he had a very hard time here at first." Then she brushed Asha's hair with her fingers to calm her.

"I don't know anything about this place. Nothing here is as I imagined it would be. In India, it was all singing the poems and dancing the stories and knowing how to cook for my husband. Here, I am a burden. Who cares about the poems here? Why would I ever dance? I am like a child. I had only hoped to be a wife."

"I understand you, Asha. I was like you are when I first arrived in India."

"If I did not have you, Denise-auntie," my aunt Asha said, shaking her head in despair, "I don't even want to think of what it would be for me here if I did not have you always at my side."

Soon enough, it would be time for my mother to gather my sister and me up from the floor. My aunt Asha always stood in the doorway in her sari to watch my uncle Sam help my mother trundle us into her car. My uncle had brought Asha to America like a doll from the store. In my uncle's house, my aunt began to fade. Her skin turned pale, she often couldn't bring herself to get out of bed. My mother was her great friend; my uncle, her husband and enemy. Asha quickly grew to hate America and everything in it, save my mother, who had become the best friend she had ever known.

The house my father found for us in the Southwest Woods section of Ridge Lawn was on a cul-de-sac ringed with stately elm trees. It was only eleven blocks from where we used to live, on Aldine, but there was space here between the homes and it was a different world. We slept in sleeping bags in the living room the night my father bought it, even before the movers arrived with our things, and my father held me to him as we slept. What did he dream of that night?

None of the women in this part of town worked, there were no other cars but BMWs, Benzes, my father's Audi, and one black Maserati driven by an old guy who wore black driving gloves. Even the oaks were tall and old, and the men spent their weekends at the country club, golfing. My father hung his Mexican painting in the bigger basement of this new and bigger house, at the end of his new and longer bar. Drinking the same tumblers of scotch down there as he had before, he'd smile to himself thinking of all that he'd achieved, this poor boy that he was inside himself who had somehow made it out of India.

The tomatoes came sometime in the night between Tuesday and Wednesday the first week of November. When my father pulled the cords to open the drapes over the picture window in the morning, the tomatoes looked like splashes of paint. One, two, three, four, five of them. My mother came bleary-eyed out of the bedroom with my sister tugging at the nipple of the breast she'd unbuttoned her nightgown to give her. Behind them in the room was the baby grand piano my father had bought because it belonged in a house like this. For a moment, they looked at that window as though it were a canvas in a modern art exhibition at the Art Institute, an unfamiliar young painter's strange masterpiece. Both of my parents fell into a dreamlike state as they took it in. Then my mother touched my father's arm, and it became real. She said, "Wash that off before you go. I don't want Francisco to see it."

My father nodded. He went out in his pajamas and blue paisley bathrobe, unrolled the hose, turned the knob on the spigot, pulled the trigger on the nozzle, and washed the tomatoes away. It was a fine autumn day, the last pair of cardinals flying away in red dashes from the juniper bushes that fronted the house, the berries on the junipers frosted and blue, the oak and maple trees all gold and purple with the season. Then my father dressed and went to work, made his calls to his clients, Motorola and Caterpillar, from his thirty-third-floor office on Wacker Drive, downtown. How could something like this have happened? How could something like this have happened in a world where he worked as hard as this? He had lunch with another client at the Italian Village, veal and martinis. The client was from Boeing, which Hinton & Thompson was very excited to be doing business with, my father explained to him. When the client was buzzed, he said to my father, "I had to go to India to deliver a prospectus to a Tata affiliate in Delhi in seventy-six. I took the train to Agra to see the Taj Mahal. Gorgeous. But at the same time, how can they let people live like that? I know you sometimes pinch yourself, Lawrence. All I could think of was Dante's hell."

In the evening, my father took the Metra commuter home. His windows were as clean as any of the other homes' were, and he knew that what had happened was not really a part of his life, that even if it had been, it was already over. He made love to my mother that night, for a change. When he opened the curtains in the morning, there were the tomatoes.

"Wash it off," my mother said, and my father went out and did that. This went on all that week, their first week as residents of Ridge Lawn's prestigious Southwest Woods. Even my mother was given pause by it. They kept quiet, washed the window, imagined it would go away. It didn't.

My uncle Sam came up with his nickname for his wife at this time, *Sita-devi,* after the Hindu goddess, Rama's wife. In other circumstances, an Indian woman might find this very flattering. But the way my uncle said it to Asha wasn't flattering at all. When my mother was at their house and on the couch with my aunt and telling my uncle in the kitchen all the amusements and museums he should take Asha into the city to see so she could begin to acclimate herself to America, my uncle would step into the kitchen doorway in his *lungi* and laugh and say, "Take her to the Field Museum? For what,

Denise? Don't you know the goddess is happiest at home? Ask the goddess herself. She is sitting right beside you. My goddess. My Sita-devi."

"Why don't you take her to the church parking lot and teach her how to drive your car? Why don't you take her to Harlem and Irving and simply walk around the shops in the mall?"

"That is what I say to him, Denise-auntie. All of these things are what I always say to him."

My uncle would smile and shake his head like laughing in the doorway. He was always kneading or stirring something, rice dough for *idli*s, gizzards and onions in a pan. "Look at her. Can you imagine her behind the wheel of a car in her *bindi*? Who has heard of a *devi* who can drive? A Sita-devi no less. She can comb her hair and braid it and wrap herself in a sari. But imagine her behind the wheel of a car? Oh my. But what she can do very well is wear a sari. My goddess, my Sita-devi. What she is very good at is wearing her goddess saris."

"You see how he treats me, Auntie?"

"Sam," my mother would say, "even Lawrence didn't treat you like a Gujarati when you first arrived, though you acted like one."

"You didn't mind how I acted then, Denise."

Then my mother would flush and shake her head, and Asha would rub her arm to console her.

"And do you know what else, Denise-auntie? He drinks. Not every day. But when he drinks, it is terrible. He shows me pictures. White women. A black woman. He says to me, 'You see what I had? You see what I had here? I was happy. I was such a happy man before I was made to marry you.' If my father knew. If I was to write a letter to my father, he would come here himself and take me home."

"He won't come here, Sita-devi. On Gore Road, maybe, and then I would have to pick him up. Your father can never come here. He can't get a visa."

"Then I'll go home myself."

"Then go."

"My father is an important administrator in Mangalore. Every ship that comes into the port, my father stamps the papers. If it wasn't for your America, you could not have a high caste like me. What is your father but a man with sons in America?"

"You see how mad she gets, my little Sita-devi?"

"He rolls on me and rolls off."

"And she lays there like a dead *bangadee*."

"I'll go home."

"Then go."

"You, Samuel. You have made my life from a dream to a misery."

"That is the problem with devis. All is dreams, is it not, my Sita-devi?"

"Don't call me that."

"You are my wife. So you are also my devi."

"Stop it!"

"Sita-devi," my uncle Sam would say, and pop a sliver of ginger in his mouth, wink, and go back to his cooking. When it was time to leave, my mother would gather my sister up in her arms, and my uncle would carry me on his shoulder. My aunt Asha would watch from the door.

As they set our sleeping bodies in the car, my mother would whisper, "You're not the Sam I know."

"I have been unhappy since I stepped off the plane."

"Be nice to that poor girl," my mother would say as she finished buckling my sister into her seat.

"Why have you done these things, Denise? Why did you go to India? Why did you bring us here? It is you. Everything that has happened has always been because of you."

"You are not my Sam."

"I am that very same."

The tomatoes came like the mail, even on Sunday. Some of the nights, my mother would lie awake to hear them. They were the quickest of sounds, at two thirty A.M., at three, like a small flight of birds who had lost their way. How could those soft sounds downstairs make this awful mess? My father snored through it every night with the scotch that put him to bed.

While my father washed the tomatoes off the window in the mornings like another of the chores in the running of this new house, my mother soon found her footing. For one, no matter who she and her husband were or where they had come from or what they had done in their adult lives that they could have done differently and now regretted, my mother understood instinctively that they were not bad people, that they didn't deserve this. Secondly, she had children.

The insulting of our house affected my father more than anything else that had happened to him in America. No matter how rigidly he constructed his vision of America and his place in it, like it or not, this was a thing that had let itself into his world. As he washed off the window, as he rode the commuter train to work in his suit and polished shoes, as he looked over the edge of his morning *Tribune* and glanced at the faces of the white men around him, all fathers, all career men like he was reading their papers, my father wondered for the first time what they really thought of him. He began to feel small among them in a way he hadn't before. He began to question his place here, as well as his self-worth.

"We have to call the police," my mother told him the Tuesday morning the week after it started, the window again dressed in seeds and pulp.

"This is kids, Denise. It will pass. This is what kids do here. You see how they throw toilet paper in the trees at other people's homes."

"That is to celebrate their football teams. That is something their families are happy to wake up and see. This isn't like that, Lawrence. This is something very different."

"I don't know what I should say to them."

"You should say that you are being harassed. You should tell them that you are being harassed, and that you have a wife and children who have been frightened by it."

"It will be worse if I call them."

"What can be worse than this?"

"We have never called the police."

"We have never had to."

My father pinched the bridge of his nose and rubbed his eyes as he and my mother stood before the stained window. He said in a quiet voice, "I am embarrassed," and though at that moment my mother saw in him the slender young man in India who had taken her for walks along the stream, had listened and laughed at the things she'd had to say to him then, had made her feel unique and loved before the man he would become in America ruined those good memories, too much now had happened between them, and she didn't allow herself to express the sympathy for him that she felt. Instead she said, "Lawrence, we are in this house because of you. No one else made us move here. We were happiest in the city. Now you have a problem that has touched your family. You are the one who has to take care of it."

My father nodded, looked through the stained window at

the brightening morning. He showered and dressed, drank his morning glass of orange juice, tucked his paper under his arm, and went out to his car to drive to the train station. At his office, he closed the glass door, with his name on it on a metal plaque, and looked through the door awhile at the busy underlings moving about in their cubicles. The day was starting, and all would soon settle down to work. And that was all that my father wanted to do, to work, to advance, to be invited to join the Ridge Lawn Country Club and fulfill the promise of the man he had been raised to be. My father's office didn't have a single Indian thing in it other than him. And all through his life here, he hadn't acknowledged that. That he hated India. That he'd wanted to leave it behind even as a child. My father stood up from his chair and looked out over the city, at the wheeling pigeons far below, at the offices across the way and the people in them, and his place in the world felt small. Then he sat down, picked up his phone, hunched his shoulders, and called Information.

"What listing please?" the woman's voice said.

"The Ridge Lawn Police Department."

"I can connect you," the voice offered, and my father agreed to that.

The line rang twice and a man answered and said, "Police."

My father rubbed his temple with his forefinger. He said into the phone, "Good morning, sir. My name is Lawrence D'Sai. I live at 1012 South Hamlin Avenue. For some nights, unknown people have been throwing tomatoes at my house."

"How many nights?"

"One full week."

My aunt Asha had said to my mother that Saturday, "My sister-auntie, please let me come and live with you at your house. I cannot stand this man. He does not respect me. I will die if I have to continue living here. You are the only one in the world who is my friend."

My mother felt my aunt Asha's tight grip on her wrists, felt India rise up in her at the sight of my trembling aunt in her sari, in the bangles on my aunt's wrists. How many of them had said this very same thing to her in her time there? *This man is bad to me. Let me come and live at your house.*

My uncle stood in his *lungi* in the kitchen doorway, his arms crossed, watching the white woman talk to his wife. An Indian man in a doorway with his arms crossed was a familiar sight to my mother as well.

Maybe it was the tomatoes that did it. Maybe it was something else. But my mother looked at my aunt Asha in her wet and awful need, and she said the thing that she felt was most true in her heart, "Your place is with your husband."

For a week, a Ridge Lawn patrol car sat outside our house at the curb like a visitor, the officer in it, a sentinel in the night. Now and again when she'd rise from bed to tend to my sister, my mother would part the curtains of my sister's bedroom upstairs to see that the black-and-white patrol car was still there. It was. My father sat in his basement and looked at his painting like looking at nothing. With that car out there in front of his house, he felt that the eyes of the world were now on him, and more than that, that he had failed. He tilted his head to pour scotch into his mouth. No one said anything about it to him anywhere. And still he felt their eyes on him as he waited on the platform for the train in his raincoat in the mornings: There he is, the Indian, the one who can't handle it here, the one who called the cops. What was there left for him to do but drink? To wish that this would pass, to wonder over and over if the world would relent and give him his life back?

The police car sat outside, and the tomatoes went away. Then the officer came to the door. No one had seen anything, this would be the last night they'd be out there. "Real sorry about it," he said, and shrugged. What could my mother do but thank him?

After she'd closed the door, my mother said to my father, "They have been nice to do this."

My father held his wrist in his hand.

"I know, Lawrence, that I haven't always been the best of wives to you. But I don't want you to think that I'm ashamed of you."

"I don't think that," my father said.

The police officer lifted his hand to my father in the morning, started his engine, drove away. My father went to work, had his meetings, and as he had been doing all of this time, he tried not to think about it. He sat a long time that night before his painting, drinking scotch, thinking of his own father, the family, everything he had been given and the others denied so that he could have all of this. He had done his best, hadn't he? He had done every small thing. He went upstairs and put himself to bed with his back touching my mother's. Maybe if he hadn't been born the firstborn son. Maybe then he could have been happy. When he opened the drapes in the morning, there were the tomatoes.

Once upon a time in India, men had come to my grandfather's house to kill him. My father and his siblings had watched with their mother from the window as my grandfather went out to meet those men. My father hadn't known why those men wanted to kill my grandfather. He only knew that he loved him. My grandfather said some words to those men that my father hadn't been able to hear. My grandfather had stood at the gate with his hands on his hips like the immovable thing that he was, and soon enough those men had gone away.

My grandfather came back into the house covered in red *paan* spit. He changed his *lungi* and told my grandmother to make tea for him. Then he sat in his chair, and my father and the others went to him.

Of all of those children, my father was the one that my grandfather had picked up. He sat my father on his lap and he kissed his hair. "Did those Hindus frighten you, my son?"

"Yes, Dad," my father had said.

My grandfather petted my father's face. He sighed and said, "I was frightened, too."

There was a thing to deal with now, the first real thing of my father's life. My mother was very quiet that morning, holding my sister in her arms. She looked at my father, and he looked at the window. There was nothing left to say. My father showered and shaved and dressed, drank his orange juice, ate a banana. He picked his newspaper up off the walkway and tucked it under his arm. Then he got in his car and drove away. My mother washed the tomatoes off the windows that morning, the first time she had done that. As she looked about her at the wakening neighborhood, its leafy trees, the large and manicured lawns that the people here paid so much to have, she did not wonder any longer who among them was doing this to them. She understood that they all were.

Of all the history that she'd brought with her from India to America in the form of my father, in his brother Sam, in the lives of her children that her body had delivered into this world, even in her own life and what she had escaped and what belonged to her now, my mother was not concerned with any of that. What my mother was consumed with that morning, as she gathered me up from my bed to wash and feed my sister and me and start the new day, was the idea that she'd made a mistake that couldn't be fixed, that she'd brought all these people here only to see them hurt. For a moment, she thought to call my uncle Sam, to tell him all that had been happening, and to apologize to him. But, too, Sam had his life now with my aunt Asha, which my mother knew she had played a hand in forcing on him.

My mother helped my father out of his raincoat when he got home, held her arms out for him to lay his tie across, his shirt. My mother rubbed my father's shoulders as he sat on the edge of the bed, and he let her. Then she led him in to dinner, which she had waiting.

"I'm sorry for every little thing, Lawrence," my mother said to my father as he ate.

"We have two fine children."

My parents put us to bed. My father worked in his new study while my mother washed the dishes. Later, she lay and read on the couch. At midnight, my father set one of the kitchen chairs in the middle of the living room and closed the drapes, and my mother in her nightgown rubbed his shoulder, kissed the top of his head.

"I love you, Lawrence."

"I know that you do."

Then my mother let my father sit there, and she went to bed.

My father sat with his hands in his lap. The clock ticked away the time. He thought about his father, about what his father would have done, about what his father would expect of him now, and he thought of my mother, my sister, and me.

How he loved every one of us. At two A.M., the tomatoes hit the window. My father sprung up from his chair, opened the front door, which he'd left unlocked, and ran out into the night in his house slippers. There were figures on the lawn in the moonlight, and the figures were men. The men began to run away. My father felt something like light come into him until he thought of nothing but the running, the capturing of one of these people. He picked one out of the group, closed in on him. For a moment as they ran together, my father's hand touched the small of the figure's back, and for the space of those two heartbeats, they were connected by that touch like friends. Then my father turned that touch into a grasp, and he had a handful of someone's jacket, and he whirled that someone onto the ground. He pounced on him, grasped his hair, and beat his face into the lawn. The man began to holler, my mother called the cops, every bedroom window in the neighborhood turned yellow. The light that had come into my father's body left.

My father was saying, *You fucking fuck bastard,* which is what people say when they've caught someone who's been throwing tomatoes at their home.

The crowd formed in its pajamas, the police car came with its sound and lights, the cops pushed through the people, and my father finally let go of what he had so far refused to. Then my father walked across the lawn to take my mother into the house by her waist.

It was a neighbor's kid of course, a high school senior, a drummer in the marching band, a tax attorney's son from three doors down. The boy licked his bloody lips in the glare of the police car's headlights as they put the cuffs on him. He was crying already. They'd only meant it as a prank. He rattled out the others' names right there. But his was the only name that would go in the *Ridge Lawn Herald*'s police blotter that week, because he was the only one who'd already turned eighteen.

His father came to my father. He asked in our living room that the charges against his son be dropped. It hadn't been about race. It was a prank that kids did at this age. The whole family was ashamed and sorry. Certainly they would punish him. They had raised this boy to be a good boy. This was only a mistake he had made. If my father prosecuted this, it would keep his son out of Notre Dame, the family's alma mater. My mother listened from the kitchen. My father nodded and let it go.

My father and mother dressed up in their best clothes in the early spring. They let the women from the country club look all around their new house. My father didn't say anything to my mother after the country club women left, and my mother didn't say anything to him. The rejection letter came in the mail.

PART 3

Sita-Devi

Now when Captain Vasco da Gama set sail with St. Francis Xavier from Portugal, my uncle would tell me as I'd sit in his lap at his house those drowsy Saturday afternoons that spring, da Gama and Xavier had been very young men. They had been young and strong in their beards, and the captain wore a sword at his side and the saint held a tall silver staff with a bronze crucifix on top of it. They had only one dream, to sail all the way around the world to India, where they knew a people were waiting for them on its coast. They knew they must take their language, their religion, and their knowledge of numbers and letters with them, and brave the terrible sea voyage. Then they would give those things as gifts to the people who waited for them, so those people could learn them and become the Konkans.

It was a new time for Portugal, a fresh time, a time of blue skies and golden wheat, of fat black grapes on the vines, and cattle herds lowing in the fields with their curly heads. All of the people of Portugal were happy, because after seven hundred years of slavery, young men like Vasco da Gama and St. Francis Xavier had charged their warhorses into battle against the Muslim Moors who had conquered their country, and the Catholic armies of Portugal and Spain had finally driven the terrible Moors back across the sea to Morocco, where they belonged.

The fighting had lasted for years and years, the fields of Portugal and Spain had been soaked with young men's blood. Every family lost at least one son. The Moors never gave up. Even when the Catholic army drove them to the top of the Rock of Gibraltar, the Moors rattled their curved swords and rained their arrows down onto them. The Catholic knights climbed up the rock on their hands and knees, even over the bodies of their killed brothers, holding their shields before them. Each of their shields bristled with arrows, and still the Catholics went on. When the king of the Moors saw the cross of the Lord Jesus Christ closing in all about him on the shields of those men, he sent his women and children across the water to Morocco in small boats. Then he did what any defeated king must do: He breathed one last sigh and threw himself from the tower of his castle. The Catholic knights took off their helmets to look down at the king of the Moors' broken body on the rocks at the edge of the foaming sea.

So Portugal was finally free, and everyone in the land rejoiced. The king called Vasco da Gama and St. Francis Xavier to him in his royal court in Lisbon, and they kneeled before him as he sat on his throne. The old king held the ruby ring on his finger out to them, and they kissed it to show their allegiance to him. The king stood up and everyone in the court bowed. He drew out his sword and held it up, and it gleamed in a ray of sunlight streaming in from a high window. Was the king going to cut off their heads? Instead, he tapped the two men on the shoulders with it. He said, "Vasco da Gama and Francis Xavier, you have been chosen by God to face the perils of the sea and journey to India, where a people will greet you on the shore. Are you brave enough to face the sea, the monsters at its edge, the terrible savages who will try to kill you on your way?"

Vasco da Gama and St. Francis Xavier looked at each other and grinned. They stood up and looked the old king right in his eye, and they said, "You have made us knights of the Lord. We are brave and ready. We will face all the terrors of the sea, just as our people have faced and defeated the Moors. We will sail to India and plant your flag and the cross of our Lord on its shore, and the people that come to us from the trees of that shore we will take into our arms and teach them all the things that they do not know. Then they will become a great Catholic people of the world, and they will forever sing the praises of you, our king, who had the goodness to send us to them."

Vasco da Gama and St. Francis Xavier were great friends, my uncle told me. The day they were to set sail, all of Lisbon came to see them off. The city was draped in colorful banners that waved in the wind, young women threw flowers down onto them from their windows as the pair rode in procession on their groomed horses to the port of Belem. Behind them came the king and queen in the royal carriage, and at the port, the soldiers had to hold the people back with the points of their lances. All of the people wanted to touch the captain and the priest and wish them good luck, and they showered them with coins and rice. On board the *Saint Gabriel,* the ship that would carry them to India, Vasco da Gama stood beside St. Francis Xavier on the captain's deck, and the one hundred soldiers and sailors who had been chosen to go with them were dressed in their new uniforms of white and purple. The wind blew their curly hair. Then St. Francis Xavier raised his staff with the crucifix on it, and the people kneeled as one. Vasco da Gama with his sword at his side, the king and queen in their crowns and robes, the soldiers, the court officials, the merchants of the city, even the peasants who had come in from the fields. The crucifix shone in the sun. St. Francis Xavier said, "May the good Lord protect us on our journey, just as He has always protected Portugal." All the people said, "Amen."

The king cut the last tether tying the *Saint Gabriel* to the pier with his sword, and the ship left the port of Belem, with its sails rippling to a cheer from the multitude. All along the bank of the River Tagus, boys ran after it. Then the sea was there, and Vasco da Gama and St. Francis Xavier stood together and looked at it. Vasco da Gama's beard was long and brown, and St. Francis Xavier's was short and black. "Do you think we'll really make it all the way to India?" Vasco da Gama asked St. Francis Xavier, and St. Francis Xavier said back, "If you believe in your heart that our mission is just, my captain, then there is no doubt that we will."

"I believe it, Francis."

"Then I believe it, too, Vasco."

They sailed for many months along the coast of Africa. For months and months and months. The sailors and soldiers were afraid sea monsters would swallow the ship if they strayed too far from the shore, and all along the beaches of Africa, naked savages as black as night came out of the jungle to howl and throw spears at them. Everyone on the ship grew lean and tired. They grew homesick for the golden fields of Portugal. They were not used to the heat in the tropics, and they went crazy from the brightness of the sun. Some of them dove into the sea to cool themselves, where they drowned and died. Others quarreled with each other over the smallest things, and they stabbed each other with knives. Still others fell ill because the food had rotted, and their gums began to bleed and their teeth dropped out of their heads. One by one, they died, and their bodies were thrown into the sea like wood. For weeks, sharks followed the ship to eat the bodies of the dead, and the men could see the fins and teeth of the sharks as they thrashed and tore at the bodies in the water. The men had nightmares about those sharks in their hammocks at night, and the ship was loud with their shouts. Because of those nightmares, no one could ever rest. No one had imagined how terrible that voyage would be.

When they reached the tip of Africa, where the sea foamed and crashed in the gorges, the last of the men wanted to turn around for home. They knew the ship would be smashed to pieces in those gorges, and that they'd never see Portugal again. They drew out their swords to kill the captain and priest. But there were also loyal men left on the ship, and they drew out their swords as well. The loyal men fought the mutineers from the captain's deck like the Catholics had fought the Moors. Vasco da Gama fired his guns while St. Francis Xavier kneeled and prayed. The ship became shrouded in gun smoke, the decks slippery with blood. The battle lasted all through the day to the setting of the sun, and the captain and his loyal men didn't stop fighting until every last one of the mutineers was killed and their bodies thrown to the sharks. St. Francis Xavier led them in a prayer of thanks, and they passed through the gorges in the night as though God Himself had guided them with His hand. By morning, they had rounded Africa.

There were barely enough men left to sail the ship now, and even the captain, even the priest, had to take their turns climbing the rigging to the crow's nest to look out for Muslim ships, because the Muslims controlled the waters of the east coast of Africa from their castles in Zanzibar. The Muslims had a rich trade in silks and spices, and they did not want Vasco da Gama to discover how much wealth they had. The African tribesmen who had seen the small Portuguese ship making its way along their coast sent runners to Zanzibar to tell the Muslims that a European ship was coming, and the sultan clenched his fists on his throne and sent out his fleet to destroy Vasco da Gama.

For some days, Vasco da Gama and St. Francis Xavier and the men still alive on the *Saint Gabriel* sailed up the coast in peace. They washed the deck and repaired the ship, and at night the captain let the men drink rum and sing the songs of Portugal. What more were they than a small Catholic ship on the great big ocean impossibly far from home? All they wanted to do was reach India, meet the people that were waiting for them, and give them the gifts of religion, language, numbers, and writing. Then one morning, Vasco da Gama looked through his glass and saw the masts and sails of the Muslim armada stretching from one horizon to the other. He called St. Francis Xavier, and he looked through the glass, too.

"This is the end for us, Francis," Vasco da Gama said. "We will die here and sink forever to the bottom of the sea, and the people who wait for us on the coast of India will never know how hard we tried to reach them."

"Did we not fight the Moors for seven hundred years?" the great saint said to the great captain. "And how many times were the battlefields red with our blood? Did we despair? Did we turn our back on our God and what He wanted us to do?"

"We did not," Vasco da Gama said.

"Then why would we turn our backs on our God now?"

By midday, the masts of the Muslim ships loomed around them like a forest. They could see the Muslim sailors in their turbans tamping charges into their cannons. The men on the *Saint Gabriel* were haggard, exhausted, frightened, and thin. Some of them looked like skeletons, as though they were dead already. St. Francis Xavier in his black robes looked down at them with Vasco da Gama in his helmet beside him. He said, "Do you see that the Muslims' sails close in about us now like smoke?"

"We see it, Father," the trembling sailors and soldiers said.

"Does any one of you believe that we will not now achieve our dream of reaching India?"

The men looked around at each other. So many had been lost, so many of those who remained were nearly dead. They did not know what to say with the Muslims' battleships closing ranks around them. Then they looked up at their brave captain, who had toiled just as hard as they had, at their brave priest, who had endured every difficulty of the journey with them. They began to murmur, and the murmur turned into a cheer, and then they began to holler just as the Catholic knights had hollered before they launched themselves in the assault on the last Moorish castle in Europe, and they said, "We will reach India! Every last one of us believes in our hearts that we will step ashore in India to plant the cross and flag of our God and king!"

St. Francis Xavier raised his crucifix, and the men kneeled. Even Vasco da Gama kneeled. St. Francis Xavier led them through the Lord's Prayer, and each man prayed as he never had before. Then St. Francis Xavier kneeled, his eyes closed, and he kissed the staff as he held it and he whispered, "My Lord God, I beseech You, come to us in our hour of need.

Look into our hearts and see our pure love for You. Take us to the coast of India, where a people are waiting for us to bring Your Church to them."

As St. Francis Xavier and Captain Vasco da Gama and all the last sailors of that little ship closed their eyes and prayed, dark clouds rolled into the sky and covered the sun, and a tremendous thunderclap broke above them, and when they opened their eyes, they saw darkness where before had been light, and they felt the first sprinklings of rain on their upturned palms. A cold fog rolled in from the coast of Africa until the *Saint Gabriel* was concealed in it and the Muslim ships could not be seen. The sultan of Zanzibar watched from the tower of his castle in disbelief, and he threw down his robes and tore out his hair. The Muslim warships became lost in that mist, and they crashed into each other and sank until not one was left.

Vasco da Gama turned the ship toward India, and the men let up a cheer. In two more weeks, they saw palm fronds and coconuts floating in the water, and then tall white birds with long yellow legs such as they had never seen before alighted on the rigging of the ship like angels. Vasco da Gama opened his glass, and through it he saw a palm-lined coast. He passed the glass to St. Francis Xavier, who looked through it, too. Then they folded the glass away, and hugged each other and smiled. Tears streamed from their eyes. Then Vasco da Gama wiped his tears away, looked down to his men, and said, "Listen to me, every one of you. We have accomplished a great feat. With the help of our Lord God, we have done something which has not been done by men. Our journey has come to an end. Tomorrow we will stand on the shore of India." The men cheered as though there were thousands of them.

My uncle Sam would pause then to see if I was asleep. If I wasn't, I would reach up to pet his smooth chin and say, "And then what happened?" I had heard the story a hundred times, told in that many different ways. But the next part of the story was the most important, and I knew I was supposed to ask him that, and I did.

"In the morning, Francisco, Vasco da Gama and St. Francis Xavier washed themselves with fresh water, put on the clean clothing that they'd kept in the bottoms of their trunks all through the voyage, and then they combed their hair. They dropped anchor near Velha Goa, which means Old Goa in Konkani, and then lowered a rowboat from the *Saint Gabriel* to the water. Vasco da Gama and St. Francis Xavier stood in the bow while the men at the oars pulled them toward shore. Their hair flew like ribbons in the wind, the wind rippled in their shirts. All along the shore, a great mass of people dressed in white began to come out of the trees. The people smiled and pressed their palms together in welcome, and Vasco da Gama and St. Francis Xavier raised their hands to them. The little boat ran up through the surf and onto the shore, and Vasco da Gama leapt onto the beach, drew out his sword, and planted it in the sand to claim India for Portugal. St. Francis Xavier planted his staff beside it. The sun shone on the crucifix like gold, and the people came to it in their sacred linen wraps and kneeled. St. Francis Xavier raised his hand and made the sign of the cross and said, 'I baptize you in the name of our Lord Jesus Christ, man and woman, parent and child, every single one.'

"'Who are you?' Vasco da Gama said to them, and the oldest one, with a long white beard, stood up and looked the great captain in his eyes and smiled. 'Vasco da Gama, we have been waiting for you since the beginning of time. We are your people. We are the Konkans.'"

My uncle Sam discovered that my aunt Asha was doing more in the world than just wearing saris and *bindi*s when he came home on a Tuesday evening that new summer, and not only was the house dark and empty, but his Sita-devi was also not in any room of it. My uncle set his keys on the kitchen table, went in and out of the bedroom twice, yanked open the shower curtain in the bathroom, and looked around in the backyard. There was nothing back there but the rows of his garden, the plants unfurling their green leaves. Where in the world was Asha? Then the thought that she had hanged herself came to him, and he hurried to the bedroom closet.

The winter had been terrible for my aunt. The incredible cold and gloom of Chicago compounded her boredom and loneliness day by miserable day, stuck in the house with nothing to do as she always was, so much so that she had even given up her letter-writing campaign. Maybe this had had to do with the fact, which my uncle had noted, that no letter covered in stamps from India had ever arrived in their mailbox, her father promising in it that he would come and rescue her from her awful husband. What arrived instead were occasional aerograms from her mother full of the banal news of the family. Everyone hoped she was happy and well in her marriage, her mother wrote, which had made every member of their extended clan proud of her. And also, could her husband not send them a little money for medicine for her arthritis? Her father had spent extravagantly on her wedding after all. It was with these thoughts that my uncle pulled open the closet door. Shirts, pants, jackets, coats all dangled from the bar. But not his Sita-devi. There was something else that wasn't hanging from that wooden bar: the Calvin Klein jeans he had bought for her when they'd first come back.

Konkan men aren't especially advanced in the world when it comes to dealing with women, and despite the influence of my mother and the other women he had known in America, when it came to his Indian wife, my uncle wasn't much developed either. To him as he had been raised, marriage was a contract between two fathers in their desire to settle debts, strengthen ties between families, apologize for old wrongs, gain prestige, or set the stage for better business. A wife was little more than a stranger encountered for the first time in any real way on the wedding night, and the only thing expected of that was the bloodstained sheet hung on a nail beside the door of the house for all to see that the contract had been sealed. My uncle had accomplished that quickly in the weeks that he'd been in India for his marriage. But now that they were alone together in America, my uncle Sam did not know what he was supposed to do with his Sita-devi at all.

Yes, in the shine of the party lights in his father's courtyard, in the endless congratulations from the men of both families, in the *roase* that covered him, laughing, head to toe in flour and eggs, in the raucous choruses of *"E puri kon achi?,"* the food, the drink, and the claps on the back until he was intoxicated with it, he had felt sure that he would love his bride. But back in America, Sita-devi in her sari and helplessness revealed herself to him for what she really was: a young Indian girl with few other skills than singing the poems and dancing the stories, someone he didn't know at all, someone he was beholden to in a way he'd never been to anyone. When my aunt would nag him in those first months to take her out into the world that was America, my uncle would look at her in her sari and try to imagine her on the streets of Chicago. Where could he take her dressed like that but Devon Avenue? All that he had to say to her shrill voice when no one else was there was, "Yes, yes. Tomorrow, Sita-devi. Tomorrow I will show you everything," and all that she had to say back was, "You are ruining my life, Samuel. Why did you marry in India when an Indian wife was not what you wanted? I myself don't even want to stay in this place any longer. I will write to my father and he will take me home."

"So write to him, what in the hell do you think I care? You, Sita-devi, what do you do but sit and complain?"

"Don't call me that!"

"But I am Rama and you are my Sita. Isn't that what your poems say?"

"Why do you have to ruin every little thing?"

"I am not ruining this dinner that I am cooking for myself. I am not ruining my job that pays for this house and the food that you eat here. You want to write to your father? Go into the bedroom and write to him. Do you think that I need a Sita-devi here? My life was full of *gopi*s before you came."

My aunt Asha would storm into the bedroom and slam the door at the mention of *gopi*s, and in there she would set paper on the dresser from the drawer, sit in the chair, and write to her father. The times when my uncle worried about what this might bring, he thought about the facts of Konkan matchmaking and gift giving and honor exchanges and marriage. Konkan marriages were never broken. No matter what she was writing to her father, wasn't his Sita-devi here to stay?

This is who my aunt Asha was: the prettiest girl of a clan of Konkans who owned a small but respectable coconut plantation called Mendonça Station, her family name, on the bank of Mulki River north of Mangalore. Her father worked at the port of Mangalore, and was not so much a father in the

bounce-the-children-on-his-knee sort of way, but another of
the men in their mustaches and *lungi*s of the extended clan
in the cluster of painted houses along the riverbank, and her
family was not so much a unit unto itself, but a part of the
larger group, as the Konkans of that very Konkan region were.
She ran in a gaggle of cousins in her youth who were each
as known and close to her as any sibling, and she swam with
them naked in the river as another of their fathers poled past
in his dugout canoe to set nets in the mangroves for *bangadee*
mackerel and crabs. She climbed the mango trees to knock
down the dangling fruit with a stick, she threw rotten figs
from the grove at the others in their game of the *Ramayana*
wars, went home again with them to be scolded, just as they
were by their mothers, for the fig seeds plastered in her hair.

Her favorite times were the early mornings when their fathers would come home from the mangroves in their canoes.
This was on weekends, when their fathers were home from
their jobs in the city and could practice this ancient Konkan
art to both keep the tradition alive, as well as for the pleasure
of being out on the water in the dark. Their fathers spent all of
their weekend nights in the shadows of the mangrove maze,
each one staking out a place, baiting his nets with fish-gut offal,
as the Mulki Konkans have always done, and then they would
sit in their canoes under the starry night, taking sips from their
bottles of Old Monk XXX rum or Two Horses cashew fenny,
and pass that quiet time with the telling of stories of Vasco da
Gama and St. Francis Xavier to whatever son they'd decided
to take with them that night. When the morning star rose
on the horizon, they'd reel in their nets and pluck off the
crabs that hung from them like crimson ornaments. The crabs
would skitter all through the canoes and nip the men's bare
ankles with their pincers, but even this was a pleasure. Back on

the bank, the sons would toss the crabs onto the shore with bailing buckets. They would holler their arrival into the dark houses, and lamps would then be lit and the children would run out from their dreams to catch the angry crabs, to collect piles of them like money.

On Sundays, their mothers would boil great pots of fresh crabs before dawn, the compound dogs crouching in close on their paws as they looked about at the humans, knowing they, too, would soon have a feast. Into the pots with the crabs, once the water boiled down, went onions and garlic and potatoes and peas, and piles of that red curry powder that made everything taste so good. Each of the children would be given a crab to pick apart and eat, and if they were lucky, the crab would be full of yellow egg sacs. The body casings they tossed to the dogs to gnaw and lick.

At this time in her youth, my aunt had been neither Asha nor Sita-devi, but "sister" and "daughter," and her father, whom she knew by the smile he saved just for her, was simply another of those men among the Mulki River Konkans who were all her fathers. Then she grew, and her mother braided flowers into her hair, and even the Hindu *harijans* who rented their fathers' canoes during the week to fill with sand from the shoals in the river and pole to the building sites of the rich Mangalorians' new retreat estates, even they would look at her in their muscled labors as they passed. Bare-chested, black from their days in the sun, glistening from the sweat of their work as though oiled, those thin men would say to her in Konkani—which was not their language—as she walked in her woman's sari along the bank, *"E puri kon achi?"* and wink.

My aunt Asha was enrolled in a convent school in Mangalore because she was beautiful, to learn to read and write, and later, to sew and type. Not because any of these men who had raised her really cared that she learned anything, but because they could all see that she was desirable, and that one day, she would make a fine match for the betterment of the family. To this end, she was also taught to sing and dance in the traditional way, the instructor coming to her room in the boarding school on Wednesday evenings, as well as on Saturdays before evening Mass, to work her through the proper foot placement of the dances, the subtle hand gestures, and more than anything, the turn of her hips in her sari, until she possessed the movements like a right. This was directed by a Hindu teacher, because Hindus still understood these things better than Konkans ever would, an old woman who had herself once been beautiful, and who corrected my aunt with quick smacks to her hands, her hips, with the ruler that was the principal tool of instruction.

My aunt understood even then that none of this was done for her own good. But because she loved her family and the Mulki River and the special smile her father had for her when he'd come back from crab fishing to touch her head in his offhand way and say, "This one belongs to me," she not only pushed herself to do well at those lessons, but to excel. Then her body filled her uniform, filled her saris on the weekends when she'd walk with her friends through the busy streets of Mangalore to have a tea and sweetmeats in a shop for fun, and when school was done, she came home from the convent with her body grown up around her. And afterward, because of her body, she passed two years mostly confined to her room. She turned twenty, which was old to be unmarried, and she understood that they were saving her for something grand. Then her father came to her room one evening with a mango sliced into slivers on a banana leaf, and he sat beside her on the bed. Her father touched her cheek, petted her hair. He was not an old man yet, but he wore gray at his temples. He was her only father in this world.

"A match has been made for you, my Asha."

"I understand, Father."

"He is a handsome boy, older than you, but that is the normal way. He is a second son of the Chikmagalurian Konkan D'Sais. They were once very successful people, and are again because they have sons in America. One of these American sons is in need of a bride. They are demanding a big dowry, which is both difficult for me, and very flattering. You should be proud of the dowry that I will pay to these people. What do you think about it, my Asha?"

"I don't think, Father. I obey as I always have."

"This man will take you to America. If you find yourself unhappy there, simply write to me and I will whisk you home."

My uncle flew in from Chicago, and with his father and uncles, he took the bus to Mulki to look at the girl. Asha sat in her room in the sari and bangles and flowers that her mother and aunts had decorated her with, and as evening turned to night, she could hear the men on their stools in the courtyard growing loud with the singing of *"E puri kon achi?,"* with the crab eating and drinking of fenny, which her father brewed himself in the still behind the house. As she sat wringing her hands, the sound of the drunken men was as terrible as the sound of feasting monsters. Then she made herself think of her childhood, of swimming in the river, of her mother's hands cutting a spiny jackfruit open on the ground with a hooked knife so that they all might eat together of the sweet yellow pulp. She thought of her father touching her head and saying, "This one is mine." She thought of the beautiful river. She loved all the people of her life, and now was her time to take her place among them. She would have her own children so that her parents would be proud, she would have her own daughters so that her own husband might lay his hand on their heads and say, "These are the ones that belong to me." Soon enough, there was a rap on the door, and her father in his suit came in to her with a smile and said, "Come, my daughter, hurry."

In the courtyard, around the circle of the lantern on its crate, were men. Most of them were old, all in suits, and then there was one young one with his eyes on her, and my aunt knew that he was her intended. Her father sat on his chair in his place among the men of his clan, and everyone looked at her. "Show them now, my Asha," her father said, and smiled.

Though there was no music, my aunt knew what was expected of her. She looked at the face of the man who was her intended, and she found that she did not hate his face. She looked again at the expectant faces of the men she had loved as a girl. There were no women around. My aunt lifted her sari to expose her bare feet, to reveal her anklets with the bells on them that would soon chime like the calls of small birds. Then she descended the three steps and entered the open space before the lantern. Looking only at my uncle, she lifted her arms above her head to the stars like the opening of the petals of a lotus blossom. Then she closed her eyes and began to dance. At first she felt the eyes of the men on her, and then she didn't. Her mind lowered itself into the shifting of her hips. She danced the harvest, and then the feast of the harvest. She danced the cycle of the sun across the face of the sky, and she danced the moon. All of these dances were punctuated with the delicate annotations of her hands. These were Hindu dances. But because she danced them as her mother had, as all their mothers before them had, they were also Konkan. My aunt Asha focused herself and became the stories of the life cycles. She wanted to impress my uncle, but she also simply wanted to get the dances right. Perspiration wet her brow, and she panted quietly. Everything was the sound of the chimes on her ankles. When she was done, she looked first at my uncle Sam, whose face was blank, and then at her father, who looked back at her with eyes that said he had never really seen her before this moment. Yes, he had been drinking. But yes, too, he now saw her for what she was. He rose and escorted her by her arm up the steps and to her room. He said to her, "Even if you never marry, my Asha, I will now be happy."

My aunt lay on her bed and breathed away her nerves. She listened to the voices of the men. They were discussing now, bartering over the bridal price. It was serious talk, like arguing. The Chikmagalurians shouted something, and then her men did. Her men shouted something, and the strangers shouted something back. What could she feel but pleased? She had caused this with her dance.

The chairs were folded with loud claps, the men hiccuped their good-byes to one another. Then all was quiet for a long time, save for the sound of the crickets. Someone rapped at her door. Her father came in with the lantern, and his eyes were bleary from the fenny. He sat in the chair with the lantern on the floor, and looked at her a long time without saying anything. Her father's eyes on her made my aunt cover herself with her hands, so she looked at her feet, at the silver rings on her toes like slivers of the moon. Her father finally said, "I wish that I could marry you myself, my daughter. All has gone well. We've agreed on a dowry."

At the wedding feast, my aunt and uncle sat beside each other in their finery in my grandfather's courtyard for all to see. My aunt was nervous and happy, and my uncle was happy, too. Then they walked in a long procession to the church, were married in it, and then they came back to the house. My aunt's mother took her aside and said, "The first time will be difficult. He doesn't know anything, just as you don't. Be gentle and be kind. Remember that he is also scared."

My uncle showered my aunt with kisses in their confinement room in his father's house, touched her body in ways that let her know instantly that he knew more about this than she did. Even as he entered her that first time in India, my aunt understood that there had been other women. Soon enough, in America, where she didn't know anything and was afraid to leave the house, he brought out a photo album and showed her the pictures of them, both white and black, smiling on my uncle's arm as only wives should, and my uncle Sam said, "You see, my Sita-devi? I was happy with my *gopi*s. Now you are here. What in the world am I supposed to do with someone the likes of you?"

My aunt did not hate my uncle, though maybe she should have. In the night, the bedroom black with the drapes drawn against this place, America, which she did not know and hated, he would lie beside her, and both of their breathing would be fast. Yes, they were supposed to sleep now, but they were married, and they both knew that there were other things that married people were meant to do. My aunt would lie still and think of the flow of the Mulki River, and soon enough she could feel my uncle's heartbeat slowing beside her. Then in the dark my uncle would rub her thigh, touch her breast, and roll on top of her. She was bewildered at these times because she did not understand why he touched her in the night when he called her "Sita-devi" all day long. When he was finished, my uncle would roll off of her again, curl on his side away from her, and sigh, and then he would fall asleep. Something inside my aunt wanted to caress my uncle's back and make it right, but another part of her didn't. In the morning, as she'd dress in her sari, my uncle would insult her casually as he put on his shirt and tie. "This is America, Sita-devi. Why do you insist on going on with these old things?"

The first months went by in this way, and then the snow-flakes began to fall. They looked to my aunt like the dust of heaven falling to earth, and for as much as she hated America, this at least was beautiful. When it snowed and my uncle was not there, she would stand in the yard and catch flakes on the palms of her hands and on her tongue. Yes, it was brutally cold here, but the snow of this place was beautiful. When she began to shiver in the wool coat my uncle had bought for her, she would go inside again to watch from the window the snow fall in its silence. What dark days those were. My aunt had had no idea that a cold such as this existed in the world.

My aunt wrote a long letter the week after New Year's to her father. She wrote it at the dresser in the bedroom, and in it, she recalled her youth, how much she had loved it when he'd touch her head, and also she wrote about how lost she felt in the steel and cement world of America, how poorly my uncle treated her, how unhappy she was here, even though she knew how much her marriage pleased all of them. She wrote, finally, that she wanted to come home. Then she put down the pen and looked at herself in the mirror.

So it has not turned out as you imagined, Asha. So what? Am I the first Konkan girl to be unhappy in marriage?

The winter relented into spring, and when it was warm enough, what my aunt did was this: She unwound the sari from her body, folded it, and put it away. My uncle was away at work, and she would have plenty of time. She unbraided her hair in the bathroom mirror, and then dressed herself in the blouse and jeans that my uncle had bought for her. Though she hated the dumpy American clothing, she turned in the mirror until she was almost convinced that she was still beautiful in them. She pulled on the sneakers my uncle had long since given up trying to get her to wear, and at the door, she put on the coat and hat and mittens that were hers. Then she went out into the drizzle of the day and began to walk. She did not know where she was going, and her footprints recorded her passage for the briefest of moments in the wet pavement behind her. Even though it wasn't cold now like the winter had been, still it stung her eyes. She walked to where the streets were busy with cars, entered the supermarket with its vast aisles of food. She looked at the white people putting vegetables into their carts, at the women paying for those things at the checkout lines. She examined how they dressed, how they walked, how they took yogurts out of the refrigerated cases, read the labels, put them back again. In this way, my aunt Asha recorded every little thing of America. Then she went back before my uncle Sam came home.

My uncle Sam said to my mother one Saturday after New Year's, "If she wants to go home, then I'll let her. It wasn't my choice to marry her. I was happier before she came."

"Try to be nice to her, Sam."

"Why?"

"Because she is your wife. What's done is done. You had to marry somebody. She's young and pretty. She's also very nice. Why not try to make the best of it?"

"Is that what it takes to be happy, Denise?"

"I don't know what it takes to be happy, Sam. But what I do know is that Asha is now your wife."

What my aunt liked best was to look at young women. Young white women her age in their ponytails and sweatpants in the supermarket, how they'd pull off their hats and their ponytails sprang to life at the back of their heads, how they moved about the aisles and world with the confidence that men did, as though the world belonged to them, too. They seemed like gods in their power. As she stared at them touching their fingers to their lips as they contemplated prices at the deli counter, as they scratched their heads before the dozens of choices of pastas, my aunt decided that she would also be who they were.

When the weather broke that spring, my aunt learned to take the bus, she used bits of the money my uncle had given her when they'd first come to ride the "L." Some days, she would walk past the downtown skyscrapers, craning her neck to take them in and wondering, "How can anything else also exist in the world?" She began to read newspapers in McDonald's as she sipped her coffee, she began to look through the want ads. Soon enough, my aunt Asha was at her first job interview.

"You have no real experience," the woman at the temp agency said to my aunt, and looked through her glasses.

"I can speak English and I can type," my aunt said back.

"There is work for you today as a maid if you want it."

"I want better work than that," my aunt said back.

All of these months, my uncle found himself avoiding his own home. He would drive past our house, past Jacqueline's apartment. He didn't know a thing about what Jacqueline's life was like now, and as far as my mother went, that was something that he felt was also fading into the past. He'd roll on his Sita-devi in the night, and as he did, he'd imagine that her body belonged to these other women. Then he would roll off her and lie on his side and wonder how he was supposed to get through this life, when this was not the life he wanted.

My aunt Asha did get a job, as a typist for a busy packaging supplier in Skokie. It was neither glamorous nor very interesting, and the temp agency took 15 percent of her wages. She took the bus and the "L" back and forth from work, and she didn't wear a *bindi*. The rough people on the "L" frightened her at first, and then they didn't. My uncle Sam left before she did, came home later.

They liked my aunt at the packing supplier, the men would ask her about India when they came in with orders from the warehouse for her to process. They were white men and black, and they made her blush with their questions about if she had ever ridden an elephant, if she wore that wraparound Indian dress when she went home at night. Even the manager in his white shirt and tie stopped to talk to her when he came in and out of his office at lunch. He was an older man, portly, and reminded my aunt of her father. Now and again he would set his hand on her shoulder and say, "You don't have to call me 'sir,' you know, Asha. This is America, not India. Everyone is equal here." Then he'd rap his knuckles on her desk and say, "Your husband's a lucky guy," as he turned to walk away.

After three weeks, they made my aunt permanent. It wasn't a cheap thing for them to do, the manager told her, but then he smiled and said, "But everyone thinks you are worth keeping around the old barn." He gave her a ring binder that explained the details of her job, office conduct, and other formalities, and as she read it leaving work that day, my aunt began to walk. There was plenty of time before my uncle Sam would get home, and she read each page again and again as she walked through Skokie, then Niles.

She would have to be there every day from 9:30 in the morning until 4:30 in the afternoon. She would have forty-five minutes for lunch. She was expected to answer the phone in a professional manner, type all memos in standard English.

Why had they all thought that she was capable of nothing more than being a bride? Why had not one of them believed that there could be more for her in the world than that one thing?

My aunt let herself think about the money she'd be making. Two dollars and ninety cents an hour. At the end of each day, she would have made $20.30. At the end of each week $101.50. My aunt had no idea what she would do with all of that money. Certainly she would buy her own clothes now, dress herself as she wanted to. In fact, that was the first thing she would do. Surely there were American clothes that she could feel beautiful in. Especially if she was allowed to choose them herself. My aunt tucked the binder under her arm. It was evening all around her in this strange and leafy neighborhood, and she understood immediately that she had no idea where she was.

My uncle searched the darkened house that night for his wife, realized she wasn't there. For an instant, he thought she'd killed herself. In that same instant, he understood that he did not want her to die. There was nothing for him to do but sit on the couch and wait. Had her letters finally reached somebody?

The phone rang. When my uncle Sam answered it, a man said, "Do you know a girl named Asha?"

"Asha is my wife."

"Well don't you think you'd better get over here and pick her up?"

"Who am I talking to?"

"Nobody. We're over at the Wally's Burgers on Northwest Highway in Edison Park. I'd take her home myself, but I'm busy."

"I'll be right there."

My uncle Sam found my aunt Asha sitting at a table in the Wally's Burgers in the Western clothes he'd thought she'd never wear. She was sipping a milk shake through a straw, and she raised her eyebrows at him to let him know she was scared. The man from the phone was sitting across from her in his apron and hat. The place was otherwise empty.

"But how can you even taste the food when there is that much spice in it?" the man was saying.

My uncle waited until they were in the car. He glanced at my aunt again and again in her clothes as he drove with his hands tight around the wheel. For her part, my aunt looked out the window.

"That was not a nice thing to do, Asha," my uncle said.

"I got fed up with sitting in the house."

"What do you do when I am not home?"

"I have a job as a receptionist."

"How can you work?"

"I gave them your Social Security number."

"It will show up on my taxes."

"I will have the money to pay it."

The headlight beams cut through the falling night. Then my uncle said, "How much do you make?"

"Enough for me."

"I will manage it for you."

"Do you think, Samuel, that I will ever let you touch a penny of it?"

All the way home, my aunt looked out the window at the passing houses, at the trees in the parkways. Now and again, she saw her own face in reflection. The reason that she kept her face turned away from my uncle was because she was biting her tongue to keep from laughing. At home, my aunt took her keys out of her pocket to let them in. My uncle took off his jacket and hung it in the closet by the door. As he did, he said to my aunt, "What about all those letters?"

"Look in the bottom drawer of my side of the dresser, Sam," my aunt said as she went into the kitchen to cut onions for supper.

My uncle went into the bedroom, turned on the light. He pulled open the bottom drawer on his wife's side. The edges of the letters poked out from under her stack of saris. My uncle lifted out the saris to see the library of letters that waited for him. He took the first one and opened it. It began,

> *Dear Samuel, How can you treat me this way when I am to be the pathway to your children? Don't you want to respect your wife, who only wants to be respected by you? It is hard for me here, but if you only guide me, I will find the way to do my part. I realize now that we will not have a fairy-tale love. But if we can only find a way to respect one another, I know that all good things will come to us in this life. Children. A sort of happiness. I don't need anything more than that.*

My uncle Sam did not roll on my aunt that night. He didn't call her Sita-devi again either.

The Peace Corps

My mother joined the Peace Corps for many reasons. The first of these was because she had suffered in the world, hated what her youth had done to her. Not only did she want to be as far away from that time as possible, but she also wanted to punish the memory of it with her good acts. But more than that, she wanted to see the world in a way she otherwise couldn't afford to, and help people less fortunate than she was, even though she felt keenly that she had grown up poor.

My mother was full of stories. There were some that she liked to tell, and others that she did not. She did not like to talk about growing up in Detroit, about the man who had come into her darkened room. But the stories from her time in India were always dancing in my mother's head. Of men on crowded buses who licked her neck, of jumping out of bathroom windows in funny hats with Lenore to escape the advances of the rich Tatas. A tale or two from her time before India when she worked in the Baby Ruth factory made her happy. But she always returned to India in her stories, as though through recounting them, she could take herself back there.

A story that made her both happy and sad came from early on in her service in India. Before she arrived in Chikmagalur, when she was still filled with dreams about making a difference in the world, she had been stationed in a small town in Karnataka named Hassan. Not far from town was an ancient temple complex called Halebid on a high hill in the forest, and the Halebid temple was seldom visited then, except for Hindu Brahmin priests who made offerings in it now and again. Every foot of its acre of black stone was covered with friezes of dancing girls, and in the great hall was a polished black granite Nandi bull. When the priests were there in their dhotis, they would burn incense and pray to the reclining Nandi.

Hassan was not far from Chikmagalur, where she would later ride an iron bicycle through the streets for twenty-two months, teaching untouchable women in the shantytown how to build smokeless ovens so they would not die of lung cancer at age forty. The untouchable women would call her "Shanti," which means "peace" in Hindi, because they could not pronounce her American name. And that was how my mother would see herself on her headiest days in Chikmagalur, as peace embodied, riding her bicycle, the wind and scents of the flowering trees in her hair.

But the story was this: Before anything ever happened to her in Chikmagalur, my mother was stationed in Hassan near the Halebid temple in southern Karnataka State with Lenore and a young man named Peter Merchant. Peter had a cot under a mosquito net in one bedroom of their house, and my mother and Lenore had their cots under mosquito nets in the other. They'd only just arrived in India, were coming to terms with the fact that not anything of India was anything like that mock village on the Stockbridge-Munsee Indian Reservation where they'd done their field training. Who in the world had come up with that idea?

This was the delicate time when many of the volunteers quit and went home in a state of shock about the grim reality of the desperate world, which they'd never really shake off, and understanding this, the Peace Corps didn't expect the ones who stayed to start projects right away, but to simply get used to the heat and poverty, the dust and noise, the languages and latrines, and to the psychological burden of being the center of attention.

My mother found that she didn't mind the people's stares, their endless waves and whistles and aggressive invitations to tea. Even their rough hands on her skin when they'd snatch touches of her arms as she moved through the cramped stalls of the Hassan market those first days didn't make her angry. In fact, the opposite was often true, the attention elated her. Yes, she couldn't get the damned sari to fit right. The way it kept falling off her shoulder made her have to all but re-dress herself completely in the middle of the road every ten feet while half the town folded their arms to grin and watch the show. And no, she didn't think she'd ever get used to the roaches on the walls of the latrine. And yes, the way that some of the men hissed at her was in fact rude. But that girl with the mole on her lip and holding the child with the long lashes on her lap in the market had smiled at her the day before, and here she was smiling again. "Is this your daughter?" my mother asked. "No, madame. My auntie's daughter." "She's very pretty." "Madame, my auntie will thank you."

Peter and Lenore were different. The heat, the dust, the chaos and danger of the rickshaws banging over the broken streets like chariot races upset them. So did the donkey carts,

the horned and humpbacked cattle, the smoke-belching Ambassador cars, the ratty and cute beggar children dashing
through all these things. The men urinating on the side of the
road, smiling and waving even as they did. The men clearing
their nostrils with hearty blasts. A woman with an empty eye
socket. An emaciated old man moving a pile of stones ten feet
up the road rock by rock, crossing the countryside in his death
pooja. Bedbugs in the bedrooms, rats in the rafters, mangy
dogs in the yard, roaches everywhere. All of those people. All
of those staring people. So Peter and Lenore left the house as
little as possible, and my mother brought provisions back for
them from the market.

They had an Indian cook who lived in their courtyard shed
and prepared their meals, a low-caste Hindu named Krishna
Arjuna, or was it Rama Krishna, none of them could ever
remember, and my mother and Lenore were altruistic Mid-
western girls, and Peter had graduated from the University
of Virginia with a degree in engineering. This was late 1966,
and though my mother and Lenore both wanted to talk about
Vietnam with him, the one time my mother found the words
coming out of her mouth, "Did you join in case they start
up the draft, Pete?" he'd looked at her with such a quickness
that she understood that he had. He was a tall boy, blond,
not ugly by any means, save for a fullness to his cheeks that
made him seem heavier than he really was. They had been
drinking Kingfishers by the light of a hurricane lamp on their
porch in the night when she'd said it. Why had she said that
when she'd already known? Peter shook his head, looked at
my mother, and said, "Fuck you, Denise."

Peter had gone into his room, and Lenore had raised her
eyebrows at my mother. Though they were on speaking terms
again in a few days, as they had to be in those conditions,

my mother and Peter both knew that they would never be friends.

Though my mother was falling for India, when she was honest with herself, there were moments when she hated it. Sometimes she wanted to shout at all of them, *Aren't you ever going to get used to me?* and she quickly learned to ignore the beggars. If she gave money to even one of them, she'd be begged by a horde the rest of the day. Even when she didn't give money to anyone, someone was always there, at every simple transaction she made in the market for bread, for candles, a filthy, hungry wretched person just paces away, holding out his hand, trying to shift into her vision, his mouth intoning dully, *Ek rupee. Ek rupee, madame. Ek rupee. Ek rupee, madame.* It got so that the old man with stumps for arms and a pail hanging from one of them who followed her from the market all the way up the road to the house in the functionaries' quarter where they lived and bleating that refrain like a wounded lamb couldn't get a paisa out of her when she had a fistful of them. When the grubby kids of the poorest of the poor ran out from the tent village along the railroad tracks where the working poor of the shantytown went to shit, she'd yell in Kannada, "Don't soil my clothing." In her first days, she had picked those children up. Even now, if she looked at their faces, it was hard, but as my mother did or didn't realize at that time, falling in love with India required being careful about what you looked at.

Lenore listened to my mother's catalog of sights at night before bed. In the dark of their room with their nets around them like curtains, my mother would talk about going into the shantytown, what the shanties were like inside, how they were cleaner than she'd imagined, how they were decorated with pictures of Bombay film stars salvaged from scraps of newspaper, how the women put on their *bindi*s and combed their hair in small shards of mirror. About conversations she'd had in the town, at the bus stand. Would madame dare to ride up here? the young men had called down to her and smiled, perched on the rice sacks lashed to the top of the bus to Belur. Of course she would, she'd called back. They'd all reached down their hands. And so Lenore would go to sleep with her head full of stories of what lay beyond the door. And more than that, she began to step out into India on my mother's arm, and when she was ready to, she went out on her own. The women of Hassan, who had trouble distinguishing between the white women, gave my mother and Lenore nicknames to tell them apart. "You are the one who walks fast," the oldest flower seller said in Kannada one day, and poked Lenore in the arm, and then she turned to my mother and told her, "And you are the one who walks slow."

"What did she say?" Lenore asked my mother, and my mother said, "That your hair is the color of amber, and my hair is the color of gold."

Lenore and my mother hired a motor rickshaw to take them out to the temple complex now and again, which was wonderful. Not only was the temple itself beautiful, with its rows of slender columns, that reclining bull, and all those dancing girls, but usually there were no other people around. In the open-air halls where living *aspara*s had long ago danced before the priests, my mother and Lenore modeled their arms like the lines of women in the friezes. Then they'd tilt their hips and stamp their feet like they'd seen dancers do in the Hindi movies. Sometimes they would mimic the latest overwrought love scene between the star-crossed young film couple, with my mother playing the man, and Lenore the woman, and my mother would dip Lenore in her arms and say in a deep voice in Hindi, *"Kya tum mujhe pyar karte ho?"* and Lenore would say back in English, "And I, too, . . . for me nothing will remain without you, but only death," and throw her arm across her forehead in anguish. Then my mother would release her and they would dance again around that room. Then just Lenore would dance, throwing her arms up to the heavens as though being soaked in a deluge, which she really would have been in the movie, the see-through wet sari scene a requisite part of every Hindi film.

Whether they knew it or not, these dances, this change in culture, were revealing to them things about their bodies that they had not known in America. After another of these silly dances in the temple, my mother and Lenore fell laughing into each other's arms. They gave themselves up to the laughter, let their eyes tear from it, and then they went and sat in their saris on the temple steps and looked down the hill and over the forest. The sky was overcast and brooding, and they could see rain falling in curtains here and there in the distance. The clamor of the town they now lived in felt like a faraway thing. The laughter passed from them the way it had come, and then they sat quietly.

My mother imagined the wet town in her mind, the thronging people. But even in this distant mood she could still imagine the color of the flowers at the market. She said, "No matter how much I like parts of it, sometimes it is incredibly difficult to be here."

Lenore looked at my mother's face. "Denise, don't you know how hard it's been for me every day?"

"The men can be awful."

"I hate it when they hiss."

"What do they think we'll do when they do that?" my mother said, and shook her head. "That they'll hiss at us and we'll suddenly go and sleep with them? Do they think we are really that loose? If that's all it took, then that's all we'd be doing our whole time here."

"Sometimes I catch a man looking at me, and I know he would pay me for it if he could."

"The whole town together couldn't afford my fee."

Lenore squeezed my mother's arm, smiled. Then she laid her head on my mother's shoulder, and my mother petted her hair.

"I am so lonely, here, Denise," Lenore said.

"You've done so good, Lenore."

"I have something to tell you."

"What is it?" my mother said.

"What would you say if I told you that I've been thinking about sleeping with Peter?"

Peter Merchant, aside from the many other things he was or wasn't, was an Eagle Scout. He'd brought the uniform with him, and the morning after my mother's comment about Vietnam, he came out of his room wearing it. It was covered in badges and beads and all of that stuff, and he wore the shorts, too. My mother understood when she saw him that it had to do with what she'd said. She looked at him, noted what he was wearing, and left for the market. If Peter had gotten whatever satisfaction he'd thought he needed by dressing up in that outfit, my mother didn't care. If it wasn't for the Peace Corps, she would have never had to meet this person.

But Peter and his uniform weren't just about my mother. It was also about his developing relationship with India. India did not do much to meet Peter on his terms, and Peter did not do much to meet India on its. He hated being touched by the people, and few were the times he attempted to go to the market that he didn't deal out a handful of shoves. Peter was also the tallest man in town. People followed him and laughed, and in the evening crowds, men lifted small children to their shoulders to point him out.

"Indians don't have a fully developed sense of respect," Peter complained to Lenore as they ate peanuts and drank away another evening in their enclosed courtyard in the early days. "What you've got to understand is that this is a caste culture that is thousands and thousands of years old. They've had these low self-esteem characteristics ingrained in them all of that time. Can't you see how the Indians have created their own conditions? At home, I thought it was because of the shortage of teachers. Now I think it's more than that."

Walking among the Indians was slow and hideous, a pot-hole every two feet, an endless minefield of cow dung and *paan* spit. Had anyone ever heard of a traffic light? How about a stop sign? Every little task in India that only required one guy to do back home took twenty here—three guys to turn the tire iron, and seventeen to look on and shout advice, and then Peter would walk by, and they'd drop what they were doing to clap and laugh. The truck they were working on was so trashed anyway it looked unfit to drive. All he had come here to do was help these people. But who could help people like this?

It wasn't long before Peter subjected himself to the torture of haggling for a bicycle. And what a torture it was. When he'd asked the merchant, "How much for that bike?" the merchant had clapped a boy on the side of the head and sent him to bring back tea.

"Sit down, my friend," the merchant had said, and smiled, patting a dirty stack of newspapers in the corner of the crowded bicycle shop.

"Can't you just tell me the price?"

"That is what we are going to find out."

But Peter had enjoyed a bit of emotional respite later as he zipped through the town, the breeze soothing his anger at the bike seller's skillful separation of him and much too much of his money. When my mother saw him on that bike for the first time, standing up to pedal, ringing his bell, kicking a cow out of the way as he whirled through the market in a blur, she, like everyone around her, felt her eyes drawn to him. What a spectacular thing that big white man was. Going that fast. Kicking that cow. And it became more spectacular yet, because Peter started wearing his uniform.

My mother said to Lenore at the temple, "Why would you ever want to sleep with Peter Merchant?"

"I feel sorry for him. He's nice to me. We talk together. I know he's awful, but I can't help it. Things aren't as easy for us as they are for you."

My mother smiled. "It's like what Steve Stewart said to me in Wisconsin. 'Are you attracted to any of the girls here?' I asked him, and he said, 'Yes, to whichever one will be stationed closest to where I'll be.' You only need to go into Peter's room, Lenore."

"Sometimes I think I might do that."

It was at this time that Peter demanded that the cook, Krishna Arjuna or Rama Krishna, a Hindu name like that, prepare American food for them. Though she hadn't been sure of his name at the time, my mother would be able to conjure the cook's face in her mind for the rest of her life. The nose so veined and bulbous that it looked like it would ooze blood if touched. The thick hair like wool. The pockmarks sprinkled across his cheeks like freckles. He was a head shorter than the shortest of them, thin with a fat potbelly. He would flash a quick and betel nut–stained smile when they'd compliment his green coconut chutneys, his thick lentil dals. But the cook was otherwise shy. My mother knew these few things about him: He was Malayali from Kerala, he had been married for a long time, he had a wife and many children in his natal village in the mountains. Who had he been? Because he had been in their inner life, inside their house, my mother had kept her distance from him.

Peter in his Eagle Scout uniform had begun to swerve at dogs, to scatter groups of children with his bicycle. One afternoon, after coming back from the market, he went into the courtyard and dressed down the cook in English. He wagged his finger. His anger made his face turn red. The Indian's cooking was the reason why Peter hadn't had a solid bowel movement since the moment he'd been here. It was the reason why all of them were always sick. How many times had they told him not to make the food that spicy? Did he think they were kidding? Was he trying to poison them?

Peter said, "From now on, you will cook only American food for us. I've been to the market. Don't tell me that the ingredients aren't there, as I know you'll try to do," and the cook saluted the American in his Eagle Scout uniform and said, "Yes, sir!" Which was what Peter needed from him, and which the old man gave him.

What followed were some funny days, with Peter spending the better part of them in the courtyard teaching the cook how to make American food. The blond American with his patches and tight shorts, dripping sweat from his chin as he stood over the cook on his stool, making him peel potatoes for French fries and mix flour and water for pancakes with his fingers, which Peter had made him wash twice with soap, the cook glancing up again and again as though to ask if he was getting it right, when he knew he couldn't possibly be, the scene looking to my mother as she smoked and watched from the porch like an organ grinder training his monkey. Why had she thought it okay then to let Peter do that?

And then there was the ultimate thing of all, hamburgers, with the buns trimmed from the centers of thick chapatis and fried, and the meat minced fine with a knife on the cutting board, and rolled into patties. The cook had never touched meat before, he had to stop the mincing now and again to stifle his gags. What could Peter do but fold his arms and sigh? He'd take a break from his frustrations with the cook to do something inside the house, and every time he did, the cook mixed spices into the meat. Then Peter would come back to taste what the cook had grilled, and he'd scowl and say, "Didn't I tell you 'no'? Why can't you get that simple thing through your thick Indian skull? No spices. Not in American food." Then he'd take the spiced meat and throw it over the gate to the waiting dogs. The dogs, in their scrawny pack, had never known such luck or gluttony as they snarled and snapped over the meat.

My mother sat on the porch in her sari with Lenore, fatigued from the heat of the day, watching what was going on with a mixture of amusement and abhorrence. She'd fan herself with a folded sheet of the day's *Hindu* newspaper, wanting to step in and stop it, yes, but also wondering how it would all turn out. Despite herself, she was eager to eat food from home. She and Lenore smoked cigarettes and drank King-fisher beers that had chilled in their butane refrigerator, and while she felt bad for the old man, she felt that Peter, no matter how much she disagreed with his choices, had as much of a right to live here in his way as she did in hers. The pancakes and burgers they would eventually eat only resembled food from home in a tangential way, translated by a boy in an Eagle Scout uniform to a Hindu in a *lungi* in impatient English, a language the cook could manage only on his best of days. It was entertaining, and it was frightening. *Look at what India could do to people.*

Peter, in his struggles, had unwittingly turned the old man into his symbol for the whole of India. Though India was a thing he could not control, the old man was something that he could. My mother understood this even as she watched it happen. Maybe it was the strange slowness of this new monsoon season, her first, its foreboding gray sky, the way it muted the colors of the flowers, the colors of the extravagant fruits piled in the market, even the women's saris, the painted horns of the cattle, the yellow and green rickshaws with their slogans about God's benevolence stenciled on them in Hindi, everything muted and made small again. But, too, it was my mother's time to settle herself in India, to sleep and wake in it under her mosquito netting, to discover again and again each morning that she really was here, and to let who she'd been at home recede into her memory. My mother herself had become muted in the monsoon, didn't anymore know who she was, if she ever had, or why she was really here or what would come of it. Nothing she knew was simple any longer. Peter demanded that the cook prepare American food, and my mother didn't say anything. So the rain fell in its first sprinkles in the late afternoon on the coals of the old man's grill, and the coals turned the rain to steam, and then the cook would carry the grill by its handles into the covered shed of the kitchen, and Peter would stand over him, wagging his finger to make sure he got it right.

"Don't you want to say something to him, Denise?" Lenore would say to my mother in the dark of their room at night, the sound of the crickets and the last oxcarts' bells coming to them from outside after the end of the rain.

"Peter will have his India, and we will have ours."

"I don't want to sleep with him anymore."

"Don't you?"

"Well, yes and no. I want to be touched by somebody is the thing."

"Then you'll be touched by somebody soon. Personally, I hope it's not Peter. But we are friends now. Even if it is him, our friendship won't be involved in it."

As she turned to her side under her netting, my mother understood that she really was Lenore's friend. The Peace Corps was a strange thing like that. As well as placing her in India, it had exposed her to all of these Americans she wouldn't have otherwise met. Certainly they didn't live in the world as she would have wanted them to, but they were also here with her. It was more now with Lenore than just making do. Lenore was the one person in the world who would ever take these first steps into this new life with her.

My mother walked all through Hassan in the mornings before the afternoon rains. The women in the market had graduated from calling her *The One Who Walks Slow* to calling her Shanti, the first word of her organization's title, which she translated for them into Hindi to explain her presence there. Among those poor people, my mother began to see herself as the embodiment of that idea. How that idea brought the blood up under her skin! Of the three of them, she spent the most time outside the compound by far, and wandering in the busy market, or into the shantytown of the working poor, where children took her fingers to lead her to their families' shacks, where she'd stand with them in the low doorways to smile down at their mothers over their pots, and also smile at the idea that she was Peace stopping by to look in. Even then she knew that India would become the singular event of her life.

The old cook stopped my mother one afternoon as she walked through the courtyard to her room. She'd just come back from another one of her aimless walks through the town, through the rice paddies of its outskirts, where the thin men in *lungi*s whipped buffalo to pull the plows until the paddies' wet clods were churned to a soupy muck for the planting, and she'd seen a handful of new things that the others hadn't: a mendicant with a long beard tying a red string around the trunk of a flowering jacaranda in *pooja*, a troop of vervet monkeys at the main temple peeling and eating the bananas left at the feet of the statue of Lord Vishnu by worshippers in the alcove inside. Her ankles were splattered with mud from the road, and she was sweaty and weary. The old man had never really spoken to her before. But this day, he hurried across the courtyard to her, took her hands in his, and said, "I know the women call you 'Shanti-devi.' You are the one becoming like us. Also more than us. Always will you be more because you are white. But you must help me. Peter is hating how I cook. He wants what I cannot do. You must come to my side. Tell him my cooking is good. Even if you feel I am stupid, you must aid me, Shanti-devi."

My mother said to him, "If I say anything to Peter, it will become worse. Peter has his way. Listen to him and do your best. Peter has no real authority over you, my uncle. If he did, you would not still be here."

"I am afraid, Shanti-devi. I do not know 'French fries.' I do not know 'pancakes.' Even now, I cannot cleanse my hands from the touching of the meat."

"No matter what Peter says, as long as I am here, you will have a job with us."

"I am not sleeping. I must not lose this job. For myself, yes, but for my family also. This job is one that does not really exist. Cooking for white people here, who has ever heard of it? I sit at your feet. I am your very own child. How can it not be so? Without this job, I have nothing. The minister gave this job to me only because the low-caste reforms have come. Afterward, he will give it to someone close to him. I hold this job in my hands like water only. Protect me, Shanti-devi. I am your child."

My mother nodded, and the cook pressed his hands together to thank her and let her go. My mother could not yet know what that conversation really meant, the commitment she'd made to him in it. Her growing love for India was as colorful as the saris she was wearing more comfortably every day, but as she enjoyed the fall of the rain from the porch, smoking with Lenore, my mother thought she could take a break from India, too, when she needed. That she was happy and existing here was enough for now. As she went on letting Peter drill the old man in American cooking, my mother felt that she would soon leave this starting place to begin her real life in her own town. Things like Peter and the cook would matter more then.

What happened was this: The old man had always been a heavy drinker. Now with the red-faced American yelling at him at every turn, he felt that his livelihood was in jeopardy. After the Americans went to bed, he assuaged his fears by pouring fenny down his gullet. Night after night, week after week. This new and heavier drinking ate into his savings, which made him ever more fearful, and so he spent even more time drunk than he had before. That he was a drunk they all knew. But his drinking at night hadn't seemed to infringe on his cooking.

One night, with the smell of the meat again on his hands and feeling very far from his religion and the family in the mountains he was working to send money to, but hadn't in a long while now, the cook sat on his stool in the kitchen shed and drank a bottle of the strongest fenny in the light of the last coals in the grill.

He had done his best to cook American food, hadn't he? Still, the American man in his uniform had nothing but scorn for him. He had done a fine job, he was a fine preparer of food. But what were these French fries they wanted from him, what was this horrible hamburger? If his wife only knew what he had to deal with, she would understand why he had not sent money. The leering face of the American above him was as terrible as a *rakshasa*. The American clearly hated him. He had even prostrated himself before the one called Shanti-devi, and while she had promised she would help him, she had done nothing. She must hate him, too. What could he possibly do now to please that angry man? He needed this job as sorely as he had ever needed anything. Why was this what life was like? Why couldn't the American see that he was only doing his best? The cook poured fenny into his mouth. He wiped his chin on his wrist, again doused his troubles with more of it. *All of that meat.* How could they eat it? How could he have touched that meat for them? Only fenny could make life bearable. One knew that there really were gods in heaven because the gods had given man fenny. And what could one do but laugh now, because fenny made even the red-faced American wagging his finger and shouting at him seem funny. Like the face of a white cow. An angry white cow's face yelling at him. Had he ever imagined that such a ridiculous thing would happen to him in this life?

The cook's heart palpitated six quick times as though trying to run up steps, and he pressed his hands to his sternum as he realized his heart really was a thing in his chest. Then it pounded one large time, and the pain of it rolled him off of his stool so that he could see the stars, which the clouds had parted to reveal. The cook remarked to himself how nice it was that he could see the stars in their thousands at this monsoon time of year, and the stars were beautiful, and their beauty made him happy. But also, his heart was not supposed to be doing what it was doing. The stone of the courtyard felt pleasant and warm under him, even though he knew he wasn't supposed to be lying on it. He thought of his job and his wife and the children and every beloved thing that made him necessary in this world. Then his heart beat one last, huge time, and the cook was dead.

My mother came out in the early morning to see Peter and Lenore standing over the cook. The cook was clearly dead, his tongue hanging out of his mouth as though he'd been strangled. A single fly worried his nose, crawling in and out of his nostrils, a busy black bug. My mother looked up at the sky. The sky would be blue soon, a hot and clear morning before the rainy afternoon. Peter touched his sandaled foot to the cook's puff of hair. He said, "No more French fries."

Peter said, "He did this just to spite us. Now the police are going to come here and cause a big stink, and we're going to have Indians poking through all of our things and in our house, and they are going to think up some reason why we have to give them money. They'll talk about all of his kids and how we have to give them money, too. Maybe if he wasn't determined to drink himself to death, he could have had a better job. A better life. And how hard was it not to burn a fucking pancake?"

My mother and Lenore watched as Peter picked up what remained of the bottle of fenny, screwed the cap on it. Then he pushed the cook's tongue into his mouth, closed the mouth with a pat of his hand, and lifted the body from the ground to hold it on his shoulder like a child. The cook's *lungi* fell open to reveal his thin and pale legs. Lenore dropped her hands from her mouth to rush to Peter and fix that.

All around them in their courtyard, the light was rising. My mother looked at the stool under the tin shed, where the cook had drunk away his last night. At home, they would have thought that stool was a toy, something for a child to play with. The cook's bed in the corner was a single sheet over a bare foam pad. The butane burner on the table, the pots and pans of the cooking stacked around it. The sacks of onions and potatoes against the wall, the big bags of rice in a tidy pile. The kitchen shed was as cluttered as a junk shop. This man had lived there. The birds in their breadfruit tree began to awaken and chirp. India had been right here all this time.

Peter lifted the latch on the big steel doors that kept their courtyard concealed from the road, banged through them with the cook on his shoulder. He carried the body through the town toward the bus stand. There were only the first morning people about, the fishmonger pushing his buckets of mackerel on a cart, the rickshaw drivers stretching and yawning as they stood from sleeping on the seats of their machines, the tea vendors with their clay cups and thermoses letting up the first sharp calls for *"Chai! Chai! Chai!"* and from the

Muslim quarter on the other side of town came the muezzin's mournful and operatic *"Allahu akbar,"* like an old man
practicing scales. But even these few people's mouths dropped
open at the sight of the tall white man carrying an Indian in
a *lungi* on his shoulder. Peter explained it by holding up the
bottle of fenny. "Ah," these people nodded, and spit. The man
was drunk. The white man's servant. The cook most certainly.
Who didn't know a cook who wasn't also a drunk? Not any
more of that good living for this one. Things would be hard
at first when he woke up, and then he would go to this cousin
or that, and find some new job, the way that people always
did. Maybe the next time, he would know better than to be a
drunk. Even the rickshaw drivers knew that he wouldn't.

At the bus stand, Peter showed the bottle to the ticket
wallah in his uniform. He'd had enough of this cook's drunkenness, he explained, was sending the man home to his family
in Mangalore. Then he handed over the fare.

"I'm going to put some money in the pocket of his shirt,"
Peter said as he looked at the ticket wallah's steel badge. "Tell
him it's in there when he wakes up. Then he can't say that I
don't have a heart. But why should I have to stand for this
sort of drunkenness?"

Peter carried the cook's body up the steps of the idling bus
to Mangalore. There was a half hour yet before it departed,
plenty of time for a drunk old man to have a heart attack in
his sleep. He arranged the cook's face against the window,
set the bottle against the wall of the bus beside him, put two
fifty-rupee notes in the pocket of his shirt. The ticket wallah
had that money in his own pocket moments after Peter left,
just as Peter had known he would. The ticket wallah tilted his
hat on his head, smoothed down the creases of his shirt, and
his mustache twitched under his nose as he thought about his

luck. Then he sat back down at his desk in the office, and his mind went on to other things.

Back at the house, my mother was throwing up in the latrine, Lenore was drinking and smoking, and Peter went into his room and began a letter to his father in Virginia. *Dad,* the letter opened, *India is the most fucked-up place on earth.*

Over at the bus stand, the 7:00 A.M. to Mangalore began to fill with people. Fat women in orange saris pulled children in trains through the aisle, looking for their seats. Old men in Congress hats clutched their folded umbrellas and sat up front. Three young men with pomade in their hair were on their way to Goa. A middle-aged man in a worn-out suit looked at his wristwatch to see about the time. Parcels and rice sacks and chickens in crates surrounded the bus on every side. Four bicycles. Hands of green bananas in a pile. Even a full-size refrigerator. Every single one of those things would be lifted to the top of the bus. The men who would do the lifting were barechested *harijans,* their hair thick and woolly, their bodies lean and black. They themselves would ride to Mangalore perched on top of the bus for their labor and half the fare.

People were traveling for all sorts of reasons, for weddings and funerals, of course, but also to place land-rights claims before a magistrate, to have a hemorrhoid looked at by a specialist, to search for an overdue husband, and the cook was traveling because he was dead. The woman who sat down beside the body of the cook chose to sit there precisely because the young men traveling to Goa had held up a rum bottle and hissed at her to come back to them. She was still nursing her very first child, and her breasts were swollen with milk. Next to the body of the cook, she pulled her green sari tightly around herself, sighed and settled her sleeping child on her lap. She looked out the window. A yellow dog humped a black bitch in the yard.

Wasn't that the way of this world? Another one was growing inside her, too. But it would be nice to sit beside her mother in the kitchen eating jackfruit in Mangalore, pomegranates fresh from the tree, as it had come again time to do. Her cousin would take her on his motorbike to set her feet in the ocean.

The refrigerator was lashed on the middle of the roof, the last packages were lifted up and lashed down around it, the *harijans* sat in a pile at the end, and the thin driver came aboard and switched on the music. The music was Hindi and loud and would play all through the nine-hour ride. They would make two stops to piss and eat. Then the well-to-do would announce themselves from the poor, because the well-to-do would eat curries with their fingers in the roadside restaurants, while the poor would crouch under trees outside and not eat. The bus lurched out of the station crammed with human beings inside and out, ten of them lactating, almost all of them breathing, and a beautiful young mother with one child on her lap, another in her womb, and the biggest set of cans in Hassan became instantly drowsy from the motion of the bus. When she woke with a start, she found she'd been sleeping on the shoulder of a kind old man who alone among these people didn't seem to mind.

Peter spent two nights in the Hassan jail. Neither my mother nor Lenore brought him any food, which meant something real, since prisoners at that time in India weren't fed by the state, but by their families. Then Peter was transferred in handcuffs to Bangalore. A crowd formed from the gate of the jail to the police car, a black Ambassador with a blue light whirling on top of it. The police led Peter through the gauntlet of the crowd, and the people spat at his feet, and somebody got him across the face with a banana peel. But mostly they had come only to look. What kind of man put a dead body on a bus like a piece of trash? *Here was the man. A man like this.*

At the same time that my mother had been crying out the story to the police captain, who demanded, "Is that right? Is that right?" as his eyes widened, a girl on the morning bus to Mangalore had covered her head with a fold of her green sari, pulled out her left breast in the tent she had made, and guided her long nipple into the mouth of her restless child. The bus turned a corner, following the road down out of the mountains, and she leaned heavily against the shoulder of the old man as it did. "Excuse, Uncle," she whispered to him, not loud enough to wake him if he was asleep, and not so quietly that she wouldn't be heard if he wasn't. In front, the driver took a swallow from his vodka bottle to clear his head, set it back down by his boot. Then he stomped the brake and wheeled the bus hard into the next curve. The dead body flopped onto the girl's lap, knocked her child to the floor, looked at her with one eyelid flapped up and its mouth wide-open beneath her fat breast, which dribbled milk into it. But even that wasn't enough. The girl jumped up screaming so her breasts flopped out from her sari, up and down, and the boys going to Goa thanked Jesus, and everyone on the bus, even the driver, turned their heads to see what was going on. But the ones who suffered most were, as always, the *harijans* up top, who neither got to see that girl's incredible breasts, nor understand why they were flying through the air as the driver slammed the brakes at the edge of the ravine, which the bus did not go over, but the refrigerator did, taking all those chickens and bananas and rice sacks and wedding and funeral gifts with it, and leaving behind it on the slope it tore down sixteen shirtless brown men without an ounce of body fat between them but plenty, now, of broken bones.

On the bus, the man in the suit stood up and said, "My fridge!"

The Peace Corps would foot the bill for that one. And gladly. Because the only man who died that day, as my mother sobbed to the police, had been dead the night before.

The U.S. ambassador, along with the Peace Corps country director, decided to let Peter spend two more days in the Bangalore prison. Then the ambassador made the necessary phone calls, and Peter flew home to Richmond. My mother and Lenore were pulled from Hassan because its residents had taken to throwing stones at their house as they passed. But not before my mother traveled with the cook's body, in a coffin she had paid for, to cremate him in his home village in the mountains in Kerala. She also paid for the wood of the funeral pyre, as well as for the Brahmin to come from the local temple and consecrate it. Once the Brahmin had left, she watched the cook's body blacken and burn in the heat of the flame, and his wife made one symbolic suttee rush to the pyre herself, only to be restrained by a touch of the cook's sister's hand.

"Rama would be honored to know that you came," the wife said to my mother in Malayalam through a man who spoke English, and the man wagged his eyebrows at my mother, smiled in a happy way, and said, "Because you are white."

Lenore never did sleep with Peter Merchant. "I hope they let us stay together," Lenore said to my mother as they sat on the bench in Bombay in their blouses and jeans outside the Peace Corps country director's office. Then the director came out with a clipboard, and he waved my mother in.

"Where do you think you should be stationed next, Denise?"

"Somewhere where there are no Americans."

The Jews of India

During the Raj, the British gave my grandfather certificates of service, pieces of parchment that conveyed the gratitude of King George VI on behalf of his subjects, and my grandfather framed the first of these and hung it on the wall of the central room of the house, next to his diploma from the Britishers' police training academy in Bombay, and below the wooden cross of his god. The central room was where family life occurred: an uncovered cement floor, blue-painted walls with the occasional crack in them, the odd territory of black mold along the edges of the ceiling. Pushed against the wall was the heavy rosewood table they'd laid my grandfather on after he'd been shot. The servants pulled it away from the wall for lunch and dinner, and on Sunday after church, when my grandfather would receive and feed guests. The room's major adornment was an ivory-and-agate–inlaid teak hutch like a dresser with a sealed and dusty bottle of Beefeater standing on it. His father's second brother had given the bottle to him for his wedding. While the Portuguese drank port in their little Goa, the British drank gin in the rest of India. My grandfather was in a British uniform now, so why not have a bottle handy in case a British officer dropped by?

Upstairs were three rooms, my grandparents' bedroom, another for the children to sleep in on mats, and the third slept in by my great-grandmother, who had lost her wits after her husband's death, and haunted the house and the room as though she wasn't even alive in it. On the wall were a cross with a blue rosary hanging from it and a picture of my great-grandfather's face, his hair trimmed, his mustache neat, not smiling, the photo black and white. When my father was four, the old woman died. Then that room became his. Everyone called it Babu's Room.

All around them lived Konkans in tidy houses, the Britishers' Konkan police officers, yes, but merchants and advocates and transportation managers, too, and their quarter was called the Christian Colony. The families' pigs slopped in its gutters, the children played rag ball in the streets. Whenever possible, the Konkans of Chikmagalur did business among themselves, and the wealthy families of the Christian Colony brought in poor Konkans from the coast to keep house. These servants were usually very young girls, who slept on mats in the kitchens, working for some years to help their fathers pay their eventual dowries. These girls would in fact grow up there. The Konkan wife's main duty, aside from having sons, was to scold her useless servants, or so it would seem from the amount of yelling to be heard in the neighborhood, especially around dinnertime.

The town itself was a bustling, commercial center just off the road between Mangalore on the coast and sprawling Bangalore in the interior, and all day railcars laden with goods passed through the district in the exchange between those two great cities. From the port of Mangalore came British steel, cement, paper, textiles, engines, and machines of every sort, and from Bangalore came the wealth of south India: hardwoods, coffee, gemstones, cardamom, pepper, silver, rubber, silk. Chikmagalur sat on that rich route like a mosquito tapped into a vein. All of that commerce was what had drawn Konkan merchants to the town from the coast centuries before, and when the British showed up, the established families collaborated and ran it.

My grandfather stole from the British and the Hindus equally, though through different methods. The British had the guns, so with them my grandfather had to nip and pluck. With the Hindus, who had no guns at all, it was simply a matter of taking.

My grandfather was a tough man. He cuffed adults as casually as he did his wife and children. Laundry washers, rickshaw drivers, fishmongers, everyone knew not to transgress against my grandfather during the Raj. And when the British left, the Hindus came to his house in the Christian Colony to kill him.

Because there was that story my uncle Sam would tell me. Of the sandalwood poachers. That my grandfather and his men had waited for the poachers, hidden in the shadows of the forest where the sandalwood trees grew. Their uniforms were wet and heavy from the mugginess of the forest, flies worried their ears, their eyes, red leeches thin as threads inched all the way up to latch on and suckle on the backs of their necks until they were as fat as slugs. Then they'd drop off to the leaf litter, leaving behind a trickle of blood, and the eventual pocklike scar. For days they did this, my grandfather and his men, four Konkans, as well as two young Hindus, because high-caste Hindus collaborated, too. The light of the morning came down through the forest in shafts. Somehow, even when it wasn't raining, rain fell in that forest. It was a world of secrets and confinement, and they knew that somewhere in it were tigers. Not one of them liked that place, but first they knew there were men in it, cutting down the precious sandalwood trees, and if they let these men cut the trees down, there would soon be no trees left.

Sandalwood never relinquishes its scent. For all the purple extravagance of freshly cut plum, as with nearly every other wood, plum smells like nothing once it dries. But sandalwood is the smell of India, and as anyone who owns a carved box of it knows, to sniff it is to step into a postcard of that place, to open the lid is to be enveloped in the land of the dancing gods. But also from my mother I knew that my grandfather and his men were not in the forest to save the rare trees from ever being cut, but only from being cut by the poachers. The sandalwood trees of India are turned into boxes, are burned in the world's incense sticks. My grandfather and his men were there to save those trees for themselves.

In the night at their camp, the Hindus boiled their rice, and the Konkans boiled theirs. They slept apart from each other in that way, too. For the Hindus, there were rigors of spiritual cleanliness. The Konkans didn't have that, but they did have their language, which belonged just to them. They sat about their fire and spoke it. The Hindus built their own fire and spoke their Kannada. The Konkans' fire leaped up in the dark of the forest, blotting out the stars, making a room for them with its light against the trees. The shadows of my grandfather's men gestured like giants against the walls of that room as they talked.

"They say these Bombay mutineers killed their white officers."

"Why didn't the British kill them when they had the chance?"

"The Muslims and Hindus will slaughter each other in Hyderabad now."

"They will slaughter each other in Kashmir."

"If the Muslims are given their own country, then we deserve our own country as well."

"We do deserve our own country. But we don't have a Jinnah."

"Jinnah is the ruin of India."

"Jinnah is a greedy Muslim bastard."

"It's different for us. Safer. The Portuguese will never leave Goa."

"Everything is madness now."

"The Sardars will kill the Muslims in Punjab until they run out of bullets."

"Or until they run out of Muslims."

"The Sardars have been sharpening their swords and waiting for this."

"Those lucky Sardars."

"At least there will always be the Portuguese."

"Those sailors in Bombay are Hindus. Nehru sees he has a navy now."

"We can always go to Goa."

"Maybe nothing will happen at all."

"Why did they ever let Gandhi come here and start all of this? Why couldn't they have simply killed him when they had the chance?"

"They say they shot their white officers."

"They should have killed him and sent him back the very first day."

"Life has become a rumor."

"We could have all thrown rocks at his body."

"It's rumored they were shot at first."

"It is too late to stop any of it now."

"What will we do if the British leave?"

"I will go to Goa."

"I say, what will we do if the British leave?"

"I have everything here. Everything that belongs to me is here."

"Have you heard this talk about a reckoning?"

"Nehru is the brain. He laughs at the old man behind his back now."

"Listen to me. What will we do if the British leave us?"

"I will go to Goa."

"Gandhi talks his foolishness. But the others know this life. The first thing they will do is close the banks."

"Don't talk all these things."

"Then they will take our guns."

"Don't talk all these things."

"I will go to Goa."

"There will be nowhere we can go."

"They will put up checkpoints."

"They will look for us in our homes."

"They will wait for us outside our churches."

"They will burn us in our churches as we kneel to say our Mass."

"I will take off my uniform and take the bus to Goa."

"They will know you by your Catholic name."

"Your neighbors will denounce you."

"They will pull down your pants and look at your dick."

"They will make you step on a crucifix."

"They will make you curse the Virgin."

"They will cut off your dick, stuff it in your mouth."

"They will fuck your wife in front of you."

"They will massacre your children."

"They will put a bullet in your brain."

"I will go to Goa."

"Your corpse will go to Goa."

"The corpses of your children will go to Goa."

"Don't talk all of this!"

"I will take my family and go to Goa."

"Your corpse will go to Goa."

"Your corpse will go to Goa with its dick stuffed in its mouth."

"And your wife will be fucked."

"And your children will be dead."

"I say, don't talk all of this!"

The youngest one turned to my grandfather. He said across the fire, "Captain D'Sai? What will you do if the British leave?"

My grandfather drew on his cigarette, scratched his knee, and looked at the fire. Then he looked across the fire at the faces of his worried men. They were sitting together on the logs like children. What more could be expected of them? Yes, they were all firstborn sons, but none of them were firstborn sons of firstborn sons reaching all the way back beyond memory. That was why he was the leader and they were the men. That was what my grandfather had inside of him.

"The British will not leave. They have the guns. Whoever has the guns has everything. Even history will belong to them. In two years' time, no one will have heard of this mutiny. At the same time, do what any sensible Konkan would do. Put some gold somewhere. Give some gems to your sisters to bury in the garden. Put some money here and there. Educate your firstborn sons. But do not ever fear. If we have to start again, we will. That is what we do. We are Konkans."

In the morning, they went on patrol through the forest, and when they heard the sawing, my grandfather put up his hand and his men crept back and hid. There were Hindus in black-and-white checkered head wraps sawing down sandal-wood trees. Five of them. One watched with his rifle while the other four worked. Sunlight came down on them in a shaft in the clearing of the fallen trees. The eyes of the one with the gun shifted from side to side. My grandfather crawled back to his men. Then they waited throughout the morning on their bellies while the poachers felled the trees. When my grandfather felt that enough trees had fallen, he waved his men in. They stepped into the clearing with their Lee-Enfields on those men. My grandfather said to the man with the rifle, "Put that weapon down!" in Kannada, and the man in his checkered head wrap lifted the rifle and shot him. Then that man was killed by all of them but my grandfather, who was sitting down. The others were easy to run down and shoot in the trees, and the one that didn't run, they clubbed to the ground and shot in the back of the head.

My grandfather's men made a stretcher of two poles and a blanket, and they ran him out of the forest on the path. As they did, my grandfather could see the blue of the sky between the leaves of the trees. Why could this world be so beautiful? But also, why hadn't he just shot him? He wouldn't be foolish like that again. And the trees had been cut down.

When I was growing up in Ridge Lawn, at the new house as well as the old, my mother and I would often take my sister for a walk in her stroller. The tomatoes on the windows the autumn before had made my mother hate what she once simply hadn't liked, but this was still her place in the world, and she was still going to live in it. My mother liked to take these walks in the evenings. The lightning bugs would rise up from the lawns like embers, and to the people we passed who said hello to us, we said hello back, and to the people who did not, we did not.

Sometimes we would walk the eleven blocks to Aldine Avenue, where we used to live. The blocks in Ridge Lawn were not very long, and it wasn't a long way to go. When we'd see our old house, my mother would say to me, "Do you remember when we lived here?" and I would say, "Yes, Mom," and then she would say, "And do you remember Nelson Street?" The times I said that I did, my mother would sigh and say, "You mustn't make up stories, Francisco. I know that you were too young to remember that."

The Bings lived on the corner of our old block on Aldine Avenue, and sometimes when we'd walk past their house with my sister in her stroller, Mrs. Bing would be on the swing on their front porch with Jason and Jenny, and my mother would stop to talk. The Bings' was the only house where we did that. As our mothers talked on the porch with our sisters on their laps, Jason and I would have a few minutes to play. We'd lift up the flagstones at the side of their house to see the pill bugs and ants underneath. The bugs would scatter, and the black ants would take their white eggs down the holes in their pincers.

My mother had explained something to me in the car one night that winter as we'd driven home in the dark and snow from the library. When we passed the Bings' house, I saw that the strings of lights on their bushes were blue. Everyone else's lights in Ridge Lawn were white. The snow around the Bings' bushes was also blue from those lights. I said to my mother while my sister slept behind us in her car seat, "Why are the Bings' Christmas lights blue?"

My mother said, "The Bings' lights are blue because Mr. Bing is Jewish. The Jews put out blue lights at Christmastime. If you see blue lights outside a house, then you know that the family inside is Jewish."

"What is Jewish?"

"It's a religion. A certain kind of people."

"Like Konkans?"

"Like Konkans. In fact, the Konkans are called the Jews of India."

"Why are the Konkans called that?"

My mother looked out her window at the snow. Then she looked at the road again. "The Konkans are called the Jews of India because they aren't really a part of India the way the Hindus are. Because they have their own religion. Because they put the education of their children above everything else. That's why I take you and your sister to the library, Francisco. When you have an education, you get to have a better life than other people do. I made myself get an education. Otherwise, I would have never gotten to go to India. And that is also why many people in India are jealous of the Konkans. Just like the Jews."

"Are the Jews good or bad?"

"Some are good and some are bad."

"What about Konkans?"

"That same thing."

"Why don't we put out different-colored lights?"

"Because we are Catholics."

"But we're different."

"Everyone who is Christian puts out white lights. Catholics are Christians. So we put out white lights."

"Is Jason a Jew?"

"Jason's not a Jew because his mother's not. Mrs. Bing is Irish. To be Jewish, your mother has to be one first. Mr. Bing is Jewish because his parents were. Don't talk about this to anybody, Francisco. Mr. Bing doesn't want everyone to know."

"Why not?"

"Because they could be mean to him."

"Then why does he put out blue lights?"

"Because he also does want them to know."

"Isn't he scared?"

"No one here knows what the blue lights mean."

"Then how do you know?"

"Because Mrs. Bing told me."

"Are we afraid to tell people we are Konkans?"

"No, Francisco, we are not."

Looking at ants with Jason that spring, I said to him, "Your dad's a Jew."

Jason looked at me. He said, "Your dad is a Hindu."

What happened to my father in the spring of that year was this: He had been at Hinton & Thompson for eight and a half years, and after watching many younger people advance quickly past him, it was his turn to be called into his boss Marshall Caldwaller's office.

My father emulated Marshall Caldwaller in every way. Marshall Caldwaller had a mahogany desk in his office. My father had a mahogany desk in his office, but smaller. Marshall Caldwaller lived in Barrington. My father lived in Ridge

Lawn. Marshall Caldwaller played golf and tennis. My father played golf and tennis. Marshall Caldwaller kept bottles of single-malt scotch on a shelf behind his desk. My father drank single-malt scotch at home.

"I'm proud of you," the older man said, and smiled, folded his hands together on his desk. "You've been my personal project all these years."

"I am grateful."

"How does junior VP, Aeronautics and Navigation Division, Chicago branch, sound to you?"

"It sounds very good to me, Marsh."

"I'm sorry you had to wait so long for it."

"That's over now."

"They're going to want you to make tough personnel decisions."

"I'll make them."

"Are you still taking those pronunciation classes I recommended you take?"

"Every Wednesday after work."

Marshall Caldwaller opened the top drawer of his desk, took out a gold-colored nameplate. On it were the words LAWRENCE D'SAI, JUNIOR VICE PRESIDENT. He handed it to my father.

My father took the nameplate back to his office. I know that my father wept.

How my uncle Sam dealt with the history of his father was a different thing entirely. There was the story he'd tell me about the poachers and the sandalwood trees and my grandfather getting shot, but there was also what had really happened. Because those Hindus had come to the house to kill my grandfather after the British left. And while my father left Chikmagalur for his education, my uncle Sam had stayed. Time had taken care of the rest. Everyone knew what everyone else had done during the Raj. They told their children, and their children told each other.

The best thing for my uncle Sam to do was to turn history into a story to entertain his nephew. Even better was to not think about it at all. Because when he did, he saw his father lying on the table in his blood-soaked undershirt, the wet wound of the gunshot when the surgeon cut the shirt off, yes. But my uncle also saw that glade in the forest, the felled trees running with sap, the brightness of the raw yellow wood, the yellow sawdust in piles, the smoke of the guns, the Hindus running through the trees, the last one burbling out Kannada even as the rifle bucked from the back of his head. And he saw all of the other times like that as well.

What my father's advancement at Hinton & Thompson really meant was that he became the Chicago branch's axman. And more than just firing people, the company used my father to fire Hispanics and blacks. They'd had to start hiring minorities because of affirmative action, and the racial lawsuits had started, even at the corporate level. So they thought it best to use a colored man to fire other colored men to take that angle away.

They flew my father everywhere that summer, to New York, yes, but also to San Francisco, Baltimore, Atlanta, and LA. In each place, they put him up in the Hilton. And in each of those cities, my father met men who were not white in the hotel's restaurant, bought them martinis on the company's dime, and fired them.

At dinner, my mother would sometimes say to me, "How do you say *no* in Konkani, Francisco?"

"*Naka,*" I'd tell her.

"And how do you say *yes*?"

"*Woyee.*"

My father would set his fork down on his plate. "Why do you insist on teaching him all of these things?"

"And how do you say *basement*?"

"*Sekla.*"

"And what is that?"

"Where Dad goes after dinner."

My uncle rented a rototiller in the spring, and he and my mother used it two weekends in a row to turn the soil for that year's garden while my sister and I played with a soccer ball in the yard. My mother wore blue jeans, and a yellow bandanna to hold back her hair. They both wore gardening gloves. Inside, my aunt Asha watched television with her legs tucked under her on the couch because she was tired from her week at work. She always wore blue jeans now. "You should plant pumpkins this year, Sam," my mother said as she kneeled in the soil to take out a stone and toss it onto a pile with the others. "They take a long time, but then the kids will get to carve them."

"This year, I will grow pumpkins and gourds. I know a man on Maxwell Street who always buys gourds to hollow and paint."

"Maybe one day you'll get Asha out here to garden with you."

"Asha is busy. The only person in the world who has ever liked to garden with me is you."

"Pretty soon, it will be ten years since I left India."

"It will soon be six for me."

"Have you heard from Les?"

"Les is fine."

"And what about Winston?"

"They've closed Gore Road."

"How are they getting in now?"

"North Dakota and Maine."

"It's got to be so strange for them to see North Dakota."

"It is strange for them to see anywhere here at first."

"And then what?"

"And then they are here."

Later, they patted seeds into the rows they'd made, corn, butternut squash, eggplant, cucumber, zucchini. Then my mother took off her gloves, wiped her face with the bandanna, called to my sister and me, and after we'd kissed our aunt good-bye inside, my mother took us home. The very next day, my uncle Sam drove to the TrueValue on Irving Park Road, came home again, and planted the pumpkin seeds he'd bought.

Every evening in the summer after work, when he wasn't out of town on business, my father would drive to the Maine South High School tennis courts in his whites, unzip his racquet from its case, chalk his name up on the board, and wait his turn to battle it out with whoever was next in line for an open court. Tennis was his new sport. The players were fathers from all over Ridge Lawn, and none of them belonged to the country club. My father often played Michael Bing, the husband of my mother's friend.

My father and Mr. Bing noticed in each other something that summer that would make them close friends for years: When they'd play against each other on the high school courts, their running and cursing and volleys and anger told them that they understood life in a similar way. The game, as with all things, was not to be played for fun, but to be won. Though neither of them was very good, they were evenly matched, and even when they were scheduled on the board to play other people, they began to defer their turns to wait and play each other. Sometimes Mr. Bing was the victor, and sometimes my father was. At the end of each one of these matches, they would hurry to the net to shake hands and say, "Nice game."

The Bings invited us over on the weekends, and sometimes we would walk there with the lightning bugs lifting off the lawns around us, and sometimes we would go in the car. Once our sisters were tucked in on the big bed upstairs and we were playing Star Wars in Jason's room with our toys, our mothers would sip their wine and look at each other with sympathetic eyes on the Bings' screened-in porch as our drunken fathers cursed politicians, the Soviets, the Green Bay Packers, and the underlings who worked for them, as well as the bosses they worked for.

"He's an arrogant prick."

"He's an insufferable ass."

"He thinks I give a shit."

"He can suck my cock."

Yes, our mothers occupied the same physical space on that porch as our angry fathers. But quick glances at each other dismissed our fathers as well.

My father would stand up with his tumbler in his hand and say, "Nobody in this world knows what I am capable of! They haven't yet made the test that I can't pass!"

And Mr. Bing would stand up, making the plates and bottles clatter on the table, and he would shout back, "You think I don't know, Lawrence? Nobody knows the things I know in this goddamned world!"

Mr. Bing worked downtown like my father did, as a claims manager for Travelers. While my father had his painting to explain his life to himself, Mr. Bing had scuba diving. Once a year, he went on a two-week diving expedition without his family to some remote corner of the world—Mozambique, Madagascar, Egypt, Thailand—and brought back the fan coral, the Emperor conch shells, that lined every windowsill in their house.

As our fathers' fury rose at all those things inside them, Mrs. Bing would lean to my mother across the table, smile, and say quietly, "We're all grown up now, aren't we, Denise?"

"And it's been a lot of fun, hasn't it, Laura?"

"At least somebody in this world knows what I go through."

"Wouldn't it be nice if that made it easier?"

Jason and I were supposed to stay in his room, to play with our toys, but not to wrestle. When we'd get tired of wrestling, we'd creep downstairs in our socks to hide behind the sofa and look at our parents.

"Your dad is a Jew."

"Your dad is a Hindu."

"My dad is a Konkan."

"Don't you know that's the same thing?"

The last week of August, Marshall Caldwaller called my father into his office. He looked at my father and said, "We've worked out a severance package for Charles Curtain."

My father sat down in the chair. He looked at the file on Caldwaller's desk, didn't pick it up. "What is this about?" my father said.

"I went to bat for him. Believe me, I'm not happy about it either."

"I hired him myself, Marsh."

"I know that you did."

"Get someone else to do it."

"There is no one else."

More than anything, my father liked Charles Curtain. My father's years in America had evolved him in some ways, and when the young man had come into my father's office with his briefcase, his smart handshake, my father had liked him. Charles only had a degree from DePaul, some internship experience at Citicorp, but his recommendation letters glowed, and he was articulate and quick. He dressed well, the raincoat he hung up was Burberry, and his yellow-and-blue–striped tie was clearly Italian. My father was able to see himself in Charles. My mother noticed my father's good mood when he came home from work that day.

"Are they sending you to London again?" she asked him as she set the table for dinner.

"I hired a good kid today."

"Good for you, Lawrence. I bet Marshall will be happy."

"This kid is different, Denise. He's a black kid."

My mother looked at my father. She said, "You did that?"

"I did."

"Why did you do that?"

"Because he is a good kid."

Now my father picked up Charles's file and took it into his office. More than anything, he was confused, and he read the memo clipped to the stack of papers. *Habitually late,* the memo said, and beneath that was a long list of dates and the times Charles had come into the office late, two pages of them dating back three years: July 2, 1976: 9:14; July 11, 1976: 9:21; July 17, 1976: 9:09; all the way up to August 19, 1979: 9:22, just the week before. My father knew that Charles had this problem, had once mentioned it to him. And while it was something that my father never would have accepted from himself, it was also something that he had always felt to be very minor.

But of course there had always been that other thing about Charles. That same thing about him that had attracted my father to him had at times also made my father nervous. My father turned to look out his window at the stone and glass of the building across the way. There were the times that Charles hadn't shown up at company social events. There were the drinks he didn't have with any of them after work.

"It's good to let people know who you are," my father had said to Charles.

Charles had smiled and said back, "They will know who I am when they read the quarterly balance sheets, Mr. D'Sai."

"Paper things are not enough."

"I know that's true. I'll try again. But I'm not sure I can do all of those things the way that you do."

And recently, they had been alone together in the elevator.

"How is your family, Mr. D'Sai?"

"My family is good, Charles. How is yours?"

"They are good, too."

Then they were quiet, looking up at the lighting numbers. Finally, Charles had said, "Sometimes I don't like what they do here."

"What do they do, Charles?"

"We don't get promoted at the same rate."

"We don't have the East Coast degrees."

"It's not just that."

Then the doors had opened to release them into the bustling atrium of people going home from work. Charles had held up his briefcase to my father in parting. He smiled and said, "Mr. D'Sai, we'll talk another time. I'm home to the wife. Thank you for being a mentor to me, by the way."

My father had held up his hand, stopped, and looked at the young man. "My pleasure," my father had said.

My father took Charles's file home with him that night, sat down with it at his desk in his study after dinner. He leafed through the pages, touching his forefinger to his tongue now and again to turn the pages easier, as was my father's way. Was he looking for an answer in those papers? There was nothing more in the file than what there was. My father switched off the green lamp above his desk, went upstairs, and sat beside my mother on the edge of the bed. My mother was propped on her pillows, reading Stephen King. She set the book on her lap when my father came in.

After a moment, my father said, "They want me to fire Charles Curtain."

"What did Charles do?"

My father shook his head. "He complains too much."

"He's right to complain."

"The world doesn't work that way, Denise."

"Why did they give it to you to do?"

"They've been giving these things to me ever since they moved me up."

"Are you kidding me?"

"I am not."

"That's awful."

My father didn't say anything.

"What are you going to do?"

"I don't know."

Then my father went down to his basement.

———

My father thought about it all of that week. On Friday afternoon, he went into Marshall Caldwaller's office. He didn't sit. He said to his boss, "What if I told you I can't fire him?"

Caldwaller sighed. He dropped his pen on his desk. He pinched the bridge of his nose and rubbed it. Then he said, "Lawrence, do you think I haven't had to do things I didn't like? Things that made me feel ill about myself? He's gone. He's out. They don't want him. Why let him take you down with him?"

"It doesn't feel right."

"Kids. House. Career. Family. What more is there to think about than that?"

That Saturday night, we went to the Bings'. The girls were put to bed, and Jason and I wrestled in his room. Then we went downstairs in our socks to spy on our parents from behind the sofa. Soon enough, our mothers came and found us, and put us to sleep in Jason's bed. Just before we fell asleep in the dark room, the shouts of our fathers called us downstairs again.

Mr. Bing was smiling as he shouted at my father, "You know what? I paid fifteen dollars for this chair. It's my fucking chair." Then he picked the chair up and whacked it on the floor. The chair broke into pieces. "Everything in this house is mine. All of this shit is mine. I can do whatever the fuck I want with it. I earned it. Smash that chair, Lawrence. Smash that fucking chair." Then my dad got up and he smashed his chair. Then our mothers stood up, and our dads grabbed our mothers' chairs and smashed them, too, and then our mothers came inside and found us while our fathers smashed things on the porch. Jason and I jumped into our mothers' outstretched arms, and they hushed us on their shoulders as they carried us up the stairs. Then my mother made me walk while she carried my sister on her shoulder downstairs, and Jason and Jenny and Mrs. Bing came with us, and we all went out to the car. My father was breaking things on the porch with Mr. Bing. I looked at them as my mother pulled me out the front door. Our fathers held the legs of those chairs in their hands like clubs as they beat them on the table, trying to kill something out there in the dark, trying to make something die.

My father tightened his tie that Monday morning, took the Metra commuter train downtown. He read the front page of the *Tribune,* and then he read the financials. He walked in a throng of people like him and pressed the buttons on the elevator that took him upstairs. There was work to do in his office, and he did it. Then he pressed the buttons to take the elevator downstairs for his appointment with Charles Curtain at Nick's Fishmarket in the First National Bank Plaza, a restaurant my father liked.

My father ordered the salmon, and Charles ordered a strip steak. "Have a martini," my father told him. Charles shook his head.

"It's because I wrote a letter to Marsh after they gave Paul Saunders the new ADM account when everyone knew it should have gone to me," Charles said.

My father shook his head. He said, "It's because you let them do it by being late."

Then my father handed Charles the papers and fired him.

The Americans

They've taken to telling me the stories again in these years after my father's death. It's as though they know that it's time to get them right. When I call my uncle in Chicago, he always asks after my mother, after my sister, whom he loves like a daughter. Then he turns to the past:

"Have I told you about when your mother and I went to pick up Winston in Vermont? He wasn't even wearing a coat. Can you believe that? From India to Vermont without a coat. How your mother and I have laughed about that. I know your father knew what we did even then. But your father never wanted to get involved in any of those things.

"There were elephants in the coffee mountains the years I lived there, have I told you that, Francisco? How I loved to look at the elephants. What is it about an elephant that can make one feel so sad? Up there, how it could rain. Everything was dark and green. One time I followed a trail to a tree, and all of its branches were covered in glass bangles. I took one. I worried all night about what I had done, and then I had a fever. As soon as I put that bangle back on its holy place, I was well again. Why did I think to do that, you know, my son? We had a difficult time respecting those people."

My mother is retired in Florida. Late one night, when we were exhausted from talking and the stories had come to an end, I said to her, "I have these memories."

"What do you think you remember, Francisco?"

"When I was very young. Memories about you. Memories about my uncle Sam."

My mother pursed her lips, looked carefully at the wine in her glass as we sat at her kitchen table. "Are they good memories?"

"They are good memories."

My mother never stopped looking at the wine in her glass. She said, "I think we remember what we need to. That each of us keeps our memories just as we need them to be. If your memories of what we did are good, let yourself remember them as good. And if they are bad, let them be that, too. Of all of our children, know that it's something that belongs to you."

"Didn't you worry about hurting them?"

"We only managed to hurt ourselves."

"And then you ended it."

"Our children began to grow."

"So you made a decision to be unhappy people."

"Not unhappy people at all, Francisco. Only people. People who understood that there were others in this world whom we cared about who had to share this life with us."

"Tell me the story."

My mother shook her head. We were quiet together in a real way for the first time that night. The story had come into the room with us.

Then my mother blushed. She lowered her eyes, smiled, and then she said, "Don't I get to keep anything for myself?

"What I remember is all that snow in Vermont. Your uncle was so skinny. We stayed in an awful motel in Burlington. I felt so happy."

This is what really happened: Vasco da Gama landed in Calicut, India, in May 1498, with three ships, the first European captain to reach India by sea.

The voyage was grueling, da Gama spent longer in the open ocean than Columbus had. The Portuguese had no idea about the riches changing hands in the Indian Ocean: pearls, ivory, silk, spices; the cheap trinkets and scarves they'd brought as trade goods led to ridicule and attack nearly everywhere they went. Scurvy began to kill off the men, and the humiliated Portuguese turned their sails for home.

Four years later, Vasco da Gama came back.

This time, da Gama commanded twenty warships bristling with weaponry the likes of which no one in the Indian Ocean had ever seen. He smashed the Arabs, he smashed the Africans, he smashed the Indians, every one. He established a direct European control of India that would last until the end of the British Raj in 1947.

And what about his friend, Francis Xavier? The two men never met.

Francisco de Jasso y Azpilcueta was born in 1506 in Spain; he would go on to win more souls for Catholicism than any other person since St. Paul. In August of 1534, Xavier, Ignatius Loyola, and five others founded the Society of Jesus, better known as the Jesuits, "those who say *Jesu* too much," the "footsoldiers of the Pope." They took vows of poverty and chastity, and simplified their names.

In 1540, Francis Xavier was ordered by the Catholic Church to India on King John III of Portugal's request for missionaries. From Goa, Xavier served as Apostolic Nuncio, converting masses up and down the Konkan Coast. Xavier made journey after journey to places few Europeans had been to at a time when sea travel killed most men quickly. He was beatified in 1619, and on March 12, 1622, he was sainted.

While acting as Apostolic Nuncio in Goa, the future saint wrote a letter to the Portuguese king asking for permission to install the Inquisition in India. He wrote that Hindu idols and temples specifically should be eradicated. Xavier himself had seen the beginning of the destruction of Goa's Hindu temples during his tenure as Nuncio, Catholic cathedrals built on the temples' sites with the rubble from their walls. The Goan Inquisition began in 1560, lasted until 1812.

The priests of the Goan Inquisition set up headquarters in the former sultan's palace. They immediately outlawed Hinduism. Sacred Hindu texts were burned, Hindu music, clothing, and foods were banned. Hindu marriage was outlawed. Violators were burned at the stake in groups in a ceremony known as the auto-da-fé, "act of faith." The strictures of the Inquisition spanned 230 pages. Hindus who confessed their crimes were granted strangulation before they were burned. So many adults were killed that orphans abounded on the Konkan Coast. The Catholic Church raised these children Catholic.

African slaves were imported to the colony. Led in gangs first by Jesuits, and later by Franciscans, the slaves descended on villages, capturing Hindus, rubbing raw pork in their mouths, thereby rendering the people outcasts from their own religion. The priests conducted a mass baptism of these untouchables on January 25 of each year, the Feast of the Conversion of St. Paul.

People who refused to convert were brought to the palace, interrogated until they confessed to heresy. Once they did, they were tried and convicted before the Inquisition's three judges. There was no possibility of appeal. The punishment was burning.

But before anyone could be burned, the necessary confessions often took torture to extract. The Inquisition had a forty-one-point manual for this. There was flogging, whipping, scalding, pressing. Fingernails were pulled out. Eyelids sliced off. Fingers and toes were removed one by one. The ears, the nose, the lips were all cut off. Legs and arms were amputated joint by joint until nothing was left but the torso, and the living head. Then the slow dismemberment began. Jews who had fled the Inquisition in Spain discovered that the Inquisition had come to India and found them.

The Goan Inquisition evolved during its 252-year length. In 1570, it was decreed that Hindus who converted freely to Catholicism didn't have to pay taxes for fifteen years. Also that year, Hindu names were made illegal. In 1684, the Konkan language was banned, Portuguese made compulsory. All books and documents written in the Konkan language were burned. In time, the original language itself would be lost. By 1812, Portuguese military power had waned, and the British invaded Goa, ostensibly to end the Goan Inquisition. At the same time, Goa was a good port from which to exploit the riches of India.

What remained on the western coast of India running from Goa south to Mangalore where the Jesuits and Franciscans executed their Inquisition was a new people forged by it. Most Konkans have never heard of the Goan Inquisition, do not know that their language is a pidgin, that their family names were adopted out of fear, that their Catholic faith was born of torture and fire. They also don't know why they like to eat pork.

But long before I knew any of that, I was a boy who loved my parents. I loved my uncle even more. We were growing pumpkins, and all of the Saturdays that fall, I helped him tend them, lifting them onto pieces of carpeting foam as they fattened, which somebody had told him would keep them from being blemished by the ground. Sometimes my mother helped us weed the garden while my sister played with dirt, and sometimes she simply sat on the grass of my uncle's yard. She'd play pat-a-cake with Elizabeth, and Elizabeth would laugh at the clapping and the sounds. My sister could say "juju," she could say "gapes." My own formal education would begin the following year at Mary, Seat of Wisdom Catholic Elementary School.

But that would be next year. Now we were watching the pumpkins grow, and my mother told me that the pumpkins grew because the leaves and vines filled them with the light they caught from the sun, and my uncle said the pumpkins' roots took their food from the soil. Either way, each time we pulled up to my uncle's house, I would run around to the garden to see if the pumpkins had grown in the week I'd been away. They had. We were going to carve them into jack-o'-lanterns, my mother promised, and I was going to be a pirate, with a beard, an eye patch, and a sword. Those things were waiting for me in my closet, ready for Halloween. Then my grandmother wrote that my grandfather was sick, and my father and I flew to India to watch my grandfather die.

India was hot and loud and yellow. There was dust, and people yelling. I gripped my father's hand as we walked through crowds of people, and people spit everywhere. In our hotel room, my father turned the air conditioner on high and wiped my face with his handkerchief. Then he wiped his forehead. He lifted me up, and we looked down from the window at all the people, at the black cars, at the men in the red turbans cleaning out people's ears with long metal pins. The big stone archway, my father told me, was the Gateway of India. The British army had come marching through that gate to conquer the whole country and make it their jewel. Men came and shined my father's shoes on their knees outside the door, they took the shirt my father had worn on the plane, and bowed, and brought it back pressed and wrapped in tissue. My father and I ate fish and chips in the hotel restaurant later, and the waiter smiled and bowed in his white jacket and said to my father in a soft voice, "Sir, is this your son?"

My father set down his fork and looked at the waiter. He said, "This is my son."

"Sir, he is handsome."

On the bus in the night, a man coughed and coughed. He coughed like that until the morning. We stopped on the side of the road in the dark, and insects whirled in the lights of the bus while everyone went into the grass to pee. There were stars over everything. In the bus, I leaned my head on my father's shoulder as I looked out the window at the stars and the dark. My father caressed my face.

"Do you miss home, my son?" he asked me.

"Yes, Dad."

"Then I want you to sleep."

In the morning, gangs of men banged on the sides of the bus with their hands as we pulled into the station. My father drank tea from a clay cup while all the people at the bus station gathered about us to look at me, and my father held my hand, and when he was done drinking, he threw the cup on the ground so that it broke into pieces. "That is what we do here," my father told me.

I could feel all those people looking at me. When I would lift my eyes to look at them, they were looking at me with their mustaches and folded arms in a circle around us. I held my father's hand tightly. Then my father took us through the crowd while men carried our bags on their heads.

In the Ambassador cab, my father said to the driver, "The Christian Colony."

The driver looked at us in his mirror. He said, "This is your son?"

"This is my son," my father said, and looked at the man in the mirror.

We passed through a dusty place crowded with people. There were cows there. The cows' horns were painted blue. The women wore colored saris. My father pointed at the passing things. He said, "That was your mother's house."

In India, I was always kept inside my grandfather's house, because I was the firstborn son of a firstborn son of a firstborn son, all the way back to the beginning. Also, I was an American boy, and nobody wanted me to get hurt in India. I was dressed in a suit all of that time, except when my father and I would go to bed in the room that had been his when he'd been my age, and we would undress from the day, and my father would wrap me in a checkered *lungi*. The windows of the house were hung with black drapes because my grandfather was dying. There were votive candles in every corner, and the servants moved about silently. The relatives were quiet and sad when they came, and my grandmother covered her face with her sari so that I cannot remember even seeing it.

Sometimes my father would burst into tears as he sat on the edge of the bed. Then I would also cry. My father's body would shake as he covered his face with his hands and cried, and I would hold his elbow in my hand and cry as I watched him. Then my father would stop his crying and look at me, and then he would gather me up in his arms and hold me tightly to him and rock us together, not saying anything. I could hear crickets. Someone was always clearing his throat in the night in one of the other rooms of the house. In the mornings, my father and I bathed with hot water from the buckets the servants heated and brought for us. It was dark in the bathing room, and my father scoured my body with a rag when he soaped me.

"I washed myself in here every day as a boy," my father told me.

"Uncle Sam lived here, too," I said.

"This is where your uncle Sam and I were children."

My father had made all of us get dressed up for a picture before we'd left America, and our family was on one side of the couch in our living room, me in my father's lap, my sister in my mother's, and my uncle Sam and Aunt Asha beside us.

"Let's do a few where we smile," the photographer had said, and then the camera flashed, and then he said, "And let's do a few where we don't."

My father had picked one of the ones where we weren't smiling, and now it was framed in glass and hanging on the wall beside my grandfather's diploma from the Britishers' police school and his citation from the king of England. When my Indian uncles came to look at the picture in their suits, they squinted at it and said, "The Americans."

Everyone wanted to talk to my father, and my father spent all of those days talking to them. My father sat back in my grandfather's chair in a *lungi*, and the men would lean toward him from their folding chairs as they talked. They drank the bottle of Beefeater that my grandfather's uncle had given to him. They dusted it with a rag as they laughed and opened it. Then they set small glasses on the floor and poured the glasses full as they talked. The men wore suits and slicked-back hair, and they all smelled like India. For a moment, when each one came, my father would push me toward them so that I had to shake their hands.

"Very fair." The men would pat my head and hold my face in their hands to look at me, and then they would say, "Babu's firstborn son is handsome and fair."

Sometimes my father would bark Konkani at the servants from my grandfather's chair, and the servants would hurry inside and take me out to the yard by the hand. There were other people in the bright yard with the wall all around it with glass shards on the top to keep the bad people out. If there were dogs there, they would hit the dogs' heads so that they yelped and went away. All of these people were Indians and dark, in *lungi*s and saris, cooking pots of curry at the fires, and they could not speak English. They all looked at me and smiled and did not talk, and then they talked a long time and laughed. They made me sit on a stool in my suit, and they brought me things and put them at my feet. There were yellow fruits with spines on them, there were flowers. There were sticks with blue strings tied around them, and Indian coins. Then there were yellow balls on a metal tray. A man came and smiled at me, and his teeth were red when he did. He stooped and lifted one of the yellow balls for me to eat. Then he took one of the sticks, lit it with a match, and smoked it.

"I am your friend, small boy," he told me.

The man puffed out white smoke and stooped to me and winked. All of those other people watched. He said something to me that I did not understand. He said something to me again, and I did not understand it again, because I could not speak Konkani and he knew that. Then he took a string of the flowers and put them around my neck. They were pink and white against my suit.

The man said something in Konkani and everyone was quiet. He touched his finger to my chest and said my name, "Francisco."

The man said the Konkani words slowly. He said, *"Tu . . . jay . . . now . . . ka . . . lay."* Then he said my name again.

"Tujay now kalay?" the man said softly, and smiled.

I said, "Francisco."

Everyone smiled and clapped.

"Tujay now kalay?"

"Francisco."

"Say to me."

"Tujay now kalay?"

"Ciprian," the man said, and shook my hand as he smiled and smoked. Then he took me by the hand to all of those people and I said, *"Tujay now kalay?"* to all of them, and they all told me their names and touched my face. Then the man put me on the stool and lifted a yellow ball to my mouth. When I took a bite from it, he blew out smoke from the side of his mouth, petted my face with his rough hand, and said, "You are Konkan."

Then they brought a white chicken, and Ciprian stepped on its neck and chopped off its head with a knife. The body fluttered around the yard while the head panted on the ground. Everyone watched what I would do. Then my father came into the yard and shouted at them in Konkani. He took the flowers from around my neck and dropped them on the pile on the ground. He brushed off the pollen from my suit, and carried me inside on his shoulder.

"Did they tease you, my son?"

"Yes, Dad."

"Then we will deal with them."

I was put on the chair beside my grandmother with her covered face, and for a long time my grandmother did not say anything to me. Then she touched my face with the gold bangles ringing on her wrist and said to me, "I see your mother in your face. But I also see us.

"What is your name?"

"Francisco."

My grandmother pinched my wrist so hard that I pulled it from her. She said to me, "What is your name?"

"Francisco."

She pinched my wrist. She said to me, "Don't you know that you have no name? Don't you know that you are a first-born son?"

"I am Francisco."

"You are Babu's son and you are Santan's son. You don't have any other name than that. Don't you know? You are the firstborn son."

"I am Francisco."

"You have no name. Don't you know that you are the firstborn son? You are the firstborn son of the firstborn son. You don't need any name but that. You are the firstborn son. That will always be your only name. Don't you know that we have all lived so that you could be this? You belong to us only. You are our firstborn son."

Then one of my uncles came in his suit, and he pinched

my face. He and my grandmother laughed. He said to me, "Are you a Konkan boy or only a white, tell me?"

When I didn't say anything, he said again, "Are you a Konkan boy or only a white?"

He held my face tightly in his hand and looked at me. My Indian uncle wagged his finger close to my face. He made his face dark and he said to me, "Don't you ever dare to be ashamed of us."

"He is the firstborn son."

"He is the firstborn white son of a Konkan."

"I want Mom," I told my father that night, and my father untied the laces of my shoes as I stood before him and he said, "Your mother says that she loved this place. That this was the only place where she was happy and that we all should have stayed here and lived in this place forever. What do you think of that, my son?"

"I want to go home to my mom."

"Now you know something of all of this."

Then my grandfather was going to die, and Ciprian and the servants pushed aside the heavy table that my grandfather had bled on when he'd been shot, and the Indian priest in his black robe and glasses and white beard came and said a Mass for us in Konkani, and the voices of the people echoed in the room in the light of the candles. For a long time, the priest read from the Konkan Bible, and I looked at his lips moving in his white beard. Then he closed the Bible and turned his face to the ceiling and said something at it, and the people turned their faces to the ceiling and said something back, and he said something, and they said something back. The priest gave them Communion on their tongues. Then he went into my grandfather's room.

"What is he doing with Grandfather?" I whispered to my

father on his lap as we and the quiet people sat in the chairs lined against the wall. My father whispered back, "He is administering the Last Rites."

"What is that?"

"He is giving Grandfather his last Communion so that he will go to heaven."

The priest came out of my grandfather's room, and we all stood up. My father held my hand. The people lowered their heads and prayed again. Then the priest sprinkled us all with holy water, and we crossed ourselves and said, "Amen."

My grandmother came to my father and held his hands. She moaned in Konkani quietly to him from her covered face. One of my uncles touched my back and began to push me and he said, "You must go into that room with Babu."

My grandfather's room was lit with candles, and my grandfather was in the bed. He looked like a great bird in his bones. He rolled his face toward me, and I could see the bones in it, too. My father took me forward.

My grandfather said to my father in English, "Is he a Konkan?"

"Father, he is a Konkan."

My grandfather reached out his arm from the sheet, touched my face with his fingers. He said, "You must surpass us."

Then he spoke in Konkani to my father, and my father said, "Woyee, Papa. Woyee, Papa." My father lifted my grandfather's hand to his lips and kissed it. Then my grandfather held his hand to me, and I kissed it.

In our room, my father held me and both of us were crying. Then my father set me down and kneeled down to me and he said, "Your grandfather was a great man. You must be greater still. Will you be a great man, Francisco? Promise me that you will be."

"I promise."

My grandfather died in the night. We knew when he did because the women began their wailing. In the morning, my grandfather was in a long casket on the table, and there were candles and flowers on the floor all around the table, and my grandfather was sleeping in the casket in a suit. They had folded a red-and-white-and-blue Britishers' flag under his hands, and wrapped his hands with a black rosary like tying them. When it was our turn at the casket, my father kissed my grandfather's forehead, and then he lifted me up and I kissed it. All day and all night, people came to kneel before my grandfather in the casket. They left money in piles on the floor where they had kneeled.

My father held me in bed until I slept, and when I woke, he was not there. Ciprian came and carried me downstairs and washed me in the dark room as he smoked. Then he dried and dressed me. He pulled my tie tight around my neck. He said, "Now he goes in the ground," and led me by the hand to where they all were.

The money was gone, the servants were lifting the closed casket from the table and onto the shoulders of my uncles and my father. My father was in the front of them with the casket on his shoulder in his suit, and they took it out of the house and into the bright day through the gate and out on the street, where many people waited for us. The men wore tall black hats and black suits and held canes, and the women wore dark saris. The priest was there in his robe with a golden crucifix on a long golden staff, and two boys in white robes were beside him, and four old men in brown uniforms carried rifles on their shoulders. The old men in the uniforms marched before my father and uncles and the casket, kicking up their legs so their heavy boots clopped on the street, and the priest went first with the crucifix, and then everyone began to walk. All behind us came the Konkans. When we left the Christian Colony, there were people in *lungis* who parted to let us pass, and as we did, they began to hiss and shout. Then I knew they were the Hindus.

All the way to the cemetery, the Hindus hissed and shouted at my grandfather's casket, and old men ran alongside where my father and uncles carried the casket on their shoulders, and they hissed and shouted at the casket as they ran, and some ran ahead and spit on the road so that the priest and the officers and my father and uncles and all of us had to walk over their spit.

Then we were at the cemetery and the priest unlocked the iron gates with his long key, and the officers stood and saluted with their rifles at their sides. My father and uncles took my grandfather's casket through the officers and the gates, and then we were all in the cemetery with the white graves around us. Men without shirts were smoking by the hole, and they pulled two more men out of the hole in their muddy *lungis* when we came to it, and they put their shovels in the pile of dirt.

The priest said something to everyone as we gathered around the hole, and everyone was serious and quiet, and the Hindus climbed up and hung their arms over the walls of the cemetery to hiss and shout while the priest sprinkled my grandfather's casket with holy water. Then the priest said a prayer and everyone said, "Amen," in one loud voice.

When the gravediggers began to lower my grandfather's casket into the hole with the ropes, the Hindus began to whistle. The priest said, "Amen," and the Konkans said, "Amen." My father wiped his eyes with his white handkerchief. The officers lifted their rifles to their shoulders to fire shot after shot in the air.

But at that time in America, it was Halloween, and people were dressing their children as ghouls and goblins and devils and demons, things the children were not, but were allowed to pretend to be on this one day. My uncle brought four ripe pumpkins to my father's house, and my mother spread newspaper over the kitchen table. Then they carved three of them, saving the last for my return. My sister sat on the table and pulled out the pulp. The seeds they washed for the oven. Then they lit candles in the faces they'd made, and the light from them was frightening and warm in the darkened kitchen at the same time.

People had set out jack-o'-lanterns all over Ridge Lawn, and laughing monsters flocked the streets. My mother and uncle took my sister out to it, and they were happy in it, too. They'd dressed my sister in a clown's motley suit, though neither of them knew what that meant, either. Then my mother put my sister to sleep in her crib.

In her room, my mother shut the door. My uncle was already in there, and she went to him. The world surrounded them, the universe. My uncle's hands on my mother's white skin seemed even darker to him than they were. He stayed until the morning, and then he went out to his car. Dawn was breaking. The last birds were waking in the branches of the elm trees before they would begin their journey south.

Acknowledgments

I'd like to thank the National Endowment for the Arts, whose fellowship made the researching and writing of this book possible.

I used many sources for the historical elements of the book. I'm heavily indebted to Dr. T. R. de Souza's *Details of the Goan Inquisition*. Also *Memoirs of Goa* by Alfredo De Mello, the writings of Kanchan Gupta, *The Hindu Holocaust Records* maintained by Aravindan Neelakandan, *The Last Days of British India* by Michael Edwardes, and various Wikipedia and *Encyclopedia Britannica* articles, notably on da Gama, Xavier, the Jesuits, and the Goan Inquisition.

Thanks to Carrie Roby, who gave me a place to write parts 1 and 2.

Thanks to Barry Spacks, first reader, and Joel Dunsany, proofreader.

Thanks to Jack Rolls, who rescued the manuscript from the Thunderbird Lodge, Redding, California, where I hid and forgot it on tour.

Greatest thanks to my agent, Liz Darhansoff, to Michele Mortimer, and everyone at the agency. Also greatest thanks to my editor, Tina Pohlman, who pushed me beyond. Thank you. Thanks to my publicist Michelle Blankenship, Lee Kravetz, Lindsey Smith, my copy editor Marian Ryan, David Hough, and everyone at Harcourt. Thanks as always to Merle Rubine, who put us all together.

A debt of gratitude to Marc Behr's fine book *The Smell of Apples,* which I pillaged for the first kernel of Francisco's voice. Thanks to Frank Nigro for the fact-check here, and for the German check in *Whiteman.* Thanks to Matt Walsh and Will Marquess for helping me out with Burlington, Vermont. There are too many people to thank gracefully . . . Please know I'm grateful.

Thanks to the readers.

Thanks and love to my mother and her wife, Irene, for putting me up from time to time and being managers. Thanks to Jessyka. Finally, thanks to my sister and family.

Phoenix and London, 2006